Amy Cunningham is a novelist who grew up in rural Hertfordshire and now lives in Cornwall. She has an MA in Creative Writing from Bath Spa University and has published novels across genres which include crime fiction, contemporary women's fiction and horror. Amy has previously worked as a concierge for luxury apartments and as a maid in a five-star hotel, and so is no longer surprised at what the rich and fabulous get up to when they think no one's watching.

THE SERIAL KILLER'S PARTY

Amy Cunningham

PENGUIN BOOKS

TRANSWORLD PUBLISHERS
Penguin Random House, One Embassy Gardens,
8 Viaduct Gardens, London SW11 7BW
www.penguin.co.uk

Transworld is part of the Penguin Random House group of companies
whose addresses can be found at global.penguinrandomhouse.com

Penguin
Random House
UK

First published in Great Britain in 2025 by Penguin Books
an imprint of Transworld Publishers

This book is a work of fiction and, except in the case of historical fact, any
resemblance to actual persons, living or dead, is purely coincidental.

Every effort has been made to obtain the necessary permissions with
reference to copyright material, both illustrative and quoted. We
apologize for any omissions in this respect and will be pleased to
make the appropriate acknowledgements in any future edition.

A CIP catalogue record for this book
is available from the British Library.

ISBN
9781804997017

Typeset in 10.5/14.5 pt Giovanni by Falcon Oast Graphic Art Ltd
Printed and bound in Great Britain by Clays Ltd, Elcograf S.p.A.

The authorized representative in the EEA is Penguin Random House Ireland,
Morrison Chambers, 32 Nassau Street, Dublin D02 YH68.

Penguin Random House is committed to a sustainable
future for our business, our readers and our planet. This book is
made from Forest Stewardship Council® certified paper.

MIX
Paper | Supporting
responsible forestry
FSC
www.fsc.org   FSC® C018179

For all those searching for justice against the untouchable.
I believe in you.

THE SERIAL KILLER'S PARTY

Prologue

October 2023

I LOOK UP FROM my laptop screen and out over the glass monoliths of London. There's a shimmer in the air, a heat haze that dances above the buildings, as if the city is underwater. The sun beats down on concrete and steel but in here I'm cocooned in frigid, artificial air. It's bliss. Or it would be if I wasn't functioning on two hours of sleep and trying to wade through some of the driest expert testimony I've encountered in my career as a barrister. It's not even my work, technically. William palmed it off on me. Even though we're doing the same job on paper, he always finds a way to boss me around. I'd say something but I don't want to become the 'difficult woman' in a male-dominated environment.

The reason for my lack of sleep sits in a frame in front of me, a picture turned face down on the desk. Every morning when I come in, the cleaners have stood the frame back up, giving me a jolt as I make eye contact with the picture and hastily lay it down again. I should really email facilities about asking them to leave it. But that feels too final. So does taking it home.

I glance back at the screen and my eyes land on the word 'loquacious'. I need a coffee. Iced, obviously. I still haven't fully recovered from my commute through the ripe, steaming bowels of the city. I find my eyes straying to the picture frame again. Even face down it's pulling me to it, unavoidable. I pick it up and slip it into my desk drawer, but I can still feel it in there – daring me to look. Demanding that I do something more to help.

'Ms Spencer?'

It's my PA, Carrie, hovering in the doorway. She's new and desperate to please so I do my best to offer her a kind smile. I remember how hard it was when I started at the firm. How intimidating I found the fast-moving, fast-talking senior staff. To be honest it's still hard for me. I know I get the dullest busywork because I'm the only woman at my level. I do wish she'd call me Amelia, but I can't bring that up again now or she'll wilt like the peace lily on her desk.

'Everything OK, Carrie?' I ask, noticing for the first time that she looks even more stressed than usual.

'Um . . . there's some police here to see you?' Carrie bites her already fairly well-chewed lip. 'They said it's a personal matter – your sister? They did call earlier while you were in a meeting and said they'd be coming but I went on lunch and forgot to leave a note.'

Just like that, I'm frozen to the bone. I reach for the edge of my desk and try to swallow the wave of dizzying panic rising in my throat, making it hard to breathe. It's not the words. It's the tone, the way her eyes flick to the floor, to the walls, sliding away from me. The fact that the police are here and not just calling back. For five weeks now I've been waiting for them to respond to my calls with anything other than a vague assurance that they were 'doing everything they could'. Now that it's finally happening, though, I want it all to stop.

'Rose?' I say stupidly. I only have one sister. One missing sister whom I've been pestering the police about for weeks. Five years younger than me and a world apart, though physically we could almost be twins. At least, we were when I last saw her. A lot could have changed since then.

I shiver.

'Bring them in,' I say, my heart racing in my chest. Good news or bad, I need to hear it. The torture might be over at last.

Carrie vanishes gratefully and two men arrive in her place. I get up to introduce myself, not caring that I had slipped off my shoes when I got in. I feel very far away from myself in the moment; as if I'm watching from outside the glass walls of my office. The hair stands up on the back of my neck and my hand shakes as I take a sip of water.

'Ms Spencer? I'm Detective Inspector Reed and this is Sergeant Michaels. I believe you two have spoken before, on the phone?'

'Have you found her?' I blurt. 'Rose. Is she . . .?' I trail off as they exchange a look. What is it? What are they about to tell me? Suddenly, despite these past months of uncertainty, I want to cover my ears. I don't want to hear it. I want them to leave.

'Since you reported Rose missing we've been trying to reach her, retracing her movements over the past few months.' He wipes some sweat from his hairline. Having only just entered the air-conditioned office, he's probably roasting in his suit, or maybe it's nerves. 'Recently her

3

landlord returned to the country and we were able to gain access to her flat. There's no sign of a disturbance. Nothing to indicate foul play. We've also found evidence that she used her passport to leave the country on a one-way ticket to Norway three weeks ago.'

I know what he's insinuating. He thinks I'm being pushy, controlling. That Rose has simply gone on an extended holiday and this has all been a massive overreaction on my part.

'She isn't on holiday. I haven't heard from her in months. She wouldn't leave the country without telling me where she was going. I know my sister. I'm her only family. Her big sister. She tells me everything.'

Used to tell me everything.

The two men exchange another glance. Finally the DI sighs and adopts a gentle tone that immediately puts me on edge. I hate feeling as if I'm being handled.

'I understand that there was some . . . friction between you and your sister shortly before you reported her missing? We found the text message on her phone . . . It looked like she hadn't been responding to you even before she left the country.'

'What?' I ask, though I know exactly what he means. 'My sister is missing. She isn't just . . . not speaking to me – she's not uploading to social media. Her boss doesn't know where she is!'

Another look passes between them. 'Yes, we checked that. Apparently she'd threatened to quit fairly often, had a number of fallings-out with another woman in the office. According to a colleague, she'd packed up her personal things several times but hadn't followed through on it – before now, it seems.' The DI rests a hand on the back of the visitor's chair I'd neglected to offer him. 'Ms Spencer, I can see that you're very worried about your sister. I want you to know that we will be willing to revisit this if any new information comes to light. When she returns to the country, or leaves Norway, we'll be alerted. However, at the moment it appears that she has gone travelling and may be taking a break from social media. It could be that because of your falling-out, she intentionally didn't inform you of her plans.'

'It wasn't a "falling-out",' I lie. 'It was just . . . We're sisters. Sisters fight – but she has never done anything like this before. She would never go travelling for this long without telling me – what about the rent on her flat? What about her cat?' I ask, thinking desperately of something that'll convince them. 'Who's looking after that?'"

The sergeant produces a notebook and flips it open. 'I believe she left her cat with a neighbour before she flew out.' He skims a few lines and looks up. 'Rose's landlord informed us that she's one month overdue on her rent. He's asked us to pass on his contact information so that you can arrange to cover it or to move her things out of the flat before he relets it.'

I stare at them, unable to put my outrage and panic into words. Yes, my sister can be flighty, full of romantic notions and prone to diving headfirst into her next big passion, but never without telling me. At least before we had our fight. Before she stopped speaking to me.

'So you're just . . . giving up?' I ask, embarrassed to find tears welling up. I try to suppress them but my throat only gets thicker, my chest aching. 'She could be in trouble! She could be . . .' The word 'dead' sticks in my throat. I'm not ready to go there just yet; as if saying it will make it real. I am never at a loss for words; it's my job to always have an answer or an angle. But in that moment I have nothing. I heave a few breaths and stare past them out towards the horizon, digging my fingernails into my palms.

'Please,' I manage. 'Please, you have to find my sister. She might have been trafficked or lured away or . . .' I can't finish the sentence. I can't bring myself to.

The two police officers look uncomfortable, but distant. The DI gives me a nod that means nothing and starts telling me to 'get in touch' if 'anything comes to mind'. Shortly after that, they leave. I return to my desk and try to pretend it never happened.

Carrie returns, asking questions, but it's as if everyone is speaking the same impenetrable language as the document still sitting on the laptop screen. I can't get a grip on the words long enough to understand them.

'I'm going home,' I say eventually, gathering my things. 'Cancel my meetings – I'll be on email.'

'But William left you some new files on my . . .'

I ignore her, ignore everything. I just have to get out of there. William stands up and calls after me as I rush past him and into a lift – I don't look back.

Only, once I'm out of the ice-cube offices and down in the exhaust-filled mouth of the nearest tube station, I don't go home. I navigate almost unthinkingly towards Rose's flat. Though we both live in London we may as well be in separate cities. My flat is in Southall and hers is in Enfield, an hour and a half away on the tube. On a good day.

I went round there for the first time three weeks after our fight. She'd been incommunicado since the argument and countless texts, emails and phone calls had gone unanswered. When she didn't answer the door I assumed she was out or still ignoring me. I went back to messaging her, sending emails. I even had a care package delivered via Amazon. Which someone probably stole off her doorstep. It was only after my third visit several weeks later that I got worried. By that point we hadn't spoken in two months, and I had my first of many meetings with the police.

Thankfully, Rose's landlord is also her downstairs neighbour and now he's back in the country it doesn't take long for him to grant me access. He squints at my ID when I tell him I'm there to go through her things. After I transfer the missing month's rent on my banking app, he gives me her key with very little resistance. I want to ask if he knows which neighbour is looking after her cat, but the building isn't pet friendly and I don't want to get anyone in trouble. I'm allergic to cats anyway, so it's not as if I could take him in. As much as I'd have liked to do that for her. The need to make amends for our argument is overwhelming.

Inside, the flat feels abandoned, like a school in the summer holidays. I feel wrong for being there without Rose – normally she'd have welcomed me in with a hug, hands still soapy from hurrying to wash up before I arrived, her signature banana muffins (which she learned to make at school and then made every time she visited me or I came over) piled on a plate.

There's a thick layer of dust on the table in the hall, more than would accumulate in only two months. Rose was never one for cleaning. When we shared a room I divided it with tape once and refused to clean her half. The room ended up looking like some weird art exhibit: 'The Half-Ruined Room' – mouldy plates and dust bunnies on one side, books ordered by height and colour-coded desk on the other. In the end, of course, I'd broken down and cleaned her side of the room for her. Rose had given me a manicure in payment.

In her kitchen/living area I wrinkle my nose at the smell coming from her fridge. Clearly she didn't clean it out before she left, but perhaps the state of the rest of the place convinced the police that it was just an oversight on her part. The rest of the room is just as dusty as the hall and very cluttered. Tumbleweeds of cat hair occupy the corners and there's a fudgy layer of grease over the cooker, dotted with a few withered chunks of onion.

Everything else looks the same as it did when I last visited her: the walls stencilled in strawberries in certain violation of her tenancy agreement; novelty cushions crowding the sofa with toadstools and stars. The tangle of pot plants by the window are now very crispy and the room is suffocatingly hot. Every inch of the place reflects the whimsy and carelessness of my little sister. But her absence lays over it all, thicker than dust.

After I force open the sticky sash window, I go to the sink, fill an empty yoghurt pot with water and douse the plants. I'm on autopilot, still trying to take care of things for her. Now that I'm here I don't know what I'm looking for. Some clue that the police didn't find? A bloody handprint on the wall; a letter made of cut-up magazines or perhaps a rope of sheets dangling down to street level. The only thing the flat contains is the unbearable absence of my baby sister.

In her bedroom I feel like even more of an intruder. The bedding is creased and crumpled, slept in and hastily made. Her wardrobe is open and there's a dent in the duvet that suggests a bag was packed there. Maybe she really did just run off for an extended holiday without telling me. Maybe she lost her phone. Rose was never good at hanging on to things, constantly misplacing her purse, tickets, keys, charging cables. In my handbag at that very moment I have a Samsung charger that doesn't fit my iPhone and a tampon I won't use, because I'm so used to her suddenly needing them. Used to being her mum as much as her sister.

The mandala wall hanging above the bed ripples in the slight breeze from the window. Her bedside table is cluttered: a sticky glass of evaporated squash fights for space with several books, a pack of paracetamol, three face creams, lube and a lava lamp. On the floor underneath it is a bed for her cat, Pimento.

I don't want to disturb the bed, so I sit on the floor. My office dress is damp with sweat, crumpled from the tube. I look up and spot a picture of Rose and her friends at some music festival or other stuck to the wall with holographic tape. We have the same dark brown hair and tortoiseshell eyes, our dad's stubby nose and our mum's full smile. Unlike me with my basic black wardrobe and millennial beige style, Rose always surrounded herself with colour. In the picture she is wearing a rainbow sequin skirt, silver bikini and had strawberry novelty glasses perched on her head. I look away from her smiling, glitter-flecked face, unable to meet her eyes. This is all my fault. Why did I have to go and upset her? If I hadn't, she'd have told me where she was going and why. Maybe she wouldn't have gone at all.

My gaze lands on a partially shredded piece of paper in the cat bed. Pimento, I remember Rose telling me, is a paper-chewer. More than once Rose has lost bills or birthday cards which it turned out he'd hidden away or partially eaten.

This isn't a bill or a card, though; it's an expensive-looking piece of creamy paper covered in calligraphy. I pick it up, some impulse that has me still cleaning up after my sister, as if she's due home any minute.

It's an invitation.

My dearest Rose,

Please forgive me for allowing so many years to pass us by. I was a fool to ever let you go. Can we begin again?

I am holding my annual get-together at my estate in Norway in a week's time. I would be honoured if you would accept this invitation to join me. Perhaps we can find some way to return to those days at Cambridge, before I committed the unforgivable sin of taking you for granted?

Yours always, if you'll have me,

Lawrence Fowley

The date of the party has already been and gone – three weeks ago. Meaning Rose got the invitation one month into our fight. Around the time she stopped posting to social media altogether. My work phone vibrates with an incoming email, but I barely register it. I can feel all those concerns about the office, my job, all of it sliding off my shoulders.

The invitation crackles as I grip it tightly. This is the only clue I have to my sister's disappearance. I have to show it to the police, to make them believe that something happened to her.

And if they still can't, or won't, do anything? Well then, I'll just have to do it myself. If this Lawrence Fowley knows anything or was involved in her disappearance . . . he'd better watch his back.

1

One Year Later

I LET MYSELF INTO the flat in Maida Vale and listen intently before allowing myself a sigh of relief. Ford isn't home yet. That means I have a little time to myself. A nice break after a long day.

I quickly slip off my wet trainers and set my purchases from Borough Market down on the black marble kitchen island. I go every Thursday to buy shockingly expensive cheese and organic figs. He likes to feed them to me, which I find about as appetizing a prospect as the figs themselves – gritty, horrible things. Once everything's put away I open a bottle of Ford's favourite red to let it breathe. He likes a glass or two before dinner.

The dishwasher I set that morning is ready to unload and I start putting things away. As I lift out our matching mugs – two unnecessarily large monstrosities with our names on them and the Eiffel Tower below. A souvenir from our first couple's trip together. So heavy and clunky that I've actually cut down on the amount of tea and coffee I drink. I put them away, resisting the urge to accidentally break one, and finish emptying the dishwasher.

Preparations for his arrival done, I take my phone into the bathroom and lock the door. Safely ensconced in what these days is my unofficial 'office', I perch on the side of the bath and review today's research notes and memos. I keep them in a folder marked 'workout plans' and if he's gone through my phone, it's deterred his attention for the eleven months we've been together.

Ford is under the impression that his fit blonde girlfriend is a personal trainer, specializing in post-partum weight loss. I'm quite proud of that part of my backstory. The personal-trainer thing was mostly to lure him in when we met 'coincidentally' on one of his jogs. The post-partum thing means Ford isn't worried about other men, and I work out of other people's homes, so he can't just 'drop by' to visit me during my fictitious working hours.

After closing my folder I set my phone aside and shut my eyes. It's been over a year since I last spoke to my sister. The anniversary of our fight passed by recently. It feels like time has stopped, but soon everything I've been working towards will come into play. Or, if things don't go the way I'm hoping, I'll know that I've wasted a year of my life but am no closer to finding my sister.

'Aimes?' Ford's voice is followed by the sound of the front door banging shut. 'Are you in?'

I open my eyes, smooth my bouncy ponytail and slip my phone into a pocket of my lilac workout leggings. 'Just freshening up, babes.'

After applying some lip gloss, I bound out of the bathroom, fully in gym-bunny mode. Ford is spread out on the corner sofa, thumbing through his phone. As usual he's still in his work suit and hasn't removed his shoes. Then again, this is his flat so he can do what he likes. His golden curls are wet from the October drizzle outside; his recently acquired horn-rimmed glasses are speckled with water droplets. He doesn't actually need them to see; they're mostly to offset his reputation as a bit of a himbo at work. An unfair reputation, as Ford isn't stupid, he just has, as Rose would have put it, 'golden retriever energy'. One of the things that have made my performance easier is that he is actually very good-looking. I've never had to pretend that I'm attracted to him, and it's not exactly a chore to spend my nights in his bed.

Ford doesn't look up as I come in but I smile anyway. The key to any good performance is consistency. As anyone in politics or PR will tell you: always assume the camera is rolling.

'How was your day?' I ask, heading to the kitchen and pouring him a glass of wine.

Ford's arms slip around my waist and I lean back against his chest, breathing in as if to savour his peppery cologne.

'Not bad, not bad,' he mutters, pressing a kiss behind my ear. 'I've been asked to take over with Ramsey since Charlie stuffed it at their last meeting. I've invited Leo and Nev down to do some damage control. I'll take them out for the night, show them a good time.'

My mental Rolodex spins and several cards flick out. Charlie I've met: he's essentially a dark-haired version of Ford. Naturally that makes them mortal enemies. Do I know Leo or Nev? Presumably one of them either is a Ramsey or works for one. Or is it a company name? I'm about to ask when the name sparks something. Of course: Ramsey, Steiner and Huntley. I read about them a few days ago on one of the blogs I subscribe to and read dutifully every morning. A tiresome process, like giving myself homework. I've never tracked the man-hours it takes me to keep abreast of Ford's work, the magazines, blogs and newspapers I scour for relevant info. Several hours per day if I factor in all the other subjects I maintain knowledge of for his sake. I may have taken a leave of absence from my old job but I'm still managing a single, demanding case. Pro bono.

Knowing all this stuff is only half the battle, of course. The other half is knowing when to be clued up and when to act vacant and impressed. Now is one of those times.

'Sounds like they're pretty important if your boss wants you on it. What sort of thing do they do?'

'I've told you,' Ford says with a sly grin that I can hear in his voice. He loves telling me things. Loves bringing out names, contracts and figures with a flourish and watching me clap my hands with delight like a child watching a magic trick. 'They're crypto brokers.'

Well, he's close. Maybe he's dumbed it down for me. They're actually developers working on new methods of encryption for cryptocurrency brokers, with dual applications for hot wallet storage. Lots of money in it anyway, which is all Ford's company cares about.

I turn in his arms and widen my eyes. 'Ooh, exciting.'

Ford presses his mouth to mine, his self-satisfied grin still firmly in place. I cosy up to him and sigh happily. If he's taking some potential clients out on the town that'll give me a whole evening to myself. Bliss.

'Speaking of excitement. You'll never guess what arrived at the office today,' Ford murmurs.

I lean back and bite my lip, painting an expression of coy concentration on my face. 'A present, for me?'

'Better.'

Ford pulls an envelope from inside his suit jacket. It's creamy white and clearly from expensive paper stock. Ford's full name is on it in familiar calligraphy.

For the first time I struggle, like an actress suddenly blinded by the stage lights. He watches me, anticipating my delight. My lines slip from my mind. My eyes freeze on the envelope – I know what it contains. I know what this is. It's everything I've been waiting for after all these months. It's finally here and I have to clench my hands into fists to keep them from shaking.

'W-what is it?' I force myself to ask.

'An invitation to the party of a lifetime,' Ford says with relish. 'My cousin, Lawrence – remember, I told you about him? Well, never mind. He throws these annual parties at his estate in Norway. His father started the tradition but Lawrence takes it bigger and better every time. It's incredibly exclusive, natch, but I'm on the list. Now I just need someone to go with.'

He grins at me, but I don't dare read into that smile. He needs to say the words.

I swallow and try to stay calm, but my heart thuds in my chest.

'Some lucky girl might get to be my plus-one.'

He waves the envelope over my head, teasing me. I jump for it obediently, giggling, back on form. Ford holds the paper just out of reach.

'Do you know anyone who might want to go?' he asks.

'I do!' I jump for the paper, my belly swooping with genuine fear. Not now that it's right here in front of me. Not after all this time. 'Take me!'

The envelope is crushed against my waist as Ford pulls me in for a kiss. 'I can't wait for you to see the family estate, meet everyone. Who knows, one day we might be moving out there, if I get a position in the family business? But, oh, you just wait – it's going to be wild. We're going to have so much fun,' he murmurs into my ear.

'So much,' I echo, slightly wrong-footed by the fizz of excitement in my belly as he kisses me. I'm suddenly eager for his touch, but I know it's just because I'm thinking of the party. Of being in the same room as Lawrence Fowley at long last. Of being in the same place Rose vanished. Finally. Yet there's a hurricane of nerves stirring inside me. Am I really ready?

After I've excused myself to change for dinner, I lock the door to the bathroom, lean close to the mirror and look into my eyes. The one thing about me that hasn't changed. It's a ritual: start with that one point of connection and the rest of me doesn't look so alien. So strange. In the month during which the police failed to gain any ground using the invitation I took to them, I started to change everything about myself. These days I'm honey blonde, sporting an expensive fake tan and about a centimetre of 'natural' makeup. I own a hundred push-up bras and have the waxing regime of an Olympic swimmer. Once I identified Ford as a convenient way into Lawrence's life, I stalked his social media and re-created his perfect woman. After that it was just a matter of tracking his jogging route via his Strava account.

I try and fail to avoid thinking about what Rose might look like now, more than a year into her disappearance. Is she being held somewhere? Has she been hurt? Is she even still alive?

I tried to tell the police about the invitation. They did contact Lawrence to ask about her, but they took his word for it that Rose barely made an appearance that night, that he didn't even remember who she was. But her invitation had been so personal – of course he knew her. He actually had the nerve to tell the police Rose had probably forged it in order to get in. The bastard. As for the rest of it, he said that she must have left and he hadn't seen her since. It became clear very quickly that if I wanted to find my sister, to get justice for whatever had been done to her, I would have to get it myself.

'I've made reservations for Pierro's at eight,' Ford calls.

'Sounds lovely, thank you,' I reply automatically.

With the tap running I get down on the floor and carefully remove the bottom drawer of the vanity unit. Underneath it the base of the unit lifts out and I remove a cosmetics case. Most of my 'kit' looks completely innocent. I've learned how many seemingly innocuous things can be used for nefarious purposes.

Much like the ritual of finding myself in my own eyes, this kit is a talisman. Touching it, holding the tools one after the other. It's a lifeline, a reminder that this is all for a reason. I think about these things every time I swallow my dignity to keep up this charade. Every time I dream of Rose's laughing face and wake with tears running across my cheeks, or smell banana muffins and patchouli and think for just a second that I'll turn around and see her.

I can do this. For Rose. I'm ready. I have to be. I won't get another chance.

'Are you nearly ready, Aimes? Don't fuss too much – you're already gorgeous.'

'Almost,' I call back, and hastily get myself put together, the kit hidden away.

As he drives us to the restaurant Ford turns to me and gives me the once-over, his eyes glittering.

'I'll have to tell Michaelson to cover next week's golf retreat. Better than having it cancelled,' he says, not sounding sorry in the least. 'I wouldn't miss this party for the world.'

'No,' I say. 'Sounds like it's a once-in-a-lifetime opportunity.'

'It is!' Ford squeezes my thigh below the hemline of my skirt. 'Oh, it really is.'

But something about the way he says it makes me pause. Beneath his excitement, his over-the-top charm, there's a flicker of unease. Is it anxiety that I might embarrass him in front of his family? That doesn't explain the hooded eyes, the creased brow. He's afraid of something. For the rest of the drive, I can't seem to relax. Ford's fear is as contagious as his excitement.

For the first time I wonder if I'm making the right decision. What does Ford know that I don't, and why isn't he telling me?

2

I PACK MY CASE while Ford's at work.

He went into a tailspin over the invitation and even took a day off to take me to buy outfits and accessories for the party. Or rather, parties. Lawrence's event is a three-day affair, with a party every night. During the day we'll have the run of his estate – cruise the fjord that snakes past his home, laze in the sauna, go hiking, climbing or enjoy his private beach. I hadn't previously thought Norway had many beaches but apparently they're world class: white sand, clear water and, thanks to the Gulf Stream, warmer than you'd think.

Too bad I'm not going there to enjoy myself.

Alone in the flat I organize outfits, designer shoes, bikinis straight off a Bond girl, evening dresses, poolside cover-ups, an enormous straw hat. I let Ford pick – he's from money and he loves to shop for himself and for me. Of course he asks me about everything, points out details like stitching and fit and loves when I join in with him. He praises me in every new set of clothes, or shakes his head and blames the designer for their ensemble not flattering me. In another life he'd have made a great personal shopper. As it is he's just the dream client for them.

Although I play along and let him indulge in a spending spree, the only things I care about are in two cosmetic cases. One holds my more innocent items – nail files and various sharp cosmetic tools. Hair pins which I've practised picking a lock with after watching tutorials online. There's a jar of magnetic face mask, but the magnet with it is not the one it came with. It's much, much stronger and far more useful.

The other case contains the more obviously unusual items – my RFID encoder for duplicating key cards, plus the blank cards to go with it. Both purchased cheaply online – the same tech used in schools, offices like my own, hotels and anywhere else with swipe cards. The case also contains my ceramic knife. If Ford saw that stuff I wouldn't be able to explain it away.

One by one I check each item, cross it off my mental list and pack it away securely. Finally I fetch my laptop and book our flights. I hadn't had to work hard to convince Ford to let me do it. He doesn't like to do the dull part of going away, all that administration and organization. On our first mini-break to Paris I'd had a minor panic that he might notice the name on my passport isn't the one he knows me by, but it had quickly become apparent that the details of his grand gestures would be up to me to iron out.

I book two return flights to Norway, knowing that if Ford notices that 'Amelia Knox' is now 'Amelia Spencer' on the ticket, I'll explain it away with my rehearsed story of my parents' divorce and pout about 'all that silly paperwork'. I'm not worried about it causing an issue at the party. Amelia's a common enough name. I'm fairly certain no one will connect it to Rose – they might not even know she has a sister. I don't know what's happened to her or if she's in a fit state to tell her captor anything at all. For all I know they've kept her in a coma or gagged all this time. Or they killed her the night of the party and never asked her a single thing.

That thought makes me feel slightly sick, but more than that I feel angry. Anger has been my constant companion for the past year. It's my armour, my refuge and my best friend, because it keeps me from breaking down, from giving up.

Once everything is packed, I sit down on the bedroom floor and remember, all those months ago, sitting in Rose's flat. This is what it has all been for. Finally, I'm going to get my answers. I'm going to expose whoever did this, and take whatever steps are necessary to bring them to justice.

I still have the picture of Rose at the music festival. I took it with me when I left her flat that day and I keep it with the rest of my kit where I know Ford will never come across it – not that I think he'll recognize her. He wasn't at last year's party – he's been cagey about why but reading between the lines he got bumped from the guest list at the last minute, a numbers thing. His loyalty to his family apparently only cuts one way. I was afraid he wouldn't be invited this year either, but I managed to subtly suggest that he get more involved with his family – essentially bribing an invite out of them with a trip of his own. Which seems to have done the trick. That or there were just fewer guests this year.

I fetch the picture from its hiding place in the bathroom and hold it in my hands. Rose grins up at me, glitter sparkling in the sunshine, an aura of youth and happiness around her. Sometimes when I look at that picture I can imagine her so clearly – blaring music in our tiny back garden, tent pitched, a cooler of alcopops for later. Rose and I dancing on the crispy summer lawn – waiting for her friends to come over. Throwing her own private festival because we couldn't afford tickets. A watery smile twists my mouth as I remember her hopping around, squealing, and me trying to pull a bee sting out of her foot with tweezers.

'I'm going to find you,' I tell her. 'No matter what it takes . . . I promise. Even if it's . . . even if I can only give you a proper burial, right by Mum and Dad. I will.'

A tear plops on to the glossy photo paper and runs across Rose's smiling face.

'I'm so sorry, Rosie,' I whisper. 'I never should've said it. I never should have driven you away.'

It all started so mundanely. We'd met up at a chain brunch place for a catch-up. Our regular Sunday morning ritual. I had black coffee and avocado toast; Rose ordered pancakes with strawberries and cream. We talked about her most recent job as an admin for a recruitment company. I told her about my new PA and how there was inter-office rivalry over who was stealing all the persimmons from our weekly fresh-fruit box. Normal basic chat. That was when I asked her about her boyfriend, David, and she said they'd broken up. She was thinking about going out with someone called 'AJ'.

'Someone from work?' I'd asked, sipping my coffee.

'No, I met him at a club. He said he wanted to take me to his dad's villa in Greece.' Rose popped a strawberry into her mouth. 'I told him I was seeing someone and he said that was OK, then he found a picture of me at work on Instagram and sent me a Michael Kors bag at the office. Elaine, the woman who has the desk next to me, nearly lost her fucking mind.'

It wasn't the first time Rose had told me a story like this. There was the department-store heir who took her to New York six months before. The stock-market broker who gave her an engraved iPhone and let her use one of his Mercedes while they were dating. I'd tried to ignore it, to discourage her. It just made me feel uncomfortable. As though she was letting herself be bought, usually by men who ended up dumping her or cheating on her. Or, in the case of 'Mr Mercedes', having their car repossessed from outside the office while she was at work. I didn't want to hurt her feelings but I must have pulled a face or something. Suddenly Rose was frowning, looking slightly pissed off.

'What?' she said, daring me to say something.

'Nothing – that's great.' It sounded lukewarm even to my own ears.

Rose rolled her eyes. 'You need to loosen up. It's not like I'm some . . . kept woman. They're just presents.'

'I don't really want to get into it,' I'd muttered, trying to steer clear of the troubled waters, but Rose was obviously more hurt than she wanted to admit. Her cheeks were burning red and she looked as though she'd been bottling this up for a while. I imagined her getting more and more upset over every vague text from me after she gushed about her recent exploits. I hadn't been hiding it as well as I'd hoped.

'You treat me like I've . . . disappointed you, and I can't stand it. So, if you're going to be like that, I just won't tell you anything.'

'It's your life – it's not for me to judge. I'm just your sister, not your mum—'

'Oh, come on!' Rose groaned, shaking her head. 'That's a big load of crap. You've been mothering me since before

Mum died. I get it, you think I'm shallow and flaky. I'm a disappointment. Maybe you should have some kids of your own and go parent them?'

That had hurt. Mum had been ill for most of our childhoods. I'd had to step up and do a lot around the house, including helping Rose with her homework, cooking our meals, and telling her to clean up her messes and when to go to bed. Mum had only passed away a few years ago when her MS progressed to its fatal stage, right before Rose headed off to uni. We'd lost Dad when we were barely teenagers. Killed in his work van on the motorway.

Rose knew how much I'd given up in order to keep things together: missing school, resitting exams, working two part-time jobs at university to subsidize Mum's tiny benefit allowance and Dad's death pay-out. Rose also knew that I'd neglected my romantic life in order to embed myself in a stable career, that I was facing the prospect of being too old for kids by the time I found someone. If I ever did find someone. I was already pushed to the brink, working fifty-to-sixty-hour weeks on the trot. Covering half of William's cases and downing coffee in lieu of sleep. I'd dropped two stone since starting my job, and I felt as if I was trapped on a hamster wheel and she'd just spun it ruthlessly.

That didn't excuse what I said, though. I remember putting my coffee down, feeling my hand shaking a little from anger.

'You want me to say it? Fine,' I said, taking a deep breath. 'Rose, you're acting like some spoiled little gold digger, flitting from one man to the next. Ever since you were at university I've only ever seen you go out with rich, privileged assholes. It never works, you always get hurt and that's because these men think they can buy you – so they don't care about you. And it makes me angry because I know how intelligent you are, how loving and how lucky anyone would be to have you. You got into Cambridge, you got a first! And you're happy to just sit in an HR office and wait for a man to buy you things instead of going out there and getting them for yourself. It's pathetic.'

Rose's face had twisted in shock and then collapsed inwards, eyes sparkling with tears. Before I'd had a chance to draw another breath she was up, angrily tossing money on to the table and grabbing her jacket.

'Rose, I'm sorry, I didn't mean—'

'You did,' she snapped, not noticing or not caring that everyone on the restaurant patio was looking at us. 'And you know what? I'm sorry. I'm sorry that after spending my whole life with your hand-me-downs, I want to enjoy myself. I'm sorry that you think I'm some whore. There's nothing wrong with wanting to be treasured after a lifetime of feeling like a burden.'

Rose yanked her bag off the back of her chair, knocking it over and jostling the table in the process. Her half-finished plate of pancakes smashed on the pavement and she turned, stalking away from me.

'Rose! Wait!' I was almost in tears, my stomach churning with regret. The restaurant had fallen silent, heads turned to watch the spectacle. It was clear from her trembling shoulders that Rose was crying as she ran towards the nearest tube station. I remember watching her go, into the crowd, without realizing I would never see her again. I got up to follow but a waitress appeared and I only had cards, no cash. I fumbled for my purse and paid as quickly as I could, but by then Rose had vanished.

I called her, texted. I wrote a long apology email about how I only wanted the best for her and I was sorry I hadn't thought about things from her side. She was right. I didn't know what it had been like for her all that time. She'd worked incredibly hard to get to Cambridge, had helped care for Mum while I was working. Who was I to tell her she couldn't take advantage of a free trip to Greece? That she didn't deserve nice things if someone wanted to treat her? I'd tried so hard to protect her and provide for her but that day I saw all the ways in which I'd let her down.

Rose hadn't answered my messages. I hadn't worried too much at first. We'd had big fights before, though nothing like this. She'd not spoken to me for three weeks once because I'd been working and had forgotten about her school's musical. She was the lead and had been desperate for me to come and see it, as by then Mum couldn't leave the flat. This was bigger than that and it would take longer for her to want to see me again. So I left it. And left it. Until two months later I was sitting on the floor in her empty flat, holding an invitation to a party thrown by the latest rich asshole, wondering if I could have saved her. Wishing I'd just told her to go to Greece and have fun instead of giving her something to rebel against, sending her all the way to Norway.

I look down at the picture of my sister. She smiles back at me. For a whole year now I've been torturing myself with what might have been, with what could have happened. Had Rose forgiven me? Had she cried out for me at the end? Or had she died hating me? Cursing my name and wishing I'd never been born?

I wipe the tears from my face and carefully dry the picture on my T-shirt. I pack it in my cosmetics case of tricks. I want to have it with me when I get my answers. I want to cling to that image of her, happy and free, when I find out what Lawrence or one of his rich friends did to her.

I zip up the case and lay my hands on its hard outer surface. Am I ready to face what's to come? I have tools for unlocking doors, opening safes and God knows what else. I have a knife and have put in hours at the gym training to defend myself. But how can I prepare for guilt? The knowledge that, were it not for me, none of this would have happened.

3

'GOD,' FORD SAYS, LOOKING out through the car window. 'I need to ask old Lawrence what's so wrong with holding a party in England. Two years since I visited and I'd forgotten how long it takes to get there.'

I make a noise of agreement, but I'm transfixed by the view outside. It's true that it's been a tiring trip, mostly because of the different stages. There was the taxi and then the flight from Heathrow to Oslo Airport – the least said about navigating Heathrow and going through security, the better. We'd been met by one of Lawrence's cars at the airport, a black BMW with the Fowley family crest on its door. The driver, smartly dressed in dark green, had loaded our bags and since then we'd been driving for over an hour.

As always when travelling outside of London, the sharp cleanliness of the air startled me when we left the airport. Inside the car all I can smell is the leather of the seats and the expensive cologne on our chauffeur. The view outside has changed from the colourful cladding and glittering glass of the city skyline to the inky pine forests and unearthly blue waters of the fjord. It's as if we've travelled into a fairy tale – small picturesque villages dot the slopes and ridges of the landscape, with the occasional manor house and manicured grounds reduced to postage-stamp size by our elevation on the winding road. I roll down the window slightly with the touch of a button and air as crisp and fresh as snowmelt rushes in to meet me, smelling of pine and sweet summer grass. Rose breathed this air, I tell myself, and my chest aches with it. I feel closer to her now than I have in over a year. She has to be here still. I can feel it.

Eventually, our driver points out the distant Fowley estate as we approach it on a private road, winding down from the hills. It's my first proper look at it, as no pictures or even satellite images are available online. Lawrence Fowley values his privacy, clearly, and can pay to keep it.

The drive beyond the first set of crested iron gates is bordered by landscaped gardens. Someone has had the place planted and maintained like the grounds of an English manor house. Trimmed shrubs and topiaries look oddly formal and controlled against the landscape of rustic pines and lichen-covered rocks.

The house itself is similarly quite self-consciously British colonial, with white columns and a grey slate pitched roof. It stands out from the dark trees like a ghost, bone white and sharply symmetrical. I imagine that the private beach Ford told me about is behind the house, where the fjord must carve its way onwards through rocky, forested cliffs.

'What fjord are we near, exactly?' I ask Ford, because our actual whereabouts are a mystery to me.

'Idefjorden,' Ford says confidently. I noticed the driver's eyes flick to him in the rear-view mirror. A crinkle of humour there. The name might be right, as he doesn't correct him, but Ford's pronunciation is clearly off. I feel a flutter of amusement at Ford's obliviousness and stamp it out.

'This house has been in the family since our great-grandfather's time. He made his fortune here, after emigrating from England,' Ford says, his voice at once proud and wistful. I can tell it means a lot to him, despite his place on the edge of the Fowley family.

I know from my research that the Fowleys are absolutely drenched in coal and oil money, but I ask Ford about it anyway. He's very proud of the business. Very knowledge-able about it too, despite his side not having anything to do with it. I don't admire much about Ford, mostly because of whom he's related to, but I do find his commitment to the Fowley name endearing. Most men in finance that I've had the displeasure of meeting would con their own gran out of her last tenner to get ahead.

The second set of gates to the Fowley estate open auto-matically, admitting the car to a circular driveway in front of the house. Ford gets out before the driver and comes around to open my door for me. An old-fashioned quirk of his that often annoys me. Today, however, looking up at the enormous house in these secluded grounds, I appreciate his presence. Even if he has no idea who I really am and why I'm here, he makes me feel less alone.

The driver is unloading our luggage when the front doors to the house open and a man emerges. Lawrence Fowley? Pictures of him are practically non-existent but as I look this man up and down I try to match him to the blurry paparazzi shots I've seen. No, despite his expensive clothes: he doesn't have Lawrence's height, and his hair isn't light enough, his curls more brass than gold. The man coming towards us is wearing a tailored suit and round glasses, his hair falling into his eyes. I note his handmade shoes and the sharkskin belt around his soft midsection. A few years at a legal firm and you get an eye for tailoring and for who spends more time at 'business lunches' than working at the office. He's definitely one of those.

Ford has been pacing around the car, stretching his legs. He catches sight of the newcomer and is at my side in moments, one arm snaking around my waist as he greets him.

'James, good to see you,' he says, all smiles. His arm around me is tense, a little too tight. I know a bit about James – Lawrence's younger brother – from Ford, but nothing about his relationship with him.

'Ford.' James nods, but his eyes are on me, the sunlight flashing over them as he descends the front steps, ignoring the chauffeur. 'I trust you and your girlfriend had a pleasant journey? We didn't see you last year.'

'Oh, you know. Work,' Ford says. Though he and I both know that he wasn't invited. Unusual, seeing as he'd been to every party religiously until then – I'd seen the proof on his social media before I decided to approach him. A yearly selfie at Oslo Airport 'off to spend time at the family estate' sort of posts – pictures at the party itself being forbidden, for guests at least.

'Aimes, this is Lawrence's brother – James,' Ford says. 'James, this is Amelia, my girlfriend. Told you she was gorgeous.'

James extends a hand for me to shake, smiling pleasantly. He's younger than me, in his mid-twenties, Rose's age. Yet he dresses and carries himself as if he's a decade older than Ford and me. There's an aura of old money around him that Ford lacks. I suspect it's something imparted by private schooling and calling this mansion his home.

'And what do you do, Amelia?' James asks as he releases my hand, making me feel like I'm at a meet-and-greet with a minor royal. Something about the way he says it makes Ford's hand tense on my side. 'A soap actress? Instagram model?' James says.

Is he trying to insult me or pay me a compliment? I actually can't tell.

'Amelia runs her own business. She's a licensed nutritionist and a fitness coach,' Ford says, giving my hip a squeeze that feels awkward and forced. He doesn't drop his hand afterwards either, but keeps it curled around my hip. Either protectively or possessively, I can't quite tell. I'm not sure why Ford is so on edge – it's not as if James is flirting or checking me out.

'Very interesting,' James says, eyes falling to Ford's hold on me, lips twitching slightly. 'Good stuff, you'll have to tell me all about it later. Well, Erling here will show you to your accommodations. Feel free to refresh yourselves before coming to meet the other guests. I believe everyone's down by the beach. Oh, and Ford, I need to talk to you later.'

James flashes a smile at Ford, then turns and leaves us alone with the chauffeur, Erling, who looks rather put out to have been left in charge of guiding us around. Nevertheless he straightens his dark green cap, picks up two bags and inclines his head away from the main house.

'This way, please.'

'Are we not staying in there?' Ford asks, speaking my thoughts out loud.

'The guesthouses have been prepared for your arrival,' Erling says. 'I believe they were only recently renovated.'

Ford's cheeks pinken and I realize he finds this insulting. He's family and yet has been excluded from the family home, apparently for the first time. I'm disappointed, too. I had been counting on staying in the house near Lawrence and his office or study. I need access to any paperwork or evidence he might be hiding in the house. If something happened here, on his estate, at his party, he has to know about it. There has to be a clue in there – CCTV footage, a list of last year's guests and who was staying where, maybe even photographs. Something I can take to the police to make them finally believe me. Still, I always knew I'd have to think on my feet. I'll have to find my own way into the manor.

Erling takes us across the drive and down a path that weaves between pine trees and soft earth dotted with wildflowers. A garden less formal than that which greeted us. The air under the trees is heavy with the scents of flowers and the lazy buzzing of honeybees. At the end of the path he shows us a chalet, picture perfect and almost twice the size of the council flat I grew up in. Beyond it several other chalets are screened by trees. I can hear fast-flowing water somewhere close, too close to be the fjord itself. Maybe a stream or river. I want to find it charming and picturesque but the shadows under the trees make my skin break out in gooseflesh.

Did Rose stay in one of these? Perhaps even this chalet? I imagine her feet on the same path I now stand on, her eyes and ears taking in this little corner of tamed wilderness. It feels as if she's out there somewhere amongst the trees, looking back at me.

I wonder about the chalets themselves. Why did they need renovating? Was it on a whim, or did something happen that made a mess, caused damage? I feel a shiver travel over my spine.

Ford helps Erling bring the rest of our luggage over and then he accepts the key card to the place. I wish it was an actual key. I've learned how easy it is to fool those readers and I had hoped for a little security while I slept. After all, I can't be completely sure that I won't be recognized, or that my prying won't attract unwanted attention. Ford doesn't thank the chauffeur and I don't want to annoy Ford so I opt for a mute but grateful smile. Erling nods at me and then departs, leaving us on the porch of our home for the next few days.

'Well, at least it's private,' Ford says as he unlocks the door with the swipe card. 'I wonder who else Lawrence has invited to this thing, besides the usual crowd?'

He goes inside but I can't seem to take my eyes off the forest. I've never been a fan of the great outdoors, which for me is anything more woodsy than Hyde Park. I'm not sure I like being this far from the main house. Out here we are wrapped up in the forest, surrounded by hiding places and shadows, without a streetlight to be seen. The trees lean over our chalet, their branches closing over us like withered fingers, holding us close. Despite the fresh air I find myself feeling smothered.

I'm about to follow Ford inside, when I hear footsteps behind me. Turning, I see two security guards in dark green, wearing the Fowley crest and marching towards me over the soft ground. My eyes immediately go to the stun guns at their waists, the cans of what must be pepper spray clipped to their belts and the guns strapped to their thighs. My mouth goes completely dry, my tongue suddenly glued to my teeth. Guns. I hadn't expected that. Very English of me, in retrospect.

'Just a moment,' one calls. 'We need to check your bags.'

My heart is immediately in my throat. Shit. I'd read that Lawrence was intensely private and security conscious. But this is somewhat excessive. I'd thought there might be security at the party, metal detectors or even a pat-down as with concert venues or protective museums, alert in case someone takes a razor to a Magritte. I had not bargained on all my luggage being searched. Even at the airport I'd been safe, thanks to Ford's insistence on paying for extra hold bags. Ford comes to the door and frowns.

'Is that necessary?' he asks, clearly annoyed. 'This is my family's house, for God's sake. I'm hardly going to blow it up.'

The two security guards exchange a look. Their expressions are hard, implacable, and I know at once that there will be no avoiding this. My heart starts to race.

'Our instructions are to search all guests and their bags. Mr Fowley was very specific,' the taller of the two guards says. By 'Mr Fowley' I can tell he means Lawrence, not James. There is only one boss in this place and it seems his will in all things is law.

'We will have to come in, thank you,' the other guard says. I realize for the first time that they have handheld metal detectors swinging from their belts. Before I was so distracted by the guns that I didn't register them. With those there's no way they won't find my hidden RFID encoder.

Ford looks as if he wants to argue but then his shoulders slump and he nods, opening the door and waving them inside. The two guards help to drag our bags in, laying them out on the floor in a line to be searched. My bags are at one end, Ford's at the other. The taller guard bends over one of Ford's cases and unzips it, then snaps on a pair of blue plastic gloves and starts to search it. A tiny wave of relief goes through me. I have a moment to think before they get to my stuff. Not long, but it's something. From the looks of things he's going to be as thorough as airport customs. More so even.

What can I do? They mustn't find my second cosmetics case. The first one I doubt they'd have issue with – it's all innocent enough, or at least looks that way. However there was no way to disguise an RFID encoder as anything that an innocent fitness instructor would bring on holiday. The best I could do was to stash a bag of cotton balls on top.

As the security guards search Ford's bags and he rolls his eyes at me, leaning against the door frame, I think quickly. My skin prickles with cold sweat.

'Babes,' I say slowly, the excuse still forming on my lips. 'Do you think I can run to the bathroom while they do this?'

'Hmm? Oh sure,' Ford says. 'Unless we're to be detained as well as searched?' he asks the guards icily.

The guards exchange a look that says 'We are not getting paid enough for this'. Then the taller one nods. 'The bathroom is upstairs.'

I brace myself and play the only card I have.

'I just . . . need my bag – I have something I need to take care of.' I pull a face, part cute pleading, part embarrassment.

The three men look at me blankly.

'A personal . . . girls' thing?' I add in an awkward ponytail twirl for good measure.

'Oh!' Ford flushes and glances quickly at the two security guards. 'She can do that, right?'

As I'd hoped, all three men look uncomfortable. Just as when I was fourteen and trying to explain my many school absences. Not one of my male teachers ever wanted to hear anything after 'cramps'.

'It's fine,' one of the guards says after a moment of silent, horrified deliberation. 'We will check your bag after.'

'Thank you!' I trill, quickly opening one of the suitcases and removing the larger of the two cosmetic cases. 'Won't be a moment.'

I rush up some stairs to the mezzanine over the living area. As I go I hear Ford comment that the security has really tightened up since he last visited. He sounds both stressed and upset about it. I understand why: this is his family after all. Yet he's being put through the full airport security treatment.

I open the door to a bedroom, laugh awkwardly at myself and try the second door, which leads to a bathroom. Inside I waste no time in opening the case and removing the incriminating RFID encoder, the blank cards and the ceramic knife. Without them, though, the case contains only a bag of cotton wool balls. Incredibly suspicious.

After a second's panic I start opening drawers in the cabinet underneath the sink. Spare toilet rolls and bars of soap, bottles of expensive shampoo and conditioner. Finally I find a huge box of tampons and a package of sanitary pads. I take a handful of each and arrange them in the cosmetics case, then hide the packages back in the cupboard. Thankfully the products aren't a local variation, they're regular Tampax and Bodyform. Products that I could have bought anywhere.

There's sweat prickling all over my body and I know I'm running out of time. Where can I put my contraband? What if the security guys do a sweep of the bathroom after I've used it? My eyes dart around but I can't see any hiding places. The vanity unit is too obvious and none of the drawers seem to come out. Aside from that the rest of the bathroom is gleaming white and empty.

My panicked gaze lands on the window and my heart sinks. I'm going to have to chuck the stuff. I quickly open the latch and look down. Behind the chalet is the source of the rushing water noise, a fast-flowing stream about two feet wide, foaming over small rocks and weathered branches.

Holding the stuff out of the window with one hand, I flush the toilet with the other. The sound of the plumbing drowns out the splash as several hundred pounds' worth of kit hit the water. I swing the window shut, close the cosmetics case and head downstairs with a heavy weight in my chest.

Back in the living area the security guards are finishing up with my cases. One of them quickly opens and closes my cosmetics case, satisfied that it only contains period products and cotton balls. I'm feeling very stupid for throwing out my RFID encoder instead of just leaving it in the bathroom cabinet, when one of them steps past Ford and, ignoring his protests, heads upstairs to the bathroom. I was right, they are going to check it. I feel both vindicated and terrified – what if he checks the vanity and finds the half-empty packages of menstrual products? What if he checks the bin and finds no empty wrapper?

I smile as pleasantly as possible at the remaining security guard and take Ford's hand as he mutters mutinously about 'respect' and 'trust'. If he notices how shaky my hand is, he doesn't comment. I wait for a shout, for the guard to emerge clutching the half-empty box of tampons.

'Are you OK?' Ford squeezes my hand. 'You look pale.'

'I'm fine. It's just a bit rude, that's all. Treating us like criminals.'

Ford nods, clearly pleased I agree with him. 'It's outrageous. I'm going to talk to Lawrence about it, don't you worry.'

We listen to the sound of a cupboard door closing upstairs. I can feel my heartbeats as painful, individual spasms. Has he found the open packets? Is he coming downstairs to check my things again? Or worse, is he heading outside to check under the window?

Ford watches me closely as the security guard walks down the stairs.

'You really don't look well at all,' he murmurs. 'Do you need any painkillers?'

'I'm . . . fine,' I manage to get out. My eyes flick to the doorway as I think of the wild woods and I wonder how far I'll get, if I have to make a run for it.

4

THE SECURITY GUARD LETS out a sigh and looks from Ford to me and back again. I hold my breath, but after a long pause, he nods to his colleague. I try not to let my relief show on my face.

They wave metal detectors over us, finding nothing, and then depart. The taller guard tosses a chilly 'Thank you for your patience' over his shoulder and tells us that they will be checking our devices for pictures before we leave, reminding us tacitly that recording or photographing the events here is forbidden. Ford looks quizzically at their retreating backs and ushers me into the chalet. Probably still offended and perplexed at the increased security measures. As the door closes behind us I let out a long breath. I've passed the first hurdle, but already I can tell this is going to be a lot harder than I'd ever imagined.

As much as I want to rush out and retrieve my contra-band – some of it is probably salvageable after all – Ford doesn't give me the opportunity. He first rants about the security protocols, the indignity of being treated like a common criminal by his own family. Then, after I've soothed him and planted kisses against his brow, he decides he wants to join the other guests. We move our cases to the bedroom and there's no excuse for me to not get ready with him.

While I change out of my travel clothes and into one of my resort outfits, I take in our surroundings. Now that the panic of the security check is over I can appreciate that the chalet really is quite luxurious. There's a lot of natural pine, sanded to a silky finish; the bed and sofas are enormous, draped in plush patchwork quilts and what look to be reindeer skins. The place has been liberally spritzed with room fragrance – pine and cedarwood hang in the air as if the wooden furniture were carved only yesterday.

Outside the bedroom a modern chandelier hangs level with the mezzanine and in the bathroom I note the rain-fall shower and bubble-jet bath. However, I'm focusing on the number of windows and doors, how well sound carries and which stairs creak when stepped on. None, which is a relief. If I have to, I'm confident I can sneak in or out of the chalet without waking Ford.

Of course that also means someone could sneak in just as soundlessly. I resolve to lay a few low-tech traps at night just in case someone gets suspicious and comes poking around while we're both asleep. Just a glass or two left on the edge of a table, where they'll get knocked over in the dark, a nail polish bottle left balanced on a door handle. Kid's stuff, but effective. Very much like the pranks Rose used to play – a cup of water on my headboard, cling film across a doorway, par-tially unscrewed lightbulbs that would turn on and off. At the time her childish games had infuriated me, but now I'd give anything to hear her laugh as I stumble into one of her traps.

With Ford in chino shorts and boat shoes, I feel compar-atively overdressed in the clothes he chooses for me. But he assures me that this is what everyone will be wearing for the welcome drinks and I'm glad to have his input. Despite my well-paid job and good education I have an inbuilt unease around the wealthy. I think he senses that. He's always sure to make me feel as if I belong when we're out with his Oxbridge friends and colleagues.

With Ford's guidance I end up wearing a black swimming costume, one piece, though it has so many cut-outs it's more revealing than a bikini. Over the top I've put on a chiffon robe that hides nothing, but wafts dramatically. I'm also wearing the ludicrous straw hat, at least five grand's worth of gold jewellery and five-inch heels.

I spend a lot of my 'working hours' at the gym, so I'm not concerned with how my body looks. I got into shape so that I'd be prepared for this party, both to impress and to defend myself. I have no idea how much running I'll have to do, or how difficult my quarry will be to subdue if it comes to it, which I'm hoping it won't.

Ford takes in my outfit, beaming. 'You look a million dollars.'

'All thanks to you.' I smile back.

'Just gilding the lily – you're perfect. Though I do think that this' – he takes a jewellery box from his pocket – 'will give you that extra something.'

My stomach drops. Please let it not be a ring. I don't want to get into it – what a mess that would be right now. I sometimes wonder what it would be like if we were a genuine couple. He's handsome and has always been good to me, but I am pretending to love him. Using him. Nothing about this is real, and I can't help feeling guilty. I usually manage to console myself by remembering that it's only for a year. It's not as if we're serious. How can we be when Rose's disappearance has coloured our every interaction? Maybe in another life we could have met under different circumstances. But in this one all I can do is keep it casual and try not to break his heart when I leave. Thankfully, when Ford opens the box it's to reveal a gold pendant in the shape of a seashell on a long, fine chain.

'That's so beautiful,' I gush, turning around and lifting my hair so he can put it on me.

'It belonged to my mother. I've been keeping it for someone . . . special.' Ford threads the chain around my throat and deftly fastens it. The cold shell lands just above my collarbone. It bobs with my throat as I swallow awkwardly, not knowing what to say. In some ways, it's worse than a ring. This necklace means something to Ford, clearly.

'Thank you,' I manage in the end, then turn and kiss him so I don't have to say anything else.

I've known Ford for just under a year and at first I had no qualms about using him to get to Lawrence. He was just a shallow City finance bro related to the number-one suspect in my sister's disappearance. Why would I care about him? But then he started to show me another side of himself, one which makes me feel increasingly guilty about what I'm doing. Somewhere inside Ford there's a sentimental guy, desperate to be loved. It's too late for me to back out now, but I hope that within a few short days I won't need to use him any more. Once I'm gone I hope he finds someone who deserves that side of him, and who wants the rest of him too.

Ford takes my arm and we walk back towards the main house together. This time I'm not distracted by James's presence and the house's sheer size. I notice the key-card lock on the door and the camera above it. I'll need to find a card to clone, if my encoder still works once I manage to get my hands on it. With the camera right there, I won't be able to risk hanging around trying to manually override the lock.

We follow a flagstone path around the side of the manor and I nearly gasp at the sight laid out before me. An elaborate knot garden of minutely trimmed topiary spirals out from a moss-covered stone fountain. The air is filled with the scents of an English rose garden, mingled with pine and the fresh sharpness of the nearby fjord.

Flaming torches light the path through the rest of the equally formal garden, and beyond the regimented topiaries a white sand beach curves away on either side of the grounds. Sparkling turquoise water laps at a crescent moon of almost blinding sand. To the far left I can just see a pristine yacht moored at a jetty. Over to the right is a larger, more elaborate fountain, and as I look I catch a whiff of chlorine. An outdoor pool probably.

On the mosaic patio between the garden and the beach (the Fowley crest in tiny ceramic tiles) there are several bars, sheltered under thatched roofs, like mini cottages. Part of the patio has been left empty as a dance floor, with more torches at its corners. A string quartet is playing on a statue plinth, all dressed in flowing white gowns.

'Wow,' I manage. 'This is . . .'

'Don't worry, it gets better later on,' Ford confides in a low voice. 'Last time I was here, they had a performing tiger on the third night – jumped through a flaming hoop. This is just the welcome spread.'

'A tiger?' I repeat, and for once my confusion is genuine. 'Is that . . . safe?'

'I don't fucking know.' Ford grins. 'That's Lawrence for you. His dad's parties were always extravagant but Lawrence takes it up a level.' He drops his arm to encircle my waist. 'Let's go mingle. I'll introduce you to everyone I know.'

In all my shock over the scene before us, I hadn't really paid much attention to the guests. Now that I actually try to count them I realize there are a lot of people in the garden and on the beach. Maybe a hundred, all dressed to impress. While the men are in linen suits, shorts or chinos and tailored shirts, the women are a real mix of formal and beach wear. Some are already dressed for the evening party in long gowns like Grecian statues. Others are more 'daytime casual' in bikinis and kaftans. I'm grateful for Ford's input. I'm right in the middle of the two categories.

Despite the month on the calendar, it's not cold. Thanks either to the Gulf Stream or global warming it's at least twenty degrees outside and there are several fire pits around as well as the torches to keep things toasty. How warm it'll be by nightfall, though, I have no idea.

As we walk through the guests I get the unsettling sense that they are watching me out of the corner of their eyes, looking away as I turn to face them. As if no one wants to be seen to be glancing in my direction. I catch the end of a head turn, or the flick of someone's hair. It feels as if I've got wine all down me or something stuck to my foot.

Ford snags us ornate cocktails from a passing waiter and I sip the cold drink gratefully, avoiding the sprig of rosemary and gold-leaf-encrusted apple slice bobbing in the glass. I know I shouldn't have more than one – I need to keep a clear head – but it's also been a long, stressful day. One which isn't over yet.

'Is it just me or does it feel like everyone's . . . looking at us?' I ask, trying to make it sound light.

Ford frowns and glances about. 'Probably just wondering who that gorgeous stranger is,' he says, nudging me. 'You look incredible tonight.'

'Thanks,' I say, disappointed that he doesn't seem to have noticed the staring. Though maybe it's just me being paranoid?

'That's Samantha – Sam – Lawrence's sister,' Ford murmurs to me, subtly indicating her with his drink. I follow the gesture and spot a young woman with long beachy brown hair sitting on a carved stone bench and sipping a glass of champagne. She blends into the background a little, wearing a relatively plain dress, dark blue linen. As she swings her legs idly I realize that her feet are bare. She looks as though she'd be more at home at a coastal pub than here, where even the most casual of the 'beach babes' are wearing diamonds.

'She's not involved with the business,' Ford tells me. 'Not like James. She's a bit of a rebel, mostly does volunteer charity work. I think she opened a hospice, or an old people's home, somewhere around here.'

'She sounds nice,' I say, genuinely surprised; from what little I've heard the Fowleys are known for their extravagance and their wealth. Not their philanthropy.

Ford grins. 'I'm sure she does it for all the right reasons and it's just a coincidence that giving money away irritates the shit out of her brothers. Stepbrothers, I should say.'

I nod, but my eyes have already left Samantha. I'm searching the crowd for any hint of the Lawrence I've seen in blurry paparazzi photographs. I only vaguely know what to expect – golden hair similar to Ford's, but on a taller, slightly older man.

'Should we greet the host?' I ask, hoping Ford will point him out.

'Wherever he is.' Ford rolls his eyes. 'No, Lawrence will make himself known when the time is right. Probably not until this evening.' Ford frowns at the guests. 'You know I've always suspected that he doesn't really like being at these things? I suppose he must enjoy something about them, but I hardly saw him at the last one. Like he was happy just to watch from up there.'

I follow Ford's gaze and notice the balcony above the garden. There's no one up there that I can see; the sun is glimmering off a set of glass doors firmly closed against the sounds of the crowd below. Is that Lawrence's bedroom? His office? Just a random sitting room? I'm about to try and tease some more information out of Ford when a couple ambles towards us, arm in arm. The man, tall and glamorous in an embroidered kurta and white linen trousers, makes eye contact with Ford and goes in for a handshake.

'Hello, I'm Zak Bakshi. This is my wife, Ingrid,' he says, in an English accent tinged with a little Norwegian. 'I don't believe we've met before, Ford is it?'

'Ford Fowley,' Ford says, stressing his last name. 'This is Amelia, my girlfriend.'

Zak smiles. 'I know, this young lady's all anyone can talk about. A new face at one of these things is cause for excitement, and on the arm of a Fowley no less.'

So I wasn't imagining the stares. I feel a shiver travel across my skin. Am I imagining things or does Ford look put out to hear that my reputation precedes me?

While Zak gives Ford the onceover, Ingrid smiles at me and indicates my necklace. 'That is a lovely pendant.'

'Thank you. Ford just gave it to me. I love your dress,' I say. It's an understatement, I'm actually in awe. Of all the dresses I've seen so far, hers is a work of art. An ankle length tulle evening dress in shades of champagne and rose with a flared skirt and a hand embroidered sari. Ingrid's arms are sheathed in nude mesh, beaded from elbow to wrist as if she has golden tattoos.

'How do you know Lawrence?' Ford asks Zak.

'I'm an executive at Henley Limited,' Zak answers hesitantly. 'Mr Fowley appointed me personally, after the takeover. I work under his brother.'

It sounds like this is a new appointment and he's a bit reluctant to talk about it. I know, as surely as Ford does, that Henley Ltd is one of the largest businesses in Lawrence's wide portfolio, almost as big as the one his family built. A green energy company he most likely acquired to try and clean up his image as a petrochemicals tycoon. I glance sideways at Ford, knowing that he very much wishes he was part of Lawrence's empire, working for such a significant family business. He would have applied for that job in a heartbeat. He probably did.

'Cool,' Ford says, clearly trying not to look as jealous as he must be feeling. 'I'm in finance, in London. Do you live in Norway?'

'Ingrid's family are from here. I moved for work and luckily we found each other,' Zak says, sharing a soft look with Ingrid. My heart momentarily aches for that kind of connection. But my life isn't about love and romance any more. That was taken from me along with my sister. For now at least.

'Are you sure you were at last year's party?' Zak asks. 'I don't think we met, and I thought I was introduced to the full family?'

'No, I was busy with work,' Ford says, the tips of his ears pinkening at this latest insult. Lawrence invited colleagues but not his own cousin last year. If I hadn't convinced Ford to invite James and Lawrence for a boys' weekend in the Highlands, I doubt he'd have made the cut this year either. Not that Lawrence had accepted the invitation; he'd been 'too busy'. To be honest it seemed as if Lawrence had forgotten his cousin's existence entirely.

'It was amazing,' Ingrid puts in. 'The welcome dinner was in a marquee on the hiking trail, themed after a medieval hunting party. On the final night we were out here with acrobats performing – one walked a tightrope over the fountain and there were fire breathers, sword swallowers . . .'

'Ingrid loves the circus, so she was very excited.' Zak laughs, but his eyes are scanning the crowd, as if he's looking for someone more important to talk to. Maybe even Lawrence himself.

'It was so lovely.' Ingrid pulls a regretful face. 'Such a shame that the evening ended so chaotically. Though I wasn't really surprised.'

'What happened?' I ask.

'Oh, you know. When there's so much excitement and non-stop champagne from breakfast until after dark, things can get out of hand,' Ingrid says. 'We've been to a few of these and there's always arguments, fights. The odd accident.'

'I bet, especially with all the drinking. There'll be some sore heads tomorrow,' I say, smiling. 'A few walks of shame too, I imagine. People hooking up with people they shouldn't.' I'm hoping to shake something loose with that remark: maybe one of them saw something last year – like Rose leaving with a man, or a well-known philanderer amongst the guests.

Ingrid only laughs musically, but I notice Zak's smile has stiffened slightly. He does his best to make it look more natural.

'Accidents?' Ford says, harping back to Ingrid's comment. Has he noticed Zak's odd reaction to my words or does he have his own reasons for steering the conversation away from the subject of one-night stands? 'What, someone knocked out by a rogue juggler?'

Ingrid laughs again. 'No! But someone did fall through a pyramid of champagne glasses. It was so loud, but afterwards he just laughed it off. Drunk, I suppose.'

'Or high,' Ford says. 'I know there's more than champagne on offer most years.'

For the first time Ingrid looks a little uncomfortable. 'Perhaps. We don't take any notice of that. It's not our thing, is it, Zak?'

Her husband shakes his head. 'I'll stick to champagne. Perhaps the odd cocktail.'

Ford toasts him with his glass, but I can see he's embarrassed at this social blunder. I smile warmly at the couple and make our excuses. Ford and I circle around towards one of the bars. I mostly nod and smile as Ford calls out to people he recognizes and greets people he doesn't. I file names and faces away in case I hear anything interesting about them later. He's enjoying being here, I can tell. I suppose he doesn't normally get to spend time at the ancestral home.

'Oh, I see James over there,' Ford says. 'He's waving me over. I should probably go and see what he wants.'

Seeing my chance, I wince a little and shift from foot to foot.

'Do you mind if I go back to the chalet for a sec? My feet are killing me – I should have put my gel cushions in before we came out.'

Ford kisses me and, in the same move, slides his empty glass on to the bar.

'No worries, I'll see you in a bit, OK?'

With that he's gone, leaving me on my own, finally. I glance up at the imposing manor house. One way or another, I'm going to get inside. For now though, I need to pay the river a visit.

I'm just leaving the party area and approaching the front of the manor, when I catch sight of Zak Bakshi again. He's walking ahead of me around the side of the house and keeping close to the manicured grassy edge of the path, muffling his footsteps. Something about the way he's moving feels off. He's walking slowly, furtively. I follow him at a distance as he trails after someone. It's one of the house staff. I can tell she's not an agency bartender, because her uniform is dark green, like the chauffeur's. She's permanent.

As she approaches a side door into the mansion under an ivy-covered trellis, Zak ducks out of her line of sight behind a topiary rabbit in a planter. I quickly follow his lead and hide behind an identical planter. The woman must use a key card, because I hear the soft beep of the reader accepting it, then the door clunks open.

Quick as a whip, Zak is out from behind the topiary and follows her inside. I hurry after him, but the door closes as

I approach. Damn it. I stand in the shadows under the trellis for a moment, glaring at the door, but there's no way in without a card. Zak got very lucky, unless he was hanging around waiting for just such an opportunity.

With no way inside I decide to leave it for now and go after my RFID encoder. Even though I can't follow him, I at least now know that I'm not the only person at this party with an ulterior motive. I just don't know if that makes Zak and me allies, or enemies.

5

I HURRY BACK TO our chalet, still wondering what on earth Zak could be up to. What is he trying to accomplish by sneaking into Lawrence's house while everyone's having cocktails? Did the member of staff know he was following her? Was she letting him in on purpose as a favour, or because they were hooking up in there?

The lawn near the chalet is soft and my shoes sink straight into it, something I need to remember in case I have to make a quick getaway at any point. I struggle around to the back of the building on my toes so as to leave no tell-tale pockmarks, keeping an eye out for any security guards, cameras or other guests. At the water's edge I find a stick and start poking about in the reeds and ferns.

'Come on . . . where are you?' I mutter to myself, alert for the dark plastic case of the RFID encoder or the pale shape of the knife. The water is fast-flowing but I don't think it's so quick or deep that it could have carried either of those away. Maybe the plastic cards for the machine but that's not an insurmountable problem. I could still steal a basic card and reprogram it for all access if needs be.

Only I can't see anything. Not a single RFID card remains, caught on a reed or a stone. No sign of the encoder or even the knife. Abandoning the stick I drop to my knees on the grass and reach my hand into the water, groping around the slick, wet pebbles. They have to be there somewhere; they can't have disappeared.

I feel a shiver pass through me. What if someone found them? They might not know what they'd found. But if security realized the significance . . . Well, if that were the case it wouldn't be long before they put the pieces together. The things were right behind our chalet after all.

My fingers brush against something thin, caught in the roots of a patch of reeds. I know what it is at once and pull the ceramic knife from the stream. At least I still have that. I'll just need to be more careful now.

I pick my way back around to the front door of the chalet and let myself in. Hopefully I'm just being paranoid and the RFID encoder and cards are bobbing in a fjord right now, not sitting on a security guard's desk. I can only hope. There's not much I can do about it.

I figure I have maybe twenty minutes at the chalet before Ford begins to wonder what's taking me so long. After hiding the knife in the lining of my evening bag I set about packing the things I'll need if I make it into the house.

It doesn't take long to retrieve the neodymium magnet from its hiding place with the magnetic face mask. I pop it in my bag and then thread several superfluous kirby grips into my hair in case I need back-up lock picks. Satisfied, I put the insoles into my shoes and check my phone's protected files while I have a moment. I might as well refamiliarize myself with Lawrence's photo before heading back to the beach.

There he is. A blurry shot taken near his penthouse

apartment in Berlin. He's half turned from the camera towards a gorgeous Brazilian model. He's also wearing sunglasses, so his face isn't that visible. There's a suggestion of a sharp jaw, pale skin just starting to tan. His hair is straight, unlike Ford's, though it's the same natural blonde. I suspect if it were shorter it would be curly. Lawrence was wearing it long back then, but I have no idea if he is now. In the picture it's swept to the side, reaching nearly past his ears.

I've looked at his picture so many times. I feel like I'm going through my revision notes right outside the exam hall. There's nothing more that this picture can tell me, but having it here, right in front of me, feels reassuring.

In the same folder as the picture are screenshots of magazine and blog articles about Lawrence. They're mostly gossip stories. I scroll the headlines: 'Fowley Heir Caught with Call-Girl' – alongside allegations of a domestic in the honeymoon penthouse suite; 'Lawrence Fowley in Hot Water over Driving Stunt' – that was when he'd allegedly grabbed the wheel during an argument with his chauffeur on the autobahn. The more interesting ones I'd circled in red: 'Guest at Fowley Manor Drops Assault Claim' – that one hinted at a payoff to a guest several years ago, who'd claimed to have been sexually assaulted at Lawrence's yearly party. I still had no idea who the woman in question was. Finally, the death of a housekeeper was reported. The obituary was dated the year before last. The year before Rose disappeared, the Fowley housekeeper had been driven home from the party (by whom remained a mystery) and once there, suffered a fatal heart attack.

Bergdis Olsen had been eighty-five when she died, so a heart attack or stroke wasn't out of the question. Still, there was something about the incident that felt wrong to me. Maybe it was just because it had happened the year before Rose vanished, also at a party, and I was desperate for a link, some kind of pattern. Maybe it was because of a Facebook post by Bergdis's niece not three months before her death – a photo of Bergdis overlooking the fjord after a weekend hike. Not the kind of activity that suggested she'd shortly drop dead in her armchair.

With my time away from Ford running out, I quickly pick up my evening bag and check my makeup in the bathroom mirror. Rose's eyes look back at me and I meet them with a silent promise. I owe it to her. After all, I'm the reason she ended up here. I'm the one who was so overbearing and protective that she never learned to fear the dangers of the world.

It had to have gone through her mind, I think as I head back towards the beach. There she was, seething over our fight. Furious that I'd essentially called her a gold digger who was wasting her intelligence. Then what should land on her doorstep? An invitation to a three-day party in Norway, hosted by the one that got away. A man she apparently had a thing with at university – when he must have been finishing his Masters. Maybe she just wanted to blow off steam. Or perhaps there was a part of her that thought she'd teach me a lesson – finding not just a rich man but one who was clearly as into her as she was him, to have remembered her after all this time with no word.

Of course, it was only later that I'd found her old phone and charged it up, gone through it, seen her pictures and calendar invites. She'd never told me about Lawrence before, maybe because they were never really together. As far as I could tell it was a short-lived thing. She'd kept a picture of the two of them together, kissing at a university ball. A blurry drunken selfie of their heads bent together, his hand with the Fowley crest on a gold ring touching her cheek. Just a quick snap, but one that she'd kept on her old phone and never posted online. As if it was too special to be splashed across her Instagram.

As I reach the gardens and look around for Ford I wonder if Lawrence invited her because he knew about the candle she still held for him. Maybe he was sincerely trying to reconnect, though if that were the case why didn't he care about her disappearance, why tell the police he'd barely seen her at the party and didn't even really know her? Perhaps he only intended to lure her to his party for a fun hook-up and somehow things got out of hand. Maybe his intentions in inviting her were more sinister still and he was covering his tracks. Perhaps he thought she was someone nobody would miss. Well, he was wrong about that. Dead wrong.

6

With Ford nowhere around I take the opportunity to try and talk to the staff. *Try* being the operative word. For a start most of them are clearly very busy, constantly circulating with nibbles or whisking away dirty glasses, like a swarm of ants in their black uniforms. There isn't really a way to catch one of them in casual conversation. I approach a waiter for a fresh glass of champagne and before I've even finished uttering a thank you, he's turning away to offer the tray to someone else.

I'm also starting to feel a bit worried about the other guests. The back of my neck keeps prickling with unease and whenever I turn to casually look behind me, I catch someone glancing away. Does everyone know who I am? Perhaps it's because I've shown up on the arm of a Fowley, but I feel uncomfortably like a common pigeon in a gilded aviary of hawks.

Still unable to spot Ford, I wander over to one of the bars for a drink. Non-alcoholic this time. I need to stay sharp and remember every detail in case Lawrence decides to make an appearance. I don't want to screw up my chances of getting him alone.

When I reach the bar there's already a woman in a pale pink dress waiting for a cocktail. I hover to the side of her and watch the bartender work. The woman glances my way but otherwise just ignores me in favour of glaring at the bartender, her arms crossed. She's obviously impatient for her drink but as far as I can see it's not taking that long to make.

The bartender sets down a champagne coupe glass and starts to pour. As she does so, the woman grabs the stem of the glass as if to whip it away as soon as it's full. She jostles it, slopping sticky-looking liquid over her hand.

'Ugh! Be careful!' The guest snatches her hand back. 'It's in my stones. Oh, for goodness' sake, they'll have to be professionally cleaned now.' She holds out a hand decorated with multiple diamond and pink sapphire rings, as if perhaps expecting the bartender to kiss them.

'Sorry, madam – I wasn't expecting the glass to move . . . Let me get a napkin,' the bartender says, her quick fingers grabbing one from below the bar. Her hand shakes as she moves to mop up the spilt liquid.

The woman in the pink dress makes a scornful noise. 'Oh, give that here, will you?'

She reaches out to grab the napkin but the bartender drops it on the floor, which only seems to infuriate her more.

'Christ. Can't you do *anything*?' In a flash she's picked up the glass. From the way she draws her arm back, it's obvious she's about to throw its contents over the poor bartender. I can't believe what I'm seeing. I've spent a lot of time in bars in London full of braying City types and never seen this level of bad behaviour.

It's instinctive. I grab her arm and twist, just slightly – a move learned on week one of my self-defence lessons. The irate guest drops the glass with a squeal and I let her go immediately. The coupe shatters across the floor. Her skin isn't even red, but she backs away from me as if I'm insane.

'How dare you!' she hisses, face flaming as she snatches up her pink clutch and storms away. 'Jumped-up little bimbo.'

'Thank you,' the bartender says quietly after the guest is swallowed by the crowd and the few curious onlookers have turned away. She sweeps up the broken glass and goes back behind the bar.

'She was being such a bitch,' I say. 'Are you all right?'

The bartender lets out a sigh, her shoulders dropping. 'I'm used to it. Can I get you a drink?'

'Do you have anything non-alcoholic?' I ask.

Her face relaxes into a smile. 'I can make something, sure. Virgin mojito?'

'Sounds good.' I watch her measure simple syrup and crush mint leaves. She's about my age, dark hair pulled back in a sleek bun. Her accent is Spanish; a gold nametag on her jacket tells me her name.

'Thank you, Elena.' I smile, accepting the drink and taking a grateful sip. 'Delicious. Sorry you have to deal with people like that. Can't be fun.'

Elena returns my smile with a polite one of her own. 'It definitely has its moments.'

'Can you tell this is my first time at one of these?' I say, going for 'all girls together' confidentiality. If she's used to it, she might have been coming to this specific event for a while. I know from my own experience, working as a hotel cleaner in my late teens, that the staff see everything. What's more, they share stories amongst themselves.

'I think there are quite a few new faces this year,' Elena reassures me. 'I hope you have a wonderful visit. I've worked at Mr Fowley's parties for the past four years and they're always special,' she adds, busying herself with tidying away mint stems.

'So you don't work here all the time?' I ask, despite having clocked the agency uniform already. Still, I can feel her opening up a little. This bar is quieter than the others and most people have begun to head down towards the beach. The more information she's willing to give me now, the easier everything will be.

'Most of the event staff are from the same company. Black Diamond Hospitality.' She indicates the discreet logo stitched into her jacket.

'What's it like, working here? Beautiful, I bet. Although you must have some stories, right? These parties are crazy.' I sip my drink. 'Accidents, affairs, you name it. I used to work in hospitality and the stuff we used to see . . .'

Elena shrugs, noncommittal. Her eyes do a sweep of the area behind me. She's on the edge of talking, I can feel it. But there's a flicker of fear in her expression. If I feel as if I'm being watched, she probably does too.

'I heard' – I lower my voice and lean in – 'that a girl went missing last year? The police came looking and everything.' I shiver, as if I'm just another guest relishing some gossip, but I'm focused on her, waiting for her reaction.

Elena's eyes flick behind me, then she dips her head and starts drying glasses. I watch her carefully, taking another sip of my drink. I'm about to press her again when an arm suddenly wraps around my waist and I jump.

'Hey, babe,' Ford says, giving me a squeeze. 'A few of us are going scuba diving before the party – might be fun, yeah?'

Behind me I hear Elena's footsteps as she leaves the bar.

She passes us, tray in hand, on her way to collect empties. I catch her glancing back at me, her expression torn between worry and interest.

'That sounds so much fun, babe,' I say, swivelling on my stool and then pouting at Ford as if in deep regret. 'I'm just worried about fucking up my hair before the party – this took me hours.'

Ford's gaze combs my long blonde hair. Well, some of it is mine. Most of it is extortionately priced extensions. I'm gambling here that Ford wants to show me off at the party tonight more than he wants me to go scuba diving. Otherwise I'm going to come off as 'too high maintenance'. It appears, however, as if I've struck the right balance.

'Good idea. We can always take a private dip later,' he purrs, pressing a kiss to my cheek, one hand fondling my hair. I simper and wave as he leaves, then immediately start scanning my surroundings. Someone else is serving drinks behind the bar now. There's no sign of Elena collecting glasses either. I step out from under the bar's shelter and catch sight of her just as she turns a corner around the side of the main house.

Hurrying as much as possible without wanting to look even more out of place, I follow her. At first when I take the corner and can't see her, I feel a sting of disappointment. Then I spot her moving through the trees nearby, the tell-tale waft of cigarette smoke filtering back to me. Perfect, she's off the beaten path and somewhere private.

The woods around this side of the house, away from the guest chalets, are wilder and denser. I stumble a few times in my ridiculous shoes, tripping over roots and stumps caked in moss. It's cooler under the trees than in the sunbathed formal gardens with all the torches and braziers. My swimsuit and resort cover-up leave me shivering. Even the air is different, the expensive perfumes and sea breeze replaced by dry earth and freshly spilled sap.

Eventually I reach what looks like a mound of dirt covered in undergrowth, the kind of thing a construction crew might pile up and leave behind. Perched nearby on a mossy rock is Elena, smoking as though her life depends on it. Her hand is shaking slightly and I feel a pang of regret for pressing her so soon. Still, I need answers and I only have three days in which to get them.

'Hey, Elena?' I say gently. She still jumps, whips round and looks at me with rabbit-in-headlight eyes. She relaxes a little when she recognizes me.

'Oh . . . hi again. How can I help you?' Her words are measured, still professional, but I can see she knows this won't be some guest–staff interaction. It's clear I've come after her, all the way out here, for something else.

I get closer, noticing as I do so that the ground is littered with cigarette ends. Hundreds of them, a risk given all the dry kindling underfoot. This must be where the staff members come to smoke. A wooden crate half lost in some ferns is cluttered with mugs, a redundant ashtray and a bug-deterring candle.

'I wanted to talk to you but in private,' I say truthfully. 'The thing is, and I don't want this spread around . . . I'm a journalist. I've read the stories about Lawrence Fowley's parties and the behaviour of his guests . . .' I pause, letting the silence convince Elena that I already know everything she has to tell me. A trick from my actual career. 'And I think it's disgusting. I want to help you, help women like you, who have to deal with this. So I need to find out about the working conditions here, the reality of what goes on behind the scenes at these parties. I mean, this' – I indicate our surroundings – 'isn't really what I expected in terms of staff accommodations.'

A chance to complain usually got people to open up, I'd found. Nothing bonded employees together faster than trash-talking their boss, after all.

'Things aren't great but . . . I don't know that I'm the one who can help you.' Elena stubs out her cigarette. 'I really need this job. I'm only here because the pay's better than back home. I have a family and if I lose this money I won't be able to go back to Seville for months.'

Money I can do. In many ways that's easier than trying to ease the truth out of her.

I dip down level with her and lay my hand on her arm. 'Elena, I promise I can pay you for your information. I'll even buy your ticket home. It's just really important that I know what Lawrence Fowley is actually like, and what happens here.'

Elena freezes. 'That's a lot of money.' She looks at me, clearly torn between wanting to help me, wanting to take the money and fear for her livelihood.

'I have it, trust me.'

When I left my real life behind to go after Lawrence I sold most of my things, including my car. Before taking unpaid leave I had a good salary and was incredibly conservative in my spending. Ford has also been generous, something I feel guilty about. But the upshot is that I have more than enough cash to pay.

'But I have to think about next year,' Elena says. 'This is good work for me.'

'You know there's something wrong with this place,' I say, taking a risk. 'Do you really want to come back here when you could just take the money and be done? Go somewhere else?'

She looks torn.

'No one has to know it was you,' I say. 'It's all confidential.' That, at last, seems to work.

'OK . . .' Elena wets her lips and glances around. Whatever secrets she's holding on to, I can tell she's afraid, though of whom or what I'm not sure. Something in my stomach rolls sickeningly. What if she knows what happened to Rose? 'But you need to send me the money first.'

I take out my phone and sign in to my banking app. It doesn't take long for Elena to tell me her details and for me to transfer the amount she's after. Once she sees the transfer has gone through, she seems to calm down a little. She lights another cigarette.

'Sorry . . . I just, I need to know that I'm going to be OK, you know?' she says.

'I understand . . . Now, what is it you want to tell me?'

Elena takes a deep drag. 'I only came here because my friend, Sara . . . she had the idea to travel out here and make money. She and I worked this party the first time, only . . . something happened.'

'To Sara?' I say, my heart thudding violently. Could it be connected? Another woman going missing or being attacked four years ago?

Elena nods, eyes downcast. 'It was on the final night of the party. This masked ball they had – that time we were in the house, but since then all the events have been out here. I don't know if it's because of what happened but . . .' She takes another drag. 'I didn't see her all night. I was serving downstairs in the banquet hall and Sara was upstairs in the gaming room, tending the bar. During the party week all the agency staff live at the old beach house down at the cove. I waited for her so we could walk back together . . . but . . .'

'She didn't show?' I interject, thinking of Rose's disappearance.

Elena shakes her head. 'She did, but she was a mess. She'd been crying and her tights were ripped. She said she'd been assaulted by a guest – someone in a gold mask.'

My insides feel cold and squirm like eels. 'And she didn't know who?'

Elena shakes her head. 'Not for sure. But . . . the Fowleys were the only ones in gold masks. It was a matching set, specially commissioned. The gods of Olympus.' Elena blinks tears away. 'She couldn't tell me anything about him, it was too dark, but she remembered the mask. They looked very similar to each other.'

So, my suspicions were right – I'm not looking for just another guest. This attack, and likely Rose's disappearance, leads straight to the Fowleys. 'How many Fowleys were at the party?'

Elena shrugs helplessly. 'I don't know. I saw them, yes, but like I said all the masks looked so similar, and other than that they wore black suits – except Samantha. I think it was a game to them, that no one knew which was which.' Elena sniffs and stabs out the cigarette on the floor. 'Before the party I saw Lawrence, and James, his brother. I think there were some cousins that year. I'm not sure how many.'

My skin prickles. 'Like the man I was with earlier – Ford?'

She nods. 'Yes, he was there. I'm positive.'

The news hits me in the pit of my stomach. Yes, I've been using Ford and yes, he was irritating on occasion. But I'd never thought he could be the same kind of predator. I shiver. I've been sharing a flat with him, sharing his bed. What if he was the one who attacked Elena's friend?

'Where is Sara now?' I ask. 'Did she go back to Spain?'

Elena shakes her head. 'She didn't want to come back here but she didn't have family at home. She stayed in Norway, running a hotel.'

'She works at a hotel?' I ask, slightly taken aback. After being cornered and assaulted by a guest, surely a hotel would be triggering for her.

'She owns it. A little bed and breakfast.' Elena sighs. 'After that night she got a lot of money from the Fowley estate and they had her sign an NDA. I told her to go to the police, but she said they'd never believe her with the whole Fowley family sticking together. So she took the money and never spoke about it again.'

I feel sick. I had my suspicions, my theories about this place. To have them confirmed so bluntly is something else entirely. What if Rose, my sweet, beautiful sister, fell into the same trap? What if she refused to take the money, was so hurt by Lawrence's betrayal that the family had to find some other way to silence her?

'Do you have a way for me to get in contact with her?' I ask eventually, unsticking my suddenly dry lips. 'She might be able to tell me who brought her the money, the NDA.'

Elena seems to consider me for a moment, then takes out a little order pad and her phone, transferring a number in shaky biro letters.

'You can call her – I'll tell her about you, but she might not talk. She won't want to lose her business or the money.'

'Thank you, Elena . . . Really, it's such a brave thing you've done and . . . I think it has helped me a lot. I'll give you my number, in case you think of anything else.'

We exchange numbers, but as I go to take the piece of paper from her, Elena encloses my hand in hers.

'If you've come here to go after Mr Fowley and his family . . . be careful. There's lots of security inside the house and I don't trust anyone. These parties are wild. He must be mad to throw them, to let people behave like that. He has secrets to protect, his and other people's. He gives me the creeps. I only come back here because I don't have to go in the house any more. I work outside; I go back to the beach house. That's it.'

I swallow. 'Listen, I need to get past the security, into the house. Is there any other way inside?'

Elena looks at me for a long moment. 'I'm not sure that's a good idea.'

'I've got to – it could be important.'

She still looks torn. 'If something happens to you—'

'Then it'll be my fault,' I assure her stubbornly.

Elena sighs, but relents. 'There is another way.' She indicates for me to turn around and I do.

The hill of weed-covered earth is not actually a hill. There's a half-rotted wooden door in a brick wall that is mostly covered in moss and lichen.

'The old ice house,' Elena says quietly. 'There's a tunnel that leads to the kitchen storeroom. The cooks and servers use it to come out here for extra breaks.'

'And no one in the family uses it?' I ask.

Elena shakes her head. 'I don't think any of them even know where the kitchen is. But listen, you really don't want to go in there. If they catch you—'

A noise in the bushes cuts her off mid-sentence. It sounded like the crunch of a twig underfoot. We both freeze, looking around to see who might be spying on us as I panic over what they could have heard.

7

We listen in silence but hear nothing more. It must have been an animal of some kind – a squirrel or a bird. After a long moment, Elena gets to her feet. 'I need to go. But don't go down there – it's not worth it.' She starts walking away but then turns back. 'If you decide to ignore my advice then . . . good luck. I hope you find what you're looking for. If you're right about a girl going missing . . . I can't imagine what she went through.'

My chest tightens and I nod.

Elena picks her way out of the woods and my mind whirls. I stare at that rotten door. Ford is out scuba diving; most of the guests are in the gardens, engaged in activities around the estate or back at their chalets preparing for the evening party. The staff are likely busy too, cooking and setting up for later. This could be my one chance. I might even stumble across Zak while I'm in there, or whatever it was he was after. Still, I hesitate.

Taking a deep breath, I step forward and open the door, revealing a small room and an arched brick-lined tunnel, lit only by faint sunlight filtering in from the woods. There's no turning back now.

I turn on my phone torch ready to step into the tunnel.

What's left of the warmth of the day under the trees vanishes as soon as I step inside. The cool, damp air is refreshing but does nothing to alleviate my nerves. It smells musty and rotten, like our flat when we were growing up. How Rose had cried when she found her 'going out' dress covered in green fur at the back of the wardrobe. She'd hate this place.

I move slowly, listening for movement up ahead. I have no idea how I'll explain myself if a kitchen porter comes the other way for a smoke break. Perhaps I could claim to be exploring the grounds, play up the drunk-guest act.

Thankfully I don't come across anyone. My phone torch lights up the dripping brick walls and the crumbling mortar on the floor until I at last reach a door. This one is sturdier but thankfully unlocked. I listen at it for several moments and, hearing nothing, slowly inch it open.

The room on the other side is almost as dark as the tunnel. I can feel that it's much, much larger, though. There's a sense of space and a draught that smells slightly musty but less like a dungeon and more like a health-food shop – all powders and grains and spices. I also don't think there's anyone in there. Shining my torch around confirms that I'm in some kind of storage room. Part wine cellar, part pantry. Rack upon rack of industrial shelving holds wine, champagne, wheels of cheese, catering-size containers of sugar, flour and every spice imaginable.

I spot the only other door and hurry over to it. I'm grateful for my forward planning as I soundlessly cross the cement floor – all of my shoes, even the high-end heels, have rubber 'anti-slip grips', making them virtually silent even on hard floors.

The door leads to a wood-panelled stairwell, too small

and undecorated to be anything but staff access. There are a few signs about workplace safety tacked to the wall and through a door to my left I can hear people clattering about and calling to each other. The smell of fish, roasting meat and herbs leaking under the door tells me that I've found the kitchen. I continue up the stairs.

My heart is in my throat as I creep around the corners of the stairwell, alert for the sounds. I listen at the next door and then carefully ease it open. On the other side there's a marble-floored entrance hall. Through the glass of the front doors I can see the backs of armed security guards. Four of them posted to make sure the guests stay in the gardens and the chalets, some of which must be divided into smaller apartments to fit everyone. The main house is clearly only for Lawrence and his immediate family.

Some quirk of the elevation means I entered the building at ground level outside, but ended up in the basement. One more flight of stairs and I'll be on the first floor. I wonder where Zak went when he got inside. Is he still here or did he get what he wanted and leave?

What I'm looking for is somewhere Lawrence would keep his private information. An office or his suite of rooms. Blackmail material if one of his guests did something: pictures, video. Deeds or rental agreements for where Rose might be being held. Invoices for building work if he had a secret cell built. A filed NDA. Or maybe in his emails I'll find him giving the order for Rose to be spirited somewhere secluded where she could be contained. My skin prickles at the thought. I've already decided that he's guilty of something – it was the creepy tone of his invitation and the fact that he started all this.

It's been easy-going so far. However, when I get to the next floor, I'm confronted by a key-card reader on the door. Clearly, though the permanent staff have the run of the lower floor, the upper floors are more restricted. Thankfully, it's a swipe-card lock so I still have a chance.

I have a few things on me that might work, but I opt for a credit card, as it's the one I've had the most success with. Up until now I've only tried it on a dummy lock at home and on a locker at the gym. This is probably going to be a little trickier.

I remove the card – an old one of mine with the information sanded off – from my bra and slide it into the card-reader slot. The technique involved is to put the card in firmly and then whip it out at the right speed to trick the lock into opening. It's not guaranteed, but it's the next best thing to having a cloned card.

It doesn't work on the first pass, or the second. I sigh through my teeth but give it another try. It's hard to get right but it only needs to work once for me to get inside. I try again – a third failure – then freeze.

Someone is coming up the stairs behind me.

My mouth goes dry. I can't get caught now, not when I'm so close. I try for a fourth time. No luck. Shit!

The plastic card is slippery with sweat. I wipe it on my clothes and force myself to move slowly, as calmly as possible. This has to work. The footsteps are gaining on me, coming up from the floor below. Soon they'll turn the corner and . . .

The lock clicks and the handle turns under my sweating palm.

I don't even stop to listen. I slide through, closing the door behind me as quickly and quietly as possible. There's still the possibility that whoever's coming upstairs will follow me through the door. I look around for somewhere to hide in the wood-panelled corridor I'm now in. The first door I try is locked and I have no time to pick it. I try a second and it opens.

Inside, my breathing slowly begins to return to normal. There are two doors between me and the footsteps. It's unlikely they'll follow me in here. The room I've let myself into is also blessedly empty. Lucky, really: given the panic I got myself into I could well have walked in on anyone.

The silence that's peculiar to old houses descends around me. A combination of thick walls, plush carpets and discreet staff. It's the sound of secrets being kept. Dust motes stirred by my sudden arrival catch the sunlight seeping in between thick curtains. The very air smells of old money – of yellowing paper, beeswax polish and leather. In front of me, a large and imposing desk dominates the room, surrounded on three sides by floor-to-ceiling bookcases. I'm in a study, and it's fairly clear whose it is.

Behind the desk, towering over it, is a portrait of Lawrence's father. A man who was not as camera-shy as his son so I have a good idea of what he looked like. He has the same curly golden hair as Lawrence and a well-trimmed beard. He's wearing a typically eighties business suit so this is clearly an older picture. In it the artist – who the hell commissions oil paintings of themselves? – has showered detail on his expensive accessories. His gold cufflinks, signet ring and watch all have the Fowley crest on them. Judging from the window in the background, this picture was painted with Fowley Senior in this very office. Had he intended for his son to sit and work under his cold painted gaze for the rest of his life?

The first thing I do is tiptoe over to the other door in the room and crack it open, peering inside. It's just a little cloak-room. Not a way into an adjoining room. Thank God. Only one entrance to worry about.

After creeping closer to the desk and not spotting any nameplate or personalized stationery – clearly too much to hope for – I start opening the drawers. There are blank reams of quality writing paper, an array of pens and office equipment. The screen on the desk is a fancy all-in-one computer similar to the ones used in my old office. I shake the mouse and a password box pops up. I doubt I'll be able to access it. I'm no hacker and this doesn't feel like the kind of place I'll stumble across a password on a scrap of paper.

I'm about to give up and go to search another room when I notice a blinking red light near floor level. My heart gives a sudden jolt. I've been keeping an eye out for cameras and hadn't seen any inside the house, and for a moment I'm unable to see the light as anything but proof I'm screwed. Then my panic subsides and I realize that the light is on a tiny keypad. A keypad on a safe.

It's disguised with wood panelling, but now that I've noticed it, squatting behind the desk, it's impossible to miss. I drop to my knees on the soft carpet and examine it carefully. Keypad means a code, not a dial lock. A shame, really, as I've learned that those can in some cases be tampered with manually. I haven't found a password for the computer in the desk, never mind a code for the safe. So I need another way in. Though unfortunately there's no clue as to the make or model on the presumably custom-made wooden casing on the safe.

If there's anything in the office of any importance, it'll be in this safe. After weighing up my options for a moment I open my bag and pull out the little velvet pouch containing my magnet.

It's a strong one, not easy to carry about with you. The pouch makes it a bit easier to detach it from anything it gets stuck to. Even so, carrying it alongside electronics or credit cards is a no-no.

As fancy as the safe looks in its special surround, I'm almost certain that it's a relatively simple home model – based on size alone. That and the keypad means that it's likely locked with a solenoid: a coil of metal acting as an electro magnet. I've watched about fifty YouTube videos about this stuff and learned enough to know that my magnet can disrupt the electro magnet and open the door – if I find the right spot to place it.

With an ear out for anyone approaching, as if attempting some kind of divination ritual, I begin to move the magnet around the front panel of the safe. I glance at the window as I work. It's mostly covered by the curtains but the sunlight seeping in is definitely turning peachy, a sign that sunset isn't far away. I've already used up so much time, I'll have to get back before too long. Frustration makes my skin itch.

Trying to open the safe is a simple process, but slow. Each minute spent manipulating the magnet feels like an hour. It's very strong and hard to move across the safe, even with the bag over it. I keep thinking about the long way back down to the tunnel, about the exposed corridors and diligent security. The woods beyond with so many places for someone to hide and watch.

I need to get moving. Ford might come looking for me or, worse, raise the alarm. The last thing I want is to have the grounds swarming with a search party.

I'm so fixated on my dire thoughts that the safe door opening makes me jump. It worked! Despite reading about the technique (and seeing it demonstrated online) I'd never attempted it before on a real safe. I quickly stash the magnet and pull out a handful of papers, revealing nothing underneath. It's all just paperwork.

Surely there's something in here? Sitting on the floor and hidden behind the desk, I open the manila folders and scan the documents inside. Invoices, projection graphs, profit-and-loss breakdowns for Lawrence's business interests. Nothing incriminating. Tension courses up my spine. If this has all been for nothing, I'll scream. I might not get another chance to get into the house.

I open another folder and find myself looking at a familiar face. My heart stutters. It's a photo of Bergdis, the housekeeper. A photo in which she is clearly dead.

My hand feels numb and a bunch of the business papers slide off my lap on to the floor. Why does Lawrence have a picture of his dead housekeeper in with his files?

Then I look past the shocking picture and realize it's on top of a printout of a handwritten form. All in Norwegian, but the word 'Politi' and the logo at the top leave me in little doubt. It's a police report. The photograph must be from an autopsy. Now that I'm looking at it properly I can see the stainless-steel background. I shuffle through the papers. Another report but this one has the name 'Tom' on it. The last name, annoyingly, is blurred by a coffee ring, which has been faithfully captured in the scan and print-out. 'S' something, Silverstone? Stockard? There's no photo attached to that one either.

Under 'Tom's' police report is a picture I know well. It's the one I gave the police and it shows Rose at her last birthday, beaming at the camera. The attached police report has her name on it.

With a shaking hand I use my phone to take pictures of every page of the report, plus the photos. I'll have to translate them later, but I'm sure I can find software to help me. My mind races.

As I gather the spilled paperwork and pile it back into the safe, I find a page with a 'confidential' watermark splashed over it. It has a familiar name on it: Henley Ltd. That's Lawrence's biggest eco energy company. The one Zak works for. Yes, there's his name in a column underneath. I follow the names up the page – just a list of men and women and their job titles. At the top is the header 'L. Fowley Information Only' and under that, in handwriting that might be Lawrence's, is just one word – *James?*

I chew my lip. Was this what Zak was after? And what is it? A list of names and jobs . . . it could be potential redundancies. If so, it looks as if Lawrence is cleaning house. Including his brother.

I go back to the profit graph I discarded previously. Things don't seem to be going too badly across the board, except Henley Ltd, which is tanking. It's no wonder Lawrence is considering axing employees. But it does seem odd, especially given that cuts usually start at the other end of the pay scale: the workers take the brunt of the loss, while management cream off the profits.

It doesn't seem connected to Rose at all, and if anything I

now have even more questions. Starting with why Lawrence has invited Zak here if he's about to be out of a job.

I put everything back in the safe and close it up. The lock, free of the magnet, resets. No one will be any the wiser. I'm pleased with my efforts and the police reports offer a tantalizing lead, but frustration and dread gnaw at me just the same. I had half hoped I'd find Rose here, somewhere.

I snap my bag closed and stand up, tense with the knowledge that I now have to get all the way back out of the house again without being spotted. The sunlight at the window is golden now. The evening's party must be starting soon.

I'm halfway to the office door when I hear the faint clunk of another door swinging shut nearby. I have half a second to consider where the noise has come from, before the door to the office begins to open, and I freeze, holding my breath.

8

I BARELY MAKE IT to the tiny cloakroom in time. I'm just easing the door shut when I hear someone come into the study, their shoes scuffing on the carpet. I'm too afraid to move, just hovering by the door with my heart in my throat and my ears pounding. Fuck.

I strain my ears and listen as whoever it is moves around, opening and closing drawers. Yet they don't sit down in the chair. It sounds as if they're searching the room. Is it Zak? Or someone else? Whoever it is, they have me trapped in here and they don't even know it.

With half an ear on the movements of whoever's outside, I take in my surroundings. No window, so no way out except the door. The cloakroom is really just a toilet and sink but it also has a vanity unit in it, as well as a wall full of photographs, all in antique silver frames.

I'm drawn to them because they seem to be from parties, both old and more recent. So I was right to assume that the 'no photo' rule didn't apply to Lawrence. Some are black and white, speaking to the long Fowley tradition of hosting these events. Immediately, I find myself looking for Rose.

The themes change between pictures: 1920s Gatsby bash to Las Vegas casino complete with showgirls. A luau with real birds of paradise flying around, bright blurs in the pictures. There's the medieval hunting party that Ingrid told us about, a stuffed and roasted swan on the trestle table, surrounded by staff in costume. Another picture shows Lawrence feeding a cube of bloody meat to a white tiger.

I examine that picture closely. I can tell it's him from the similarities to the paparazzi shot, but in the framed photo I can see more of his face. He's handsome in a sharp-edged, Scandinavian way – icy eyes and blonde hair around a bone structure as rugged as the cliffs around the fjord. He isn't smiling in the picture, doesn't even seem to know it's being taken. I know he has a fiancée from my research, so maybe she took it, or one of his siblings did.

I go back to the medieval banquet. Didn't Ingrid say that was last year's theme? After scanning all the faces and not spotting Rose I feel a stab of frustration. Maybe she wasn't at the welcome party, or Ingrid mixed up the themes. She said they'd been to more than one. Wasn't there something about acrobats on the final night?

There aren't many pictures after the tiger one. They don't seem to be hung in date order either. I keep one ear out for movement behind the door. A drawer slides closed and something rustles – they must still be searching the desk.

Finally I spot a firework going off in one and, silhouetted against it, is the shape of a tightrope walker, hovering over the fountain. I examine the people in the picture. The foreground is another candid, this time of an incredibly beautiful woman. Her waist-length hair catches the light like a mirror and her light brown skin is flawless, glowing. I only recognize her by the ring on her hand, dazzling the camera lens. That is an absolutely enormous diamond engagement ring, too big to have been bought by just anyone. Lawrence's fiancée, Cecile.

My first thought is that she looks too sweet to be with someone like him. It's hard to tell in the picture but there doesn't seem to be anything mean or unkind about her face. No faint frown lines, no haughtiness. She's smiling warmly and looks fully engaged with the person she's talking to, someone with their back to the camera. My second thought is that she wouldn't be the first woman not to realize the love of her life wasn't who she thought he was. Lawrence charmed my sister and no doubt he can charm everyone else as well.

I glance at the next picture and for a moment I think I'm mistaken. I'm thinking of Rose so perhaps I've somehow tricked myself into thinking I've seen her. But it's not an illusion or wishful thinking. My sister is in the background of that photo. She's at the very edge, cut in half by the frame. Only her arm, her back and a small slice of her face have made it into the image, but it's clearly her. I recognize the crooked heart shape of the hairline at her nape, created by a rollerblading-related accident and subsequent scar. I can just about see the tiny mole near her top lip. From the looks of things, she was smiling as the picture was taken, talking to someone just out of frame. The only part of them on show is an arm in a black suit jacket, gold cufflinks flashing and a pale hand on her elbow. It could be Lawrence, his brother, or just another guest. It's impossible to tell.

Despite coming to the conclusion that Rose vanished from Lawrence's party, seeing concrete proof of her being here sends a shiver through me. She was here, on this estate, at the final party last year. I am right where she disappeared and I am beyond certain that she is still here, somewhere. I can feel it. My stomach churns as I imagine all the places they might have put her.

I reach out and press my fingers to the cold glass over Rose's picture. I want to climb right through it and into the past, to put my arm around her and tell her I'm sorry. Tell her that I'm here to take her home.

My arm falls to my side. I can still bring her home. Too late, perhaps, to stop everything that's happened, but I can still make things right.

I take my phone out from its hiding place in the cup of my swimsuit and snap a picture of the framed photo. I try zooming in on the arm, looking for anything distinctive. That's when I notice that the cufflinks are the same as the ones in the portrait in Lawrence's office. The Fowley crest cufflinks. The person with my sister was wearing what seemed to be Fowley Senior's cufflinks.

A notification pops up, making me jump. I always have my phone set to silent, no vibration. I also don't get a lot of notifications these days as I've cut off everyone from my old life. But the message isn't from Ford. It's from an unknown number.

I think someone heard us talking in the woods. They might be following me, what should I do?

Elena.

My thumb is hovering over the reply window when the cloakroom door suddenly opens and I nearly cry out in shock. I've let myself be distracted and didn't hear anyone approaching. But there he is – a man I've never seen before, dressed in a Black Diamond uniform.

86

'Who the hell are you?' he asks.

'I was looking for a bathroom,' I lie, going for the dumb blonde angle. 'Thought I'd locked the door . . . should you be here?' I ask, realizing that if he's in an agency uniform he shouldn't be in the house at all.

'I work here,' he says flatly.

We both look at each other, assessing. Even if he's on the kitchen end of things, that doesn't explain why he's upstairs. Let alone going through the drawers in the office.

'I'm sorry,' he says, clearly still being cautious but not wanting to be rude to a guest. 'This floor is off limits. The entire house is, actually. Can I ask how you got in?'

'Oh, I followed some woman with a tray.'

'Who?'

'I don't know,' I say with a little laugh, as if the names of staff are completely beneath me. 'A woman.'

He sighs and turns to look back into the room. I read the name on his badge. Charlie. He's quite attractive in a wholesome way – sandy-haired and freckled but too old to be called 'adorable' any more. He looks uncomfortable in his uniform and I notice the creases in his shirt, a tell-tale sign that it's new from a package. He doesn't seem to be a seasoned employee like Elena. Unfortunately that doesn't mean he's naive.

'You just . . . walked in from outside and came up here, past a security door?' Charlie says, eyes narrowing.

'It must have been stuck open a little. I just pushed it, and I'm not that strong!' I pout.

'Hmmm,' Charlie says, as if trying to decide what to do.

I go on the offensive. 'What are you doing up here anyway? Shouldn't you be outside with the other waiters?'

Charlie blinks. So he's not so innocent either. I wonder what he's come up here looking for. Perhaps I'm not the only one here with a vendetta against Lawrence.

'I'm not a waiter, I'm a cleaner,' Charlie says, glancing around the office as if looking for anything out of place. 'I'm . . . uh . . .' He shakes his head. 'Look, never mind – you shouldn't be here. So . . . you know – leave.'

'OK,' I say, still trying to work out what his angle is here. 'I'll head back down to the garden then. Sorry.'

I edge my way past him and out of the door. As I reach the office door I can feel his gaze on me, but I don't look back.

I fast-walk down the empty corridor towards the stairs, listening carefully in case he tries to follow. Ford will be getting ready for the evening party. I'm out of time, but I've gained a little ground and have leads to follow, questions to answer.

Once I'm in the stairwell I tap out a quick text back to Elena.

Don't stay for the party. Go, pack and leave asap. It's better if you're gone before anyone catches on.

A few steps later she responds with a thumbs-up emoji and a quick: *I will. Thank you. Be careful.*

I feel bad for costing her a job and possibly putting her in danger, but once she gets on a flight home I won't have to worry about her any more. She has more than enough in her account now to get home safe to Seville. I just have to hope Charlie doesn't reveal my secret for fear of exposing his own. I'm starting to realize just how many layers of lies this place is built on.

9

FORD IS ALREADY DRESSED and waiting when I arrive at the chalet. My trip back through the tunnel was uneventful but when I reached the woods and found the gardens and beach set up for the party, with guests already returning in their evening things, I realized I'd pushed my luck too far.

'Where have you been? I was worried you'd got lost,' Ford calls down from the mezzanine, brows furrowed. His hair is slightly damp and his face is flushed from being in the sun all afternoon. I, on the other hand, feel clammy with sweat and in need of a shower and an early night. My nerves are strained already.

'I did. I went for a walk and got a bit turned around in the gardens,' I explain, the excuse weak even to my own ears.

'In those shoes?' Ford sounds incredulous, looking at my heels. 'Your poor feet!'

'Yeah . . . that was really silly. I ended up having to stop and have a sit-down and those cocktails must have been stronger than I thought because I lost track of time.' I climb the stairs and stop just in front of him, pouting regretfully. 'I'm so sorry, babes, I know this is important to you.'

'It is,' Ford stresses, clearly still a little het up about it. My insides churn. I'm usually so good at handling him. It's as if coming to this place has shaken both of us up, made him easier to irritate and me scrambling for the right things to say and do. My plans and tricks are starting to fail when I need them more than ever.

'How can I make it up to you?' I purr, batting my expensively extended eyelashes.

He softens. 'No time for that, I'm afraid. More's the pity. Go get ready – do you need any plasters for your feet? I can call up to the main house?'

'I'm fine – or I will be once I've changed my shoes. Help me pick something lovely out, won't you? I want to look incredible.'

'As if that'll be difficult.' Ford rubs his hands over my upper arms, petting me to show he's not too angry now. 'I took the liberty of laying out a few options – we can still be fashionably late.'

I give him a quick kiss and then hurry into the bedroom. I've had a year of practice at being 'trophy girlfriend Amelia', so the routine is second nature now. I refresh my makeup and change my eye look for something smoky with a bit of sparkle. Fresh lip gloss, a spray of perfume and a quick outfit change has me 90 per cent ready. Ford has laid out five dresses and some accessories to make getting ready easier. I pick the flashiest thing.

I spend ten minutes fucking with my hair, trying to get it mussed but not too messy. When Ford gets bored and wanders off I get the magnet out of my bag and pop my phone, credit card and a handful of other useful things into it instead.

My chosen dress is stupidly garish– strappy, long and backless, made of gold sequins the size of two-pound coins, held together with gold jump rings like chainmail. I look as if I'm about to present someone with a car on an eighties game show. The shoes are equally ostentatious – five-inch heels, also gold. The necklace that completes the outfit is practically mayoral regalia: a heavy gold chain with a lion's head pendant the size of a fist. He might have excellent and expensive tastes, but it seems he's not immune to the lure of the gaudy on occasion.

'You look amazing,' Ford says when he comes back into the room, phone in hand.

'Thank you.' I smile, though I already feel nervous about the party. All the staring earlier has sort of eroded my confidence, both in myself and my act. I'm half hoping Lawrence will be there and half praying he isn't. I'm not sure I'm ready to meet him face to face. But there's no going back now.

Arm in arm, Ford and I walk from the chalet back to the gardens. Since I dashed back to the chalet the staff have been busy – the way is lit by fairy lights in the trees and newly placed candles along the edge of the path: the day drinks atmosphere easily transformed into something more intimate and luxurious. I only hope Elena managed to make her escape. The last thing I need is to have to worry about her being questioned.

Several large white tents have been set up on a wide lawn between the formal gardens and the pool. Each one has its two long sides tied open so the guests seated at the tables inside can see the fjord reflecting the stars overhead. The bars from earlier have been moved up to the poolside, where a clear Perspex cover has transformed the backlit aqua water into a dance floor. Out on the fjord several speedboats and jet skis are lined up, perhaps for the evening's entertainment. Night-blooming jasmine drenches the air and the sound of silverware on crockery underscores the live band playing jazz on the patio.

His arm in mine, Ford escorts me to a table in one of the tents. The inside is strung with more fairy lights and on the shorter, enclosed sides a banquet of seafood has been laid out on ice. White-jacketed staff stand to attention, poised over stuffed lobsters, fresh oysters and prawn cocktails. One chef steers a gold serving cart over to a table nearby and proceeds to prepare moules marinière tableside, adding white wine and garlic to the night air.

While Ford looks over a menu card I take stock of the guests seated around us. No sign of anyone who might be Lawrence, though I do spot his brother, James, at a table with Ingrid. The two of them seem to be in polite conversation but Ingrid catches my eye and smiles warmly. I finger-wave back, wondering where Zak is and why he's abandoned his wife at what both of them seemed to think would be a wild party.

'I thought you said these parties were crazy,' I say to Ford, lightly teasing in the hope of drawing out some hint of what to expect.

He smiles slowly, apparently amused by my question. 'Just wait – each party's like a warm-up for the next. By the final bash people have really come out of their shells.'

I try to read between the lines on that one.

'I'm thinking about having the *fiskeboller* – what about you?' Ford asks.

I haven't even looked at the menu yet. I glance down. *Fiskeboller i hvit saus*. Fish balls with béchamel. One of the only Norwegian dishes on offer. More importantly, an opportunity to ingratiate myself by flattering Ford's tastes.

'Sounds like a great choice – same for me.' I smile. 'I'll have whatever you're having for the main course as well.'

Ford nods and flags down a waiter and puts in for two of everything he's decided on – the fish balls, tuna carpaccio and *tilslørte bondepiker* for dessert. I'm hoping that this is the one non-fish item available.

Across the tent, on the opposite side to James and Ingrid, I spot Sam, Lawrence's stepsister, sitting with his fiancée, Cecile. Both women look at ease, sipping white wine and chatting. In profile Cecile is still stunning, especially tonight in a creamy satin dress which makes her almost luminous in the intimate lighting of the tent. Sam is still wearing her linen shift from earlier, though she has put on some espadrille wedges instead of staying barefoot. A heavy abalone necklace dangles over her tanned and freckled chest.

'No sign of Lawrence,' Ford says. 'I'd thought he'd have put in an appearance by now. I wonder what he's doing that's more important than this?'

'Maybe work,' I offer, mostly just to keep Ford talking.

He snorts. 'Everyone who works under him is here. I'm starting to think we might not see him today.'

That makes me feel uneasy in the extreme. What if Lawrence has decided to give tonight a miss? Perhaps tomorrow too? I might not get the chance to meet him, to feel him out. Rose went missing at his party and he's my prime suspect. Either he took her, or he knows who did. My skin prickles as I consider for the first time that he might be occupied with Rose, perhaps busy making another girl go missing.

'What do you feel like doing tomorrow?' Ford continues, wrenching me out of my dire thoughts. 'I thought we could try out the sauna.'

'I haven't seen one of those – is it in the house?' I ask, hoping for another opportunity to look around.

'They're over there, in the orchard.' Ford gestures to a point over to the far right of the house. 'One of the blokes I went diving with . . . Ethan something, he said he tried it last year and it was phenomenal. Apparently Lawrence has the charcoal made on site out of local wood. It's meant to be very relaxing.'

'Sounds amazing.' I smile at him, knowing I can't relax here, even if I wanted to. Sitting there waiting for our food, the back of my neck is hot and I can feel eyes on me. Hear whispers and muffled laughter. It's not just the Fowleys I have to worry about. None of these people are my friends. I have to remember that, no matter how pleasant they might be to my face, they're here to party, to indulge.

'There are some lodges over that way as well apparently,' Ford continues. 'Bigger than the chalets. I would have thought Lawrence might have put us up in one, considering I'm family.'

The dip into resentment is cut off by the arrival of our appetizers. I consider the long rectangular plate of fish balls, presented with a smear of béchamel and two neatly crossed baby carrots. I've always hated this kind of thing; what Rose used to call 'play food' when we hate-watched *Masterchef* on our ancient TV with Mum. Rose had such a scornful way of saying 'smears of things' and making fun of the foams or orbs of flavoured gel. I'd once taken her along as my plus-one to a work Christmas do. The dinner had been exactly like this: turkey five ways with about half a bite of each. Christmas pudding 'air' and an eggnog crème brûlée that had admittedly been delicious. It was a just a shame it was the size of an egg yolk and served under a cloche full of vanilla smoke.

It had taken everything in me not to burst out laughing as I watched Rose's reaction to every course. When the chef came out for a round of applause at the end she'd looked ready to have him forcibly sectioned. I remember now how she'd grabbed my arm as we were leaving, dragging me away from the black cabs waiting outside. We'd ended up following the map on her phone to a Burger King. We were the only people there, in full evening dress, laughing almost too hard to gobble our bacon cheeseburgers.

My chest aches, thinking of Rose like that. Carefree and full of laughter, a smudge of ketchup on her cheek, lipstick half destroyed by a burger bun.

'Are you eating that?' Ford asked, gesturing to my plate. I've been toying with the starter for several minutes and his plate is empty.

'Saving myself for the main,' I manage and offload several fish balls on to his plate. They smell delicious but I'm suddenly not hungry.

Somehow I manage to get through the main course and dessert. I eat half of everything and he probably thinks I'm worried about my figure. After the meal is over we rise and our table is immediately cleared – other guests are waiting to dine.

Ford walks me over the Perspex-topped pool to a bar and fetches me a dark and stormy. My favourite cocktail. I feel a stab of guilt. It's easy to forget sometimes that from his perspective, we have been together for nearly a year: a loving couple with so many shared interests. He remembers my likes and dislikes – or at least the ones I have created to go with my new identity – and he tries so hard. One day, soon, he's going to make someone a good husband.

Though of course, I remind myself, he might be putting on just as much of an act as I am. After all, he was at the party Elena's friend was assaulted at, wearing a gold mask just like her assailant.

'Are you all right? You look a bit out of sorts,' Ford comments after I've downed my drink.

'It's probably the journey catching up with me,' I say as he touches my back.

'It's been a long day.' Ford looks around, to where some guests are now dancing. 'Do you want to get an early night? Start fresh tomorrow?'

I do, but at the same time I'm too wired to sleep. There's also the possibility that Lawrence will still make an appearance. I might miss my only chance.

'I think I just need to get a bit of air, somewhere quiet,' I say, hoping that I can shake Ford for a while and do a quick circuit of the party. 'But if you want to mingle . . .'

'I should probably do my duty, but I'll come and find you later – go have a sit and a drink, rest your feet for dancing.' He kisses me quickly on the cheek and watches with a smile as I walk away.

Once I'm out of his eyeline, I do a circuit to satisfy myself that Lawrence isn't anywhere in the gardens and grab another drink from a passing waiter. I look up at the balcony that hangs over the party and notice that the glass doors behind it are open, yellow light spilling out into the darkness. He's probably up there, watching us. My insides twist at the idea. I wonder how many cameras he has set up to watch the crowd. He could have already recognized me and be planning his next move. If he has a file on my sister, he might put two and two together and work out who I am. My palms feel sweaty despite the cool evening air. Lawrence has taken on the attributes of a mythical monster in my mind: everywhere and nowhere, all-seeing and all power-ful. Perhaps he's less of a monster and more of a god. Here I am, trapped in his own private Eden.

Not wanting to stand out in the crowd by myself I navi-gate my way down to the beach. There are only a handful of people on the white sand and I soon leave them behind. I've shed my shoes and the sand is cool under my bare feet as I wander into the darkness, breathing in the crisp night air. It's cooler still down here by the water, but not by enough to be uncomfortable. I'm refreshed as I let the fake smile slip from my face and allow my shoulders to hunch slightly. It's a relief to not have to worry about my movements or how I look from all angles.

Aside from a few flaming torches at the edge of the beach there's no illumination. All the better to see the light display taking place on the water. The speedboats and jet skis are now in motion, decked out in coloured lights, pulling water skiers behind them, also outlined in lights. Fireworks go off in the background, briefly illuminating a large yacht, from which shadowy staff members are letting off the explosives. As the embers fall and die in the water, a shiver of dread creeps up my spine. I feel as if I'm being watched again, even here, away from everyone. Away from the woods with their shadows and row upon row of trees to hide any number of spies.

That's when I hear the soft tread of footsteps on the sand behind me.

I freeze, unable to turn, my body refusing to do what I want.

Another firework lights up the sky.

'Beautiful, aren't they?'

The voice is as cold as the breeze coming in off the sea. It sounds oddly familiar, but I can't place it. Maybe it's just because he sounds like his brother, like his cousin. That same well-bred, accentless voice, sharp and clear as glass.

I finally turn, my movements slow and clumsy. Standing not five metres away, leaning against the wooden post of a tiny jetty, is Lawrence Fowley.

10

I KNOW IT'S HIM immediately. Even in the dark, even with-out having ever seen an entirely clear picture of him. It's not his appearance that gives him away, it's his voice. His manner. There can be no question that the source of that velvety, slightly bored voice could be anyone but the owner of everything around us. His lazy lean against the jetty, his nonchalant smile. He's not trying to impress anyone; every-one is trying to impress him.

He takes a drag on a cigarette and his sharp bone structure is thrown into harsh relief in the red glow of its tip. His hair is even longer now than it was in the picture. Not ratty and uncared-for, but healthy and the colour of fresh sawdust. I knew from reading about him that he was attractive, but that's different to seeing him in person. He is breath-taking – practically hewn out of marble. I can't understand why he's so camera-shy when he could be an A-list actor with looks like that. His cheekbones are high and his skin is so perfect I almost think he might be wearing makeup. He's wearing a classic dinner jacket, but his tie is undone, hanging over his slightly unbuttoned shirt. His bare feet are half buried in the loose sand.

'They are,' I manage finally, recovering from the shock of seeing him. 'Clearly our host spares no expense.'

He sighs, as if I've disappointed him. 'Don't do that.'

I tense. 'Do what?'

'You know who I am,' Lawrence replies, sounding bored but not annoyed. 'Everyone does. It's quite exhausting.'

I let a beat of silence pass. How to handle him? He's clearly more complex than Ford. I can feel him toying with me but I can't quite guess at his purpose. The fact that he so blandly batted away my first attempt at getting round him has unnerved me. I'm used to flattery working, but perhaps the head of the Fowley family doesn't need his ego stroking. Maybe he's craving someone a little more genuine?

'I'm . . . sorry. I wasn't sure if you wanted to remain anonymous, as you're all the way over here and not at your party. I can leave, if you like?' I take half a step backwards, nibbling my lip and playing the shy outsider.

'No need,' Lawrence replies, sounding breezier now. 'I'm quite glad it's you, actually. Finally, a chance to meet the famous Amelia.'

I'm already on the edge of chilly in my ridiculous gold dress, but his words send a shiver over me. He sounds as if he knows exactly who I am, and why I'm here.

'Ford has told me all about you, of course,' Lawrence continues. I relax a little, but with the relief comes disappointment. 'He was most insistent on bringing you along this year. You've clearly made a big impression on him in the months you've been together.'

It's hard to decode the minute stresses in his light tone. There's an edge of suspicion, but it could just be that I'm dating his cousin – a humble fitness instructor with a Fowley. He's bound to have some concerns.

'Well, thank you for inviting me. And Ford. He told me it had been a while since he'd seen you all,' I say blandly.

Lawrence draws on his cigarette, watching me. 'That is unfortunate. Sadly I'm often so busy with the business that I forget to reach out to the less immediate members of my family. I was unable to take him up on his invitation to the Highlands, though James had an excellent time. I understand that was your idea?'

Again I feel as though he's picking at the edges of me, as if I'm a stubborn sticker and he wants to see what's underneath. 'I just know how important family is. To Ford. How much he was missing you all.'

Lawrence nods again, as if he knows this all already and I'm boring him. My heart is beating too fast; I'm glad it's dark and he can't see how tense I am. How hard I'm trying to keep up a front in his presence. At least, I hope he can't see.

'It is indeed important, which is why I'm willing to offer you half a million pounds to drop this charade and leave my cousin alone.'

My heart nearly stops beating. 'I . . . I don't know what you mean.'

He sighs. 'My cousin is not overly wealthy, merely comfortable. I guarantee you that anything he's offering you won't match what I'm willing to hand over as a one-off payment. Your . . . arrangement with Ford can end tonight if you just admit why you're really here and take the money.'

He thinks I'm a gold digger. That I'm using Ford for his money. I have prepared for exactly this kind of accusation. Drawing myself up and putting my shoulders back, I adopt an expression of outrage and hurt that I've practised in the mirror.

'How dare you?' I say, softer than the waves lapping at the shore. 'I don't want your money. Or his.'

'But you are wearing quite a lot of it,' Lawrence says flatly. 'Three-quarters of a million – final offer.'

I laugh, removing the heavy gold necklace from around my throat. I hold it out to him. 'Ford might not be a billionaire, but he works hard and, yes, likes to buy me things, but he can return it. Return all of it. I'm perfectly happy with just him – and you can take your money and fuck off.' I toss the necklace at his feet and storm off, but I only get two paces before Lawrence calls me back.

'Amelia?' He doesn't yell, just calls my name and waits. I turn and watch as Lawrence stubs his cigarette out on the jetty's railing and returns the end to a metal case.

I glare at him as he walks towards me, unhurried. When he gets close enough he offers me the cigarette case.

'I don't smoke.'

'Me neither, in the house. Makes the staff unhappy,' Lawrence says. 'Can I offer you a drink instead, to . . . apologize for my little test?'

He steps to the side and I spot the shadowy shape of a basket on the sand. The neck of a bottle poking up out of it. Heedless of his expensive suit, Lawrence sits down on the jetty, legs dangling in the fjord, trouser cuffs and all. He pulls the bottle out of the basket and pops the cork, catching it deftly and tossing it into the basket.

'That wasn't funny,' I say stiffly. 'You can't just try and buy people off like that.'

'I'm sorry. It just seemed necessary, given how fond Ford has grown of you, and so quickly.'

I take a seat beside him. He helps me down with one

hand, then offers me a glass of cold champagne. 'Please for-give me. I sometimes take my role too far, but I would do anything to protect my family. Which, from the way Ford has spoken of you, may well include you, before too long.'

This wasn't what I was expecting. I'd imagined the rich and notorious Lawrence Fowley to be grand, imposing. A titan of industry with no time for fools and an ego the size of his estate. There's something non-threatening about him now, as if his steely, impossibly beautiful exterior was just a show. And beneath it he's a charmer who's out of place at his own party. If it's an act, it's a good one. My stomach tightens as I realize it's just the kind of act that would have worked on Rose. Like me, she'd have found him charming, romantic. Was this how he lured her too? I hold the glass of champagne but don't take a sip.

'I saw your fiancée, Cecile? She's very beautiful,' I say inanely, still playing the part of the nervous girlfriend.

'She is, isn't she? I sometimes wonder what on earth I've done to deserve her. It was probably something in a past life.' Lawrence smiles slightly. 'She's one of very few people who tell me the truth, rather than what I want to hear. One of my oldest friends.'

'Are you planning to have the wedding here?' I ask, slightly thrown by his response and how self-deprecating it was.

'Most likely. Cecile loves this place. I expect it'll all happen very soon.'

He sounds as though he's discussing someone else; as if he's a guest at this party and Lawrence Fowley's marriage is no more a concern for him that it is for anyone else here. Less so, even.

'You don't sound too excited,' I say, going for cheeky but sounding more accusatory than I'd intended.

He waves a hand airily. 'Oh, it's hard to maintain excitement for an occasion that's been so long in coming. Cecile and I had been scheduled to marry before we were scheduled to be born. Lots of history between our families. A lot of promises.'

Time to push a little. 'You've got a lot of history yourself, I hear.'

Lawrence laughs politely. 'I am not unfamiliar with the gossip about myself. James takes great pleasure in keeping me informed . . . What did you happen to hear about me?' His tone is still light but there's a sharpness to it now. He turns to look at me as if he's seeing me in a new light. The hair on the back of my arms stands on end in the cool night air and my skin crawls with the fear of being found out.

'I suppose most of it's just magazine filler,' I say with a shrug. 'That stuff about you grabbing the wheel from your driver . . . and I heard from one of the other guests that someone at one of these parties got attacked a few years ago. A waitress? That must have been awful.'

He's still watching me, eyes sharp and unblinking.

'Miss Knox, I'd heard you were a personal trainer – but you have truly missed your calling as a police sergeant. Or a journalist perhaps. Sorry to say that the rumours about me are mostly made up by money-hungry strangers. Though some do have a sliver of the truth about them. On the autobahn, for example, I was forced to grab the wheel when my driver suffered an absent seizure. Apparently he'd had the condition for years, albeit undiagnosed. He's now medicated and on indefinite paid leave.'

'Generous of you, since he nearly cost you your life,' I say, not believing a word of it.

'And his as well. Ford will be very happy you're taking such an interest in the family lore.'

I notice that he's made no attempt to address the other 'rumour' I brought up. Perhaps he didn't feel the need to, or perhaps he has no excuse for that one. I can't tell. In fact as the conversation continues I'm having a hard time marrying the idea of Lawrence that I've formed over the past year with the man sitting beside me, sipping champagne with his feet in the water. He's certainly lying or, at least, not telling the complete truth. But I have no idea why.

'You're not what I'd pictured,' Lawrence says, interrupting my train of thought.

'Neither are you.'

'I'll admit the impression James gave me of you earlier was a tad on the insensitive side, but you don't quite match with Ford's glowing report either.'

'Sounds very complimentary,' I say, injecting just a tang of acid into my words.

'Oh, it is. Very. James took you for a standard piece of arm candy – though the term he used was not quite so polite. He's a suspicious type, that's why he's such a good accountant. Ford calls you sweet and incredibly kind. But that's not you either, is it?'

I swallow, speechless, as for once I have no idea what to say. What to do.

Lawrence abruptly gets to his feet, leaving the champagne bottle on the decking beside me. I'm reeling from his words and when he offers his hand to help me to my feet I take it before I can think better of it. It's soft, which I was expecting, but there's a strength in his fingers that surprises me. The scent of his cologne, warm and expensive, curls through the air. Tobacco and juniper.

'You and Ford must join the rest of the close family on my yacht tomorrow. I expect you'll find it most interesting. Seeing us all together. One big happy family.'

As much as the prospect fits into my plans to get closer to Lawrence, I keep my cards close to my chest. 'I'll ask Ford.'

'You'll be there,' Lawrence says, not angrily but in a tone that leaves no room for dissent. 'Family is the most important thing, after all. Don't forget that. Goodnight, Amelia.'

With that, Lawrence strides away over the sand, his black suit quickly swallowed by the darkness. I stand there, a bottle of champagne and two untouched glasses at my feet, wondering what's just happened. There was definitely a skirmish, if not a full battle. But I honestly can't tell which one of us has won. Though I have the sneaking suspicion it wasn't me.

Family is the most important thing. Don't forget that.

My thoughts trouble me as I pick my way back to the party, unsteady on the sand. Not much has changed in my absence. Everyone is still drinking and dancing. Yet as I work my way through the crowd I am more aware than ever of how the other guests stop talking and look my way as I pass. As if I am not really a guest so much as a tame animal that has been allowed to roam amongst them. I can feel eyes on me as I accept a glass of champagne and try to find a suitable spot to stand, searching for Ford.

I'm sipping my drink, trying to make it last, when a hush spreads that has nothing to do with me. A wave of quiet that passes over the crowd of guests like a spell. I look on in confusion while they turn towards the manor as if on some signal that I can't hear. When I follow their gazes I freeze. My grip tightens automatically on my champagne flute.

There's a figure at an open sash window on the second floor. The man – because it is a man, I can tell from the suit trousers, dark against the white stone – has his legs dangling out and over the ledge.

Someone, possibly a staff member, must move one of the spotlights because suddenly the figure is lit up clear as day. It's Zak Bakshi, squinting and shielding his eyes from the bright light.

The silence has dissolved into whispering. Some panicky; some clearly intrigued, even entertained. Do they think this is part of some show? I don't think it is. My skin is crawling with unease. Something about the crowd seems strange. It takes me a moment to realize that it's the absence of phones being held up and flashes going off. If cameras weren't banned at this party I know everyone would be recording, wanting to catch whatever happens next.

For my part I'm wondering if Zak has been in the manor house since I saw him sneak in by the side door. That was during the welcome drinks. Surely he can't have been there that long. I hadn't come across him. Perhaps he lifted a swipe card and went back in during the party, hoping to find the place emptier?

'Zak!' I jump as Ingrid's voice flies up from the crowd, sharp with anxiety. 'What are you doing?!'

Zak looks down at us as if he's not really seeing the crowd below. His expression is so dazed that I'm not even sure he's aware of where he is or what he's doing. He leans forward, swaying on the ledge, and the crowd gasps as one. A wave of tension ripples through the people around me as they realize what's happening. Though looking at their expectant faces, I'm not sure they're hoping for a good outcome for the man above.

'Zak . . .' Ingrid says again, and this time I spot her in the crowd, looking up. Her face is a mask of horror, her eyes wide. She screams; the crowd sucks in air all at once. I see a flash of movement. Everyone takes a half-breath. Then I hear a noise like nothing I've ever heard before or want to hear again. The crunch of a body hitting flagstones from two manor-house storeys up. Bones breaking, a skull shattering.

Someone, far back in the crowd, cheers drunkenly. As if Zak's fumbled a cafeteria tray. They're quickly shushed but there follows a smattering of laughter, smothered and guilty. I only hope Ingrid, sobbing and fighting her way to her husband's body, doesn't hear it.

The crowd around me starts to move as staff direct everyone away. People rush to Zak's side and the guests either gather to watch or wander off to some other distraction. I look up at the window. There's no one there, though if Zak were pushed whoever did it wouldn't have hung around.

Slowly, feeling as if I'm trapped in a nightmare, I approach the gaggle of people on the patio. Ingrid is wailing and I can see blood smeared over her clothes, already soaking into the stones. None of the staff seem to know what to do. One calls for a tablecloth and two more try to haul Ingrid away. A waiter, his face grey with shock, feels for a pulse. Even though Zak's whole face is caved in.

Finally I find myself standing close enough that I can smell the alcohol wafting from Zak's body. Bourbon or

Scotch, I'm fairly sure. Was that what had him reeling, hanging out of a window for some air without seeming to know what he was doing? Or is there more to it?

I came to the Fowley estate to find my missing sister, but in doing so, I may have made myself a witness to a murder.

11

'AMELIA!'

I flinch as someone wraps their arms around me, pulling me away. It takes a second for me to recognize Ford's voice, his cologne wrapping around me, reassuring and familiar. I am feeling numb and shaken to the core. A man just died in front of me. I heard his bones crack.

'My God, I can't believe . . . Jesus Christ, what a nightmare!' Ford babbles. 'Come away, you shouldn't have to see that. I'll get you a drink. You're probably in shock.'

I must be, because I let him lead me away and park me on a bar stool. The person manning it must have hurried off to help with the crisis. Ford fumbles with the bottles and hands me a glass of orange juice heavily mixed with vodka. I down a good amount before remembering that I'm meant to be keeping a clear head. Especially now that there's been a death right in front of me.

'What the hell was he doing in the house?' Ford mutters to himself, stroking my hair absently. 'How did he even . . . God, Lawrence is going to lose his mind.'

'Did you see that?'

I twist and catch sight of Sam, still gaping at the house as she leans against the bar as if for support. The scent of weed wafts off her like musky perfume.

'That was . . . What the fuck happened?' she mutters, blinking erratically. 'What do we do?'

'I don't know . . . Where's Lawrence?' Ford asks.

Sam shakes her head helplessly. 'No idea. Inside maybe?'

I can't quite manage to put the words together to tell them that I just saw him down on the beach. He could be anywhere by now, though. I peer past Ford at the guests who have mostly resumed their chatter, gathering in little knots and occasionally glancing at the activity on the patio. As if Zak's sudden, gory death is just another amusement to be discussed.

'They don't care,' I mutter, so numb with shock that I can barely feel my lips move.

'Hmm?' Ford follows my gaze and shakes his head. 'They're probably all too drunk to really grasp what's going on. Come on, let me get you to bed. You're shaking.'

'I'll find James and . . . try to get the staff organized,' Sam says, and hurries off.

Ford shepherds me away from the bar and along the path towards the front of the manor. We don't meet anyone on our way to the chalet and I'm barely present as Ford helps me out of my clothes and into my nightwear. He tucks me into bed and brings me water along with the packet of sleeping pills from the bedside drawer. I actually got them prescribed in case I needed to knock him out with them, but I pretend to take one for his peace of mind.

'I should go and see if they need help.' Ford sighs. 'The family should be together on this. Will you be all right here?'

I nod, and he gives me a small smile of reassurance. 'I'll see you later. Sleep tight.'

I listen as he heads downstairs and leaves the chalet. After spitting the pill out and flushing it, I lie back down and try to get hold of myself. Maybe it was all just an accident, but I can't deny that it feels sinister. Not to mention how strange Zak had looked when I joked about affairs earlier. And what was he after when he snuck into the manor? Both of us broke the rules today and went out of bounds. Now he's dead.

I can't quite see the whole thing: there are too many unanswered questions. I have the sudden thought that this may mean this whole thing will be cancelled, the guests sent home. As awful as it makes me feel, I find myself hoping that things don't go that way. I've done so much to get here, I'm not ready to leave yet.

The vodka and the exhaustion that follows the adrenaline rush slowly lull me to sleep. At least without the pill in my system I'll be able to wake up if someone comes in. Or so I hope.

In practice, I wake up the next morning with Ford in bed beside me and no memory of him returning. If anyone had come to kill me in the night I'd probably have slept right through.

'Hey,' Ford says sleepily, sitting up with a wince. 'God, last night was a nightmare. Thank fuck it's over.'

'Over?' I frown. 'What happened?'

Ford, already climbing out of bed, shrugs as he finds his robe. 'Ambulance came, confirmed what we already knew – Zak was dead the moment he hit the ground. Poor bastard. They took him away and last I saw the staff were hosing the patio down while Sam, James and I got the guests to keep their distance.' He sniffs. 'Bunch of ghouls, that lot.'

'Did Lawrence help?' I ask.

'I didn't see him.' Ford finishes tying his robe. 'I image he was inside by that point. I didn't see Zak's wife, so maybe he was calming her down.'

My stomach twists at the idea of poor, devastated Ingrid being left alone with Lawrence. Like handing a crying child to a boa constrictor. He might have been charming when we met but he was hiding something. I don't want Ingrid to be next.

A thought occurs to me. 'They hosed off the patio? What about the police? Won't they need to see where it . . . happened?'

'Police?' Ford's eyebrows shoot up. 'It was an accident. We all saw what happened – he was drunk and he fell.'

'But even so . . . isn't it normal to call the police?' I ask, knowing full well the answer. Even if it wasn't legally required, surely it was as ingrained an impulse as calling an ambulance. But then these people are a law unto themselves. Wealth does that.

Ford just shrugs. 'I wouldn't know. Anyway . . . hopefully that's all behind us now and things can carry on as planned.'

I'm sickened by the relief that floods through me when he says that. I have a mission here and I can't give up on it because of Zak's death, even if that makes me feel as ghoulish as the rest of the guests. Maybe I can even find out what really happened up at that window. After all, it may well be related to my own reasons for being here.

'Right . . .' I say, rallying myself and climbing out of bed. 'By the way, I met Lawrence last night and he invited us out on his boat today. For cocktails.'

Ford looks at me, dumbfounded. 'He . . . what?'

Just then someone knocks at the door downstairs. Ford's attention splits between me and the sound, but after a second he dashes off and I hear him talking to someone. He returns with a breakfast tray and sets it on the bed, his expression still somewhat awed.

'You're sure he invited us?' Ford asks as if I might be playing a trick on him.

'Yes, he definitely said we were both invited, but I mean . . . it'll probably be cancelled now, right?' I say, picking up a fork and toying with some fruit salad. My stomach is grumbling but I'm still not feeling great.

'No! It won't be – if it had, Lawrence would have let us know. A card with breakfast or a message from the maid. No, it's still happening. OK . . . fuck.' Ford jumps up off the king-size bed and starts pacing the room. 'What shall we wear? We haven't brought anything for this! Cocktails, on a yacht? What is that, casual, resort . . . formal?'

He's almost cute, panicking like this, I think, despite myself. Dress codes and etiquette always seemed so natural to him; now he's worried because it's Lawrence. Though to be honest I feel it too, a gnawing inside me as though I'm about to go on stage in a half-rehearsed role. That added unease on top of the residual shock of Zak's death makes my throat constrict and I put down my fork.

'They're your family: I'm sure casual is fine. Besides, if Sam is going to be there you won't be the only person dressed down. She was very casual last night and no one batted an eye.'

Ford nods but still looks anxious. 'But Sam's Sam. You know? She's not . . .'

He wants to say 'rich' but doesn't want to look like an asshole. I can tell.

'As versed in etiquette?' I substitute.

Ford nods, looking grateful. 'Exactly! She rocked up to the party last night in her day clothes. She's not playing to the same rules as the rest of us. Which is fine for her – she's Lawrence's step-sister. But I'm a guest here. There are standards.' Ford chews the side of his thumb and looks me over. I'm still in the white silk cami and shorts pyjama combo he put me in last night. God, how I miss sleeping in flannel bottoms and roomy T-shirts. These days I'm almost always cold.

'What do you want to wear?' Ford asks.

'Whatever you want me to,' I say without thinking, and he looks a little put out that I don't want to play the game with him and conspire over my wardrobe.

Ford dives into the bathroom for a shower and I take the opportunity to find my 'day bag' – a wicker clutch – and hide my ceramic knife and a few items inside: a nail file, credit card and a few pins just in case I get the opportunity to go exploring. There, I've also picked a bag and I show it to Ford when he returns.

'I'll find an outfit that goes with it – great choice,' he says, and I take the bag with me, discreetly, so he can't look through it.

By the time I've used the bathroom, Ford has wolfed down most of the breakfast tray and laid out an outfit for my approval. It's casual, but perversely also one of the most expensive. The ragged jean shorts are designer and cost just shy of two grand. The cropped T-shirt is Alexander McQueen and the ankle-length crochet cover-up was handmade for the runway at last year's London fashion week. My outfit is worth over ten grand even before adding half a pound of twenty-four-carat layering necklaces, a handful of matching gold rings and the Vivien Sheriff straw hat. It feels wrong to be dressing up and planning a fun day out less than twelve hours after watching a man fall to his death.

Finally, once Ford has dressed in a striped shirt, chinos and designer shades, we leave the chalet and head to the beach. The yacht, previously far out on the fjord, is now waiting at the larger jetty. There are several figures already on deck and I can pick out Sam, Cecile and James among them. However, there's no sign of Lawrence.

'Ford, Amelia – Lawrence said you'd be coming,' James calls down to us as we cross the ramp on to the deck. James looks fresh from the pages of *Brideshead Revisited* in a cream-coloured waistcoat and trousers, though his severe modernist specs ruin the effect somewhat.

'Good to see you both after last night's debacle,' James says casually as we reach him.

'I don't think we need to rehash it,' Ford says, clearly irritated.

'Right, sorry. Well, you've met Sam, I believe – our step-mother's bonus baby.' He smoothly redirects to introducing her, gesturing upwards.

'Morning!' Sam calls from the upper deck. My cheeks flush at the awkwardness as she's clearly unaware that James referred to her as a 'bonus baby'. Maybe I'm being too sensitive but I didn't like the way he said it.

'This lovely lady,' James says, ignoring Sam and gesturing down the deck of the yacht, 'is Lawrence's fiancée, the pearl before the swine, Cecile.'

Cecile is either too far away to hear his comment or is ignoring him. She's leaning on the rail at the far end of the deck, looking out over the fjord, her long hair and dress catching the breeze. I can't work out if she's just coincidently turned herself into an Instagram post, or if she's aware of how perfectly posed she is.

'Well, I'll leave you two to find the drinks,' James says, brushing past me. The scent of Scotch reaches me seconds later. James has started rather early, possibly explaining his overt rudeness.

After he leaves for the other side of the boat, Sam comes down the steps from the upper deck. Once again she's in a casual, beachy outfit. More fit for a tourist than a party guest – a muted green playsuit, flip-flops and a baseball cap.

'Please accept my apologies for my stepbrother,' she says, 'he's only like this when he's awake.'

OK, so maybe she isn't as clueless about James's attitude towards her as I thought. Maybe it's just sibling rivalry. After all, Ford said last night that they worked together. Rose and I used to snark back and forth in the same way, albeit when we were teenagers.

Ford laughs at her joke and I smile politely.

'Ford, why don't you get some cocktails from upstairs and I'll introduce Amelia to Cecile?' Sam says.

Behind me I hear a thud and realize that the ramp has been withdrawn and we're about to start moving. I glance up and just manage to make out the outline of a bearded man in the bridge overhead, wearing a white uniform.

'Is Lawrence not piloting the boat?' I ask.

'Oh no, he's not here.' Sam pulls a regretful face.

'He's not coming?' Ford sounds disappointed.

Sam nods. 'Said something came up. Business or some-thing to do with last night. I didn't ask. He seemed stressed out enough. Anyway, come and meet Cecile. She's his better half anyway.'

Perhaps their eagerness to get on with things as normal is just a type of 'stiff upper lip – keep calm and carry on' attitude. As if the Fowleys were trying to emulate the royal family in these unfortunate circumstances.

Sam tows me along by the arm, leaving Ford behind. As we approach Cecile she turns and smiles at me. My opinion of her, although based on a photograph, was apparently accurate. She exudes a friendly vibe and there's nothing hard or aloof about her appearance. If I had to pick an occupation for her, it'd probably be nanny, or perhaps a teacher at a quaint girls' school. She looks as if she grows her own flowers and takes spiders outside instead of crushing them with a slipper. Then again, appearances aren't everything. I probably don't look like I have a knife on me.

'Cecile, this is Ford's girlfriend, Amelia,' Sam says, waving between us. 'Amelia, Cecile has made the questionable decision to marry my big brother.'

Cecile rolls her eyes fondly, but smiles at me. 'It's lovely to meet you, I hope you're enjoying yourself . . . despite the awful accident yesterday.'

Cecile is seemingly exempt from the Fowley facade. I glance sideways at Sam, who doesn't react to Cecile's words, her pale grey eyes watching the fjord flow past, a crease between her brows.

'It's been . . . interesting,' I say. 'I feel awful for Ingrid, though. I met her and Zak yesterday; they seemed very happy together. I can't believe he just . . .' I wave my hands, unable to articulate my horror.

Cecile nods sadly. 'Lawrence still isn't sure how it

happened. None of the guests have access to the manor – it's very clearly out of bounds – and yet . . .' She shrugs.

'Can we please not talk about it?' Sam finally says, sounding strained. 'Last night was hard enough.'

I feel a wave of empathy for her. After all, while I was tucked up in bed she was out there in the gardens with James and Ford, corralling guests while staff hosed blood off the flagstones.

'Of course,' Cecile says gently. 'Well . . . Amelia, the final party is really going to blow you away. Lawrence has been planning it for months.'

'She won't tell us what it is, so don't even try,' Sam says, relaxing slightly.

'I already told you – it's . . . a surprise,' Cecile says, mustering a semi-believable cheeky smile.

Sam lightly slaps her arm and I feel the tension in my shoulders ratchet down a notch or two. Even if this casual atmosphere feels as fake as it is, I'm at least glad to not be trapped in an awkward conversation. Although it makes me feel horrible, I know that if everyone were to remain stuck on the Zak topic, I'd have few opportunities to find out more about Lawrence.

Ford arrives with a tray of cocktails and the four of us drink and admire the view as the yacht cruises down the fjord. For a while it's peaceful: Ford talks about work; Cecile reveals that she is a qualified paediatrician – just as wholesome as I'd assumed but demonstrating how clever and well educated she is too. She admits that she doesn't practise at the moment but doesn't go into why. Perhaps she's put all her eggs in the 'being the next Mrs Fowley' basket? Then Sam tells us about her new charity initiative to bring abandoned cats and dogs into the retirement home she runs and Cecile laughs because apparently Sam is allergic to pet hair. Sam cracks a smile at the irony.

Unfortunately, James comes to join us after about an hour, drunker than he was before. His method of dealing with yesterday's incident is to get plastered. He's unsteady on his feet, clutching a fresh drink, and Sam catches my eye, nodding her head slightly towards the upper level.

'Um . . . Sam, would you show me around?' I ask quickly, guessing her meaning and wanting some time alone with her to ask about Lawrence.

'If you insist. 'Scuse us, Ceecee, Ford,' Sam says cheerily.

'Oh you little . . .' Cecile hisses, then plasters on a smile, voice sweet with concern. 'Hi, James, do you want me to find someone to make you a coffee?'

Sam giggles as we hurry to the upper deck. Once there she motions me to a ladder and we climb up to a shaded viewing platform with panoramic views. The fjord really is beautiful. I find myself wondering if Rose got the chance to experience it like this, if she can see it from where she is now, and feel tears start to creep into the corners of my eyes. I blink them away. This isn't the time to dwell on the past; it's Rose's future I need to concern myself with.

'You don't mind me stealing you away, do you?' Sam asks, depositing herself on a padded bench that runs around the platform. 'I just can't take another minute with drunk James today.'

'He does seem like . . . a lot,' I say.

Sam laughs. 'Oh yeah – you don't need to be polite. I grew up with the pair of them and they're my brothers, but damn, sometimes I can use a break from being part of the Fowley circus, you know?'

I take a seat on the bench beside her. She's kicked off her flip-flops and pulled herself up to sit cross-legged. The shorts of her playsuit expose a lot of tanned leg and the edge of a large sticking plaster on the side of her thigh, clearly freshly applied. Around her ankle there's a faded friendship bracelet which looks handmade, with a few beads dangling from the end. A far cry from the gold and diamonds everyone else is sporting.

'Have you met Lawrence yet?' Sam asks after a moment's silence. 'James said he invited you today, but I wasn't sure if he meant he'd invited Ford and his plus-one or you specifically.'

I nod. 'I met him last night, on the beach. Before . . .' I stop myself, unwilling to bring it up again.

Sam sidesteps my slip-up. 'Let me guess, he was dossing around doing his poor-little-rich-host routine?' She snorts, rolling her eyes. 'He does the same thing every year. Honestly, I think he hates all the mess and gladhanding that goes along with it. He was never the most sociable. Even when we were kids he was hard to get to know. I never even saw him hug his dad. Not that you'd want to.'

'What was he like?'

'My stepdad? Oh . . . busy, rich, distant. The usual. Gave Lawrence grief constantly about how he was going to be the head of the family and that it was his duty to steer the ship.'

Not exactly specific. 'Was he the one that got you into charity work?'

Sam snorts. 'Nah, he wasn't too hands on with that. Just wrote big cheques for his pet charities. I kind of like that it's my thing, you know? That it's not something Lawrence or his Dad's money bought me. I did that. Lawrence's father mostly donated to environmental causes. God knows his business caused enough damage, so I suppose that makes sense.'

'The oil and gas stuff? Ford told me. Business must be booming.'

'Uh-huh. He's trying to go a little bit more "green" now. Wind farms and hydroelectric – all that stuff. But I'm not sure how profitable it is. Fossil-fuel prices are skyrocketing so I guess he's doing well.'

'Hey!' Ford calls up to us. 'Fancy a swim?'

I look down and spot Cecile unwrapping her dress to expose a sleek tankini set, before diving into the fjord. It's a reasonably warm day, but not warm enough for my British self to go jumping into the water. Though now I understand why Ford had me put a bikini on under my clothes.

'My hair,' I pout, and Ford laughs, then looks to Sam. 'You coming in?'

'No,' Sam calls back. 'You're all right.'

'Come ooon, don't be such a—'

'She said no,' said James.

'It'll be fun. We can—'

'Just . . . leave it, will you?' James interjects, surprising me. He sounds annoyed on Sam's behalf.

Ford quickly strips down to his trunks, the back of his neck scarlet with embarrassment. I look down on James curiously. I hadn't really pegged him as being the type to leap to anyone's defence. Especially not Sam's, given the current of rivalry between them.

'Not feeling the water? Me neither,' I say with a shiver, turning my attention back to Sam.

I'm surprised at how dark her expression has turned. She takes a slug of her drink and frowns over my shoulder at the rippling blue waters of the fjord. Something passes through her, a shudder that makes the ice in her glass chime.

'Are you . . . OK?' I ask.

She swallows and avoids my eye. 'I used to hate coming out here.'

'On the yacht?'

'On the water,' Sam corrects, turning to face me again. 'I used to have a panic attack if I so much as stepped on to a boat – and swimming? Forget it. I still can't.'

Sam's devil-may-care attitude has faded slightly. I can see the deeply unhappy woman underneath now. Her tone suggests she's waiting for me to make a glib comment or change the subject out of second-hand embarrassment.

'Oh no . . . how come?' I ask, sensing that I need to encourage her a bit, let some sympathy smooth the way. Which is easy because I feel bad for her in the moment, so obviously ashamed and hurt.

Sam sucks in a shaky breath. 'We were really just kids at the time. My mother had recently married their dad and they were trying to get the three of us to "bond". Yeah, right. I think he just didn't want me cramping their style,' she says, clearly meaning Lawrence's father. 'He had Lawrence and James take me into the grounds to play. This was back in England, at his country house. There was this river at the bottom of the garden where you could swim in summer. Lawrence got me to swim all the way out. Out of my depth.'

Sam necks the rest of her drink, looks at her glass for a moment as if considering the merits of tossing it overboard, then sets it down on the railing.

'It was silly, really. I don't think he did it on purpose. He was older but we were all kids, he was just . . . joking about. I didn't have to do it,' she continues, voice cracking slightly with emotion. 'He had the plans and the games. We just followed him. Me and James. That day, though, I . . . I couldn't swim back against the current and I went under. I was trying to get up for air and I could hear him every time my head came up – laughing. Like it was some big joke. I don't think he even realized how scared I was, how close I was to drowning.'

I want to say something, to comfort her. But my instincts as a barrister keep me quiet. I know there's more. I can see her bracing herself, getting ready to tell me. As much as she's defending her brothers, I can tell she's not entirely convincing herself. Maybe her loyalty to them isn't as blind as Ford's. Maybe I can use that, make her my ally.

'He eventually came in to save me, but when he was dragging me out I got my foot caught in a branch underwater. He'd left it so long that by the time I got out I still nearly died. Had to go to hospital, developed pneumonia. I missed months of school, couldn't see my friends . . . He was really sorry, and his dad gave him hell over it. He was meant to be looking after James and me. I think his dad beat him with a belt for what happened. After that Lawrence took being the eldest really seriously. Always watching out for us, no matter what.'

Sam snaps out of her reverie, offering me a brave half-smile. 'When I got to uni I decided it was time to start facing my fear of the water. I hadn't done anything more strenuous than taking a bath since it happened. So I joined the boat club – stayed in it all three years, even got the tattoo. But I still can't bring myself to swim in open water. I don't think anyone besides Lawrence and James knows, so don't be mad at Ford about it.'

I let the silence hum around us for a moment, then sense that she's done. She blinks slowly and I can tell that even with the alcohol making her hazy, she's worried she's said too much.

'I'm so sorry that happened. That's just awful . . .' I gently place my hand over hers where it lies on the bench, trembling slightly. 'Thank you for telling me,' I say honestly. I feel as if I've just had my first peek behind the Fowley family facade, and there are murky waters there to explore. Sam might just be my way in.

12

SAM AND I TALK a while longer, though not about anything of great importance. I can tell she's embarrassed to have shared so much with me. James isn't the only one who's been hitting the bottle since boarding the yacht and she doesn't get herself any more drinks. Sam tells me a bit about the boat club, the races they won and the places they competed. After a while she gets up, seemingly recovered from our heart-to-heart, and suggests we rejoin the others.

Down on the lower deck I find Ford and Cecile dressed, their hair wet, talking about her father's investments. James is nowhere to be seen.

'Where's my darling little brother?' Sam asks brightly. 'Not throwing up over the poop deck, I hope?'

'I'm not sure,' Cecile says, pulling a regretful face. 'He went off to get another drink and didn't come back.'

All three of us eye Ford and he turns slightly pink. 'I suppose I should go check on him then?'

'Would you? Thank you so much,' Cecile says, beaming.

Ford raises his eyebrows at me and I smile slightly as he leaves on his mission.

'Sorry if Ford was talking your ear off about non-fungibles. I know from experience that is non-fun,' I joke weakly. Cecile laughs politely. I'm finding her quite hard to read, beyond the surface: what side of things she falls on – whether or not she knows about Lawrence's reputation, whether she likes the family or not. Though, like Lawrence, she's too perfect and charming to be real.

'It was fine. He's obviously very passionate about his work. What were you two ladies chatting about?'

I glance at Sam, who is looking out over the water again, ignoring the question. I shrug.

'Just boats and sailing. Sam told me about her time rowing at university.'

'Ah,' Cecile says, a slightly sorrowful look passing over her face. 'I see.'

From her reaction I think there's a possibility she knows about Sam's story. Sam didn't seem to think that anyone else knew, so that means Lawrence must have told her. I'm puzzled as to why someone who seems so outwardly kind and friendly as Cecile would be with Lawrence if she knows he nearly caused Sam's death. Then again he wouldn't be the first sociopath to twist the past in his favour. Perhaps in his version he leapt in to save Sam immediately, after she accidently got out of her depth. I can imagine him laying on the guilt and talking about how awfully his father punished him for something that wasn't his fault. Perhaps Cecile likes that poor-little-rich-boy routine.

'James is passed out on a sofa upstairs,' Ford reports, making me jump as he puts his arms around me from behind. 'What did I miss?'

'I meant to ask you,' Cecile says, neatly changing the subject, 'you said you met Zak Bakshi yesterday? Did you talk to him?'

Ford nods. 'Yeah. He seemed nice. He said he worked for . . .' He clicks his fingers.

'Henley Limited,' I say, obediently filling the gap.

'Yeah, that's right,' Ford says.

'Did he seem all right to you? Generally speaking, I mean. He wasn't upset or . . . stressed?' Cecile asks.

Ford frowns and I jump in before he can waste the opportunity to press her. 'You mean . . . because of what happened? You think maybe he . . . that it was intentional?'

Cecile winces regretfully. 'Lawrence told me there was something going on at the company. Something to do with losses recently . . . I don't know. He's just worried that Zak had gotten wind of it somehow – that he was depressed. Apparently there was an empty decanter up in James's room – that's where he jumped from.'

'Or fell,' Ford says. 'God . . . maybe he just got drunk because of what he'd found and didn't mean to . . .' Ford clears his throat and deflects the conversation my way. 'You didn't get a vibe off him, did you, Aimes?'

'He seemed perfectly friendly when we spoke. Not stressed or anything. Do you think he was worried about redundancies?'

Cecile sighs. 'It's not been a good quarter for renewable energy in general, but Henley has had just . . . awful losses. I don't know why. Maybe the green side is taking hits because there are so many hurdles to getting the energy we're generating into the system. Take your country, for example – last year the National Grid paid over two hundred million to turn *off* wind production, because it was overwhelming the infrastructure and they couldn't get the power to where demand was highest. It's madness.'

Ford whistles. 'Didn't I hear James ranting about some guy at Henley? Not this year but . . . a while back?'

Cecile looks nonplussed for a second, but Sam chooses that moment to re-enter the conversation. 'You mean Tom Slazenger?'

'Oh, Tom!' Cecile's expression clears. 'No, that was before the market problems. James and Tom just didn't get on. Let me think . . . that would've been about three years ago now. Four maybe?'

'Three,' Sam corrects. 'Tom brought it up at the party, remember?'

'Yes, you're right. I miss Tom. He was always fun.'

'I haven't heard much about him. Is he not here this year?' I ask, suddenly paying more attention.

Cecile looks regretful. 'It was terrible. He had an accident, right after the party. He brought his climbing gear along and went on to a solo trip afterwards. He never came back.'

'I remember Zak wasn't too crushed about it, though,' Sam says, raising her eyebrows as she sips her drink.

'Sam!' Cecile chides.

'Why's that?' Ford asks.

'Zak was pissed off that year because Tom made a move on his wife,' Sam explains. 'I went out with Tom when I was, like, fifteen and he was always a terrible flirt. Nothing serious, but Zak didn't take it that way.'

I remember the way Zak's face changed when Ingrid was talking about the parties getting out of hand. People having affairs. Despite Sam saying that it was nothing serious, I wonder if there's part of the story she's missing out on. I am, however, less interested in a marital squabble than in the fact that Tom apparently 'disappeared'. And I remember the police reports I photographed in Lawrence's safe: that blurry last name could have been Slazenger.

'And you're sure he went on this trip?' I say, trying to sound upbeat and humorous. 'Zak didn't just clobber him over the head and dump him in the fjord?'

Sam and Cecile both laugh, but Ford gives me a disapproving look.

'I doubt it – Zak never struck me as the violent type. I'm not just saying that because of . . . Well, let's put it this way: I expect Tom had a strongly worded email waiting for him that he never got to read,' Sam says. 'Besides, Lawrence would have noticed if he left all his climbing stuff lying around in a guesthouse. He's a very uptight man when it comes to clutter.'

I want to ask if they ever found his body, but that's definitely a step too far for polite conversation. Perhaps I can google him later or translate the police report – surely the answer will be in there? Or – a sudden flash of inspiration strikes me – I can ask Elena. She might be long gone from the estate but I still have her phone number. She was working that year.

I'm desperate for more info on Tom and his disappearance, but there's not much chance of me getting a moment alone to call Elena. At least, that's what I tell myself. However, only a few minutes later, Sam offers to go and get another round of drinks and Ford excuses himself to the 'heads'. Cecile and I are abruptly left alone, so, after denying the temptation for a few moments, I clutch my bag and sigh.

'Sorry, my work phone's buzzing – do you mind if I take this?'

'No problem.' Cecile smiles. 'I expect all your clients are missing you.'

I excuse myself with a gracious smile and take my phone out as I wander down the deck, towards the bow of the yacht. There I waste no time in finding Elena's text and tapping the call icon beside her number.

Looking out over the icy blue fjord I listen to the tinny sound of my call trying to connect. When there's no answer after four rings, I frown. Given how alert she was to the prospect of repercussions from the family, I'd expect her to pick up my call immediately. I might be trying to check in on her, or warn her even. Perhaps Elena is on a plane right now and can't answer? That seems the most logical answer, even if she must surely have reached Seville by now. Our flight to Norway from Heathrow only took two hours or so, after all.

The phone beeps and a robotic voice asks me to leave a message. I hesitate but then feel prodded into action by the silence on the other end of the line.

'Hi, Elena, it's me, Amelia? I'm just calling to make sure you got home OK and to ask a favour. I'd like to know anything you remember about a guest – Tom Slazenger. He went missing right after the party three years ago. On a climbing trip? Let me know, OK?'

I ring off and look down at my phone, annoyed at myself for babbling. I'll have to try and get hold of Elena later on.

'Who are you calling?'

I turn round, startled by the voice. James is standing a few feet away, bloodshot eyes narrowed at me. There's a wet patch on his shirt, probably from the drink in his hand, which is half full, the glass dripping on to the deck between us.

My insides are a twisted-up ball of nerves. I don't know how much he heard, or what he's thinking. How could I have been so stupid?

'I'm waiting, Amelia,' he says, looking at me like a half-starved guard dog. 'Who are you calling?'

13

'I WAS . . . I JUST rang one of the staff members I met yesterday. Elena.' I swallow, trying to generate some saliva. My
mouth feels dry as bone and it's entirely because of the way
James is looking at me.

'I'm glad you said that,' James says, transferring his weight
to his other foot, posing casually as if this isn't the interro-
gation it feels like. 'Because at least that's half true. I heard
you say her name. Very good. So, why do you have Elena's
number and what are you calling her about that can't wait
until we're back on shore?'

I can feel my cheeks turning red. So, Lawrence isn't the
only person here suspicious of me. He as good as told me
that James thought I was a gold digger; maybe he thinks I
have another boyfriend on the side?

I take a breath and give him an unimpressed look. 'Firstly,
I got her number because I made friends with her – she's nice
and she was going to send me a link to her bronzer. And I
wanted to have a point of contact for if I needed a tampon
in the middle of the night. It's not like we're in a hotel and I
can just call down to reception, or pop to the shops. In case
you hadn't noticed, we're not in the main house like you.

Secondly, it's none of your business what I might need. What the hell is your problem?'

It's a gamble, I'll admit, going on the offensive, combined with the period trick again. I'm hoping that it'll make me seem more authentic, this defence of my privacy, and that it'll get the others on the boat on my side if James decides to make a scene.

James's eyes are so narrowed now that they're just creases under his glasses. 'If you think I'll let you make a fool out of Ford—'

'Amelia!' Sam breezes past James and hooks her arm through mine, offering me a cocktail with her free hand. 'I was wondering where you'd got to. Is my little brother bothering you?'

I glance from James to her, trying to put on a decent act as a cornered bumpkin overawed by her betters.

'I was just calling one of the staff to ask about getting some supplies for the room and . . . uh . . . not sure if James is thinking too clearly,' I say, softly enough that it at least looks like I'm trying to keep him from hearing.

'That's because he's hammered, aren't you, James?' Sam says with the air of someone used to making excuses for him. 'Cecile'll get you a coffee, if you ask nicely.'

James looks as if he wants to out me to her, but stalks off without a word. He staggers a little as he reaches the steps to the upper deck, but styles it out and soon disappears. I feel bad, to be honest; he's just trying to look out for his cousin. I'd be suspicious of me too.

'Sorry, he's being abnormally shitty today.' Sam sighs, leaning on the railing around the side of the boat. 'I have no idea what he's so twisted up about. Must be last night or just the time of year. He's always uptight around now. I think the only time I've seen him enjoy himself at one of these was . . . two years ago? When poor Bergdis died.'

The housekeeper. 'Who was that, his girlfriend?'

'Oh my God! No!' Sam looks appalled and amused in equal measure. 'She was Lawrence's housekeeper. Well, actually she was the housekeeper when I lived here too – she was in her eighties. Pride keeps a lot of people going at that age, I find. There's something about having a reason to get up in the morning that gives older people a lift, even when their health isn't what it was.' Sam looks out towards land and chews her lip. 'When she died I was quite shocked. It seemed like Bergdis would always be here. A fixture. But, sadly, we lost her.'

'And James was *happy* she died?' I ask, not entirely surprised that James wasn't cut up about her death, but to be happy about it seemed too evil, even for him.

'Oh yes.' Sam sighs. 'They had the worst time with one another. Even when we were kids. She was always on at James to straighten up, take his muddy shoes off, to not steal cake between meals. You know, typical stuff. James didn't like being told what to do, especially not by a staff member.' She shrugs. 'Not much has changed in that regard. Though obviously he doesn't get back at the staff by salting their tea or hiding their umbrellas any more. As far as I know!' She laughs.

'Sounds fairly innocent. I can't imagine celebrating someone's death over that,' I say, mentally urging her to let the rest of her story spill out. There has to be more to it than that.

Sam pulls a regretful face, sobering slightly. 'I think it was more to do with St Jude's. When James was about fifteen things sort of escalated. He was only getting more awkward and messier and Bergdis was getting more exasperated. One day she picked up all his comics and said she'd thrown them away – it was a shock tactic, she'd just hidden them, but James was kind of understandably furious that his stuff had been thrown out, so . . . he locked her in the freezer.'

'The freezer?' I repeat, not having to feign horror. I've seen pictures of Bergdis Olsen before she died: she looked like a wizened little apple in a flowery blouse and apron. A beaming smile from ear to ear as she tickled her latest grandchild. I can't imagine anyone shutting her in a freezer.

Sam winces, as if she wants to defend him but can't quite bring herself to. 'I know. It was such a stupid thing for him to do. We had one of those walk-in things, like in a restaurant? She went in there for something and James shut her in. Of course, after the incident Lawrence's father had it removed. She was in there for less than half an hour but obviously she had no way of knowing when, or if, James was going to let her out.' Sam shudders, clearly imagining being in that situation herself. 'She was so upset –and his father was so angry – a week later James was sent away to school in England. St Jude's. That's where he met Tom.'

'Tom . . . Slazenger?' I ask, feeling my chest tighten when Sam nods. The missing man has a connection to James, and Cecile already told me James hated working with him. I play dumb. 'They were school friends?'

Sam actually laughs. 'Oh God, no! James and Tom hated each other. Probably because they were so similar. You know, spoiled little rich boys who cry and throw things if there's skin on their custard. Like something out of a German fairy tale – one where a goblin comes to cut off your toes for being bad.' She chuckles, then glances around as if afraid she's going to be overheard. Interestingly, her loyalty seems less extreme than Ford's. Maybe because she knows James and Lawrence better.

'I thought you said you went out with Tom?' I can't resist asking.

'I did – but only to piss off James. I was fifteen, so it seemed like a good idea at the time. Worked, too.' Sam laughs again. 'Hell, it's probably why Lawrence started inviting Tom to the parties, gave him a job – to get at James. I always got the sense that Tom and his friends used to bully James at school – he probably deserved it. But yeah, I think that's why James latched on to the thing with Zak's wife. Don't get me wrong, Tom was being a creep and he deserved repercussions, but James doesn't normally give two shits about sexual harassment. It was all about trying to get rid of Tom.'

I feel cold, right down to my bones. James had a history with the dead housekeeper and now with another person who 'went missing' around the time of one of these parties. If Sam is right about him, he could be the one who attacked Sara and made Rose disappear. Maybe I've had the wrong brother in my sights this entire time?

'Are you all right?' Sam asks. 'You look a bit white.'

'It's just the boat, I think. I'm not used to being on one. Especially not while drinking.'

'Oh, no. Do you want a mint? I find that helps sometimes.' Sam digs a packet of Tic Tacs out of her pocket and hands them to me. She glances to the side. 'We're on our way back now anyway.'

We are, I realize, heading towards the jetty. Our cocktail voyage at an end. I'm glad. The idea of being trapped on a boat with James suddenly fills me with dread. I need to get some time alone to google Tom Slazenger and find out if his body was ever found. Translating that police report is also a must. Maybe dig a little deeper on the subject of James and the housekeeper. Was he just a moody teenager or is there something more to it? My pulse is rushing with adrenaline. Yesterday I was so sure Lawrence knew something but now I'm not sure.

Today is the second of three days of events. I'm already halfway through my time at the Fowley estate and I have so many leads to follow.

As I suck a mint and allow Sam to 'distract me from my seasickness', I begin to wonder if there isn't a third suspect I need to be aware of. Perhaps Tom's disappearance isn't relevant at all. James wasn't the only one who hated him; Zak did too. I was trying to solve Tom's disappearance to get to Rose's abductor, but what if that secret died with Zak? Tom made a move on his wife, Ingrid, after all. Perhaps they'd even had a liaison at the party.

As the yacht draws up to the jetty, I feel as if my thoughts are getting away from me. I stepped on to the yacht with a clear plan but now I am anything but certain. As I walk along the jetty, I feel eyes on me. I glance round and catch James watching me from the edge of the boat, a strange smile on his lips. I smile back, but his expression doesn't change and as I turn to face the woods, I can feel his gaze lodged between my shoulders like the tip of a knife.

14

FORD JOINS ME ON the jetty and I try to ignore the continued pressure from James's stare. I glance down at my phone. It's only just gone one. There's a full afternoon ahead of us before the second of Lawrence's parties. Time is slipping through my fingers. I have so much I need to do.

'Fancy going for a soak in the hot tubs by the pool?' Ford asks me. 'Or maybe we could go for a hike, explore the woods.' He scans the wooded hills beyond the manor and points to what looks like a lodge or cabin in the distance. 'We could go up there – get some alone time.'

I smile flirtatiously, scheming for a way out of this. The thought of being out there in the forest makes me shiver. This estate is miles from anywhere – it sits on a peninsula cut off from civilization by steep mountains and cliffs. There are wolves and bears out here, I think. But right now, the thing that scares me most are the two-legged predators, like James. He hated Tom and then Tom disappeared. Hated Bergdis and then she was dead. What if he took a dislike to my sister as well?

And now he seems to be on to me.

Out of the corner of my eye I spot James himself coming up behind us. He's not weaving; perhaps he wasn't as drunk as he looked. That or he vomited and has sobered up a bit. Still, he looks more in control of himself now and he's heading right for us.

'Why don't we all go to lunch together?' James says with a smile, his glasses flashing in the sun. 'I'll have a private table set up in the Japanese garden.'

The chance to get to grips with those police reports slips through my fingers. Damn it. There's no way Ford's going to turn him down, not based on his previous behaviour.

'Sounds great,' Ford says weakly. 'We'd love that, wouldn't we, Aimes?'

'Sounds lovely, thank you so much,' I say, injecting some pep into my voice.

James steps forward, forcing me out of his path, and I watch him leave, trailing after him with Ford.

'I suppose it'll give us a chance to see more of the grounds,' Ford says, still not sounding thrilled but apparently trying to force himself to put a positive spin on it.

'Should we not change?' I ask, hoping for just a few minutes alone where I could at least google Tom Slazenger.

'I don't think there's time . . . You look perfect anyway,' Ford says and kisses me on the cheek. I smile at the compliment but inside I'm seething. As soon as lunch is over I'm going to have to feign a migraine or something so I can get some time to myself.

'Hurry up, it's this way,' James calls back.

The Japanese gardens are on the opposite side of the manor to the chalets and far enough from the fjord that the air there isn't so much beachy and fresh as damp and earthy with moss and the surrounding trees. Beyond the gardens, through an arch in the surrounding hedge, I can see the orchard Ford told me about before, where the sauna is. Or rather saunas. I can just about spy four plank cabins with turf roofs, covered in wildflowers. It's like something out of a luxury spa brochure – the sun-baked planks, thin streams of smoke rising from the chimneys and the apple trees heavy with fruit, surrounded by pristine white beehives.

In the small Japanese garden there's a sunken lily pond with a bamboo water feature, clunking every few minutes as it fills with water and empties. A small stone bridge leads over the pond towards a meandering path up a slope. Between the red maples and stone lanterns there's a pagoda, painted glossy black. James is already seated in its shade at a wrought-iron table.

Ford and I take our seats inside the pagoda. I feel very much as if this is James's private kingdom. A tiny piece of his brother's estate that he has control over. There's something about the precise nature of everything, the secretive and shady pagoda in the midst of the rest of Lawrence's bacchanalian gardens, that matches James's severe and haughty attitude. He reminds me of the posers I used to meet at work: white guys with Zen gardens on their desks, practising their Duolingo Japanese vocab on each other and making snide comments about 'Western women'.

Moments after we sit down a black-jacketed waitress appears and sets down a tea tray. In contrast to our surroundings, it's a strictly English afternoon tea menu. The cucumber and tomato sandwiches are laid out a precise centimetre apart and the bone-china teapot and cups are accompanied by sugar lumps, slices of lemon, and a tower of bitesize cakes and miniature crumpets. I can't tell if this is meant to intimidate me, as the 'commoner' Ford has brought along, or if this is genuinely the kind of thing James prefers.

'What a lovely selection.' I smile at the waitress and she smiles back, albeit nervously, her eyes flitting to James as if awaiting permission to leave.

'Is this Assam?' James asks, voice sounding sharper than ever in the almost silent garden.

'I . . . it's an English breakfast blend,' the waitress stutters. 'I can check . . .'

James dismisses her with a wave of his hand and she scuttles away.

The bamboo pipe clunks and releases a gush of water.

'This is nice,' Ford says, after a painful pause.

'I wanted to apologize,' James says, somewhat stiffly. 'I'm afraid I made an arse of myself earlier. Last night was . . . trying, and I reacted poorly to the shock and the sleepless night. Amelia, I'm sorry for snapping at you.'

Ford glances at me, a question in his gaze, but I shrug slightly to deter him from asking questions. Maybe James is being sincere, or maybe he's just trying to put me off guard.

'Where exactly did you two meet?' James asks pleasantly. He selects a cucumber sandwich and transfers it to his plate with a pair of ridiculously small silver tongs. I feel as though I'm eighteen again, being interviewed by a panel at university. Expected to justify my existence, the space I planned to take up. Only this time I'm not eighteen and I have something more important than my education to pursue. Lawrence didn't intimidate me with his attempt to buy me off; I won't let James get to me.

'I was out for a run and I just bumped into Amelia in the park. Couldn't resist chatting her up – you know what I'm like.' Ford laughs easily. 'We had a coffee at the pavilion, didn't we?'

I nod. 'You put your fleece down on that bench for me to sit on. Very gentlemanly.'

Ford grins. 'I was just trying to show off my abs.'

'Sounds like you were lucky to meet when you did,' James says, glancing my way. 'You use Strava, don't you, Ford? I've seen some of your posts.'

'Yeah, I do.' Ford frowns, clearly unsure what to make of this sudden deviation.

'It's a great app, but I do sometimes wish it wasn't so public. Don't you?' James asks.

Ford shrugs, his eyes remaining firmly fixed on his food.

I keep my face neutral and try to control my breathing. James is poking at my web of lies, gently at the moment, but who knows if he's got enough to tear the whole lot down.

'And where do you come from?' James asks me. 'Your family, I mean.'

'London. I've always lived in London,' I reply breezily. I know my backstory forwards and backwards. Just because he thinks I'm lying doesn't mean he knows what I'm lying about, I tell myself. To him I'm just a gold-digging gym rat, but they are easy to underestimate. Even if his voice sends a shiver through me, making me wonder if he brought Rose here. If this is where he might have decided what he was going to do with her, after she 'wronged him' the same way Tom and Bergdis did.

'Where in London? Golborne?' James asks, probably just naming the most deprived area he can think of.

'Woodberry Down.'

'Ah . . . sounds lovely.'

Ford clears his throat and reaches for the teapot, possibly because his mouth is as dry as mine is right now. I'm focusing hard on the conversation, on James's mannerisms, trying to intuit what I can from them. James laughs and edges the pot out of his reach, as if Ford is a naughty child trying to steal still-warm cookies.

'It's not brewed yet. You've no patience, have you?' To me, James says, 'You're a personal trainer then – how much does that make, yearly?'

I sense the chance to counterattack instead of parrying his assaults.

'About thirty K. More than enough for me. You work for your brother, right?'

He nods, his expression blank, as bland as paper. 'Where did you go to university?'

'I didn't. Apprenticeship with "Totally Fitness" in Hackney.'

'Didn't they close down three years ago?' James asks, and I realize he's been doing some googling of his own.

'After my time. That was a shame, though – the owner, Rhoda? She was so much fun – I really miss her. She moved to Spain after she sold the business. Good for her, I say.'

I've stalked her online; he could ask me her preferred brand of tea and I'd be able to answer in seconds. I watch as he frowns, trying to find a new avenue of attack. Ford has leaned forward in his seat, his shoulders tense.

'What is it you do for Lawrence?' I ask.

'Accounting,' James says, eyes flashing as he takes a bite of a crumpet. Perhaps James is trying to poison Ford against me. Lawrence was the carrot and James is the stick; they're quite a pair.

'Sounds stressful,' I say. 'Sam was telling me you went to school in England, is that true? Like a special school for "bad boys".' I laugh. 'Not many "bad boy" accountants, I can imagine.'

James doesn't answer and I feel Ford shift uncomfortably beside me. It's clear he wants to de-escalate things but I'm fairly sure he doesn't know how. He can only watch as James tries to stare me down and I meet his eyes with a smile, forcing him to speak or face the unrelenting silence.

'I did – it was a boarding school.' He sighs. 'Very English and very dull. Where did you go to school? Your social media doesn't go back that far.'

'I didn't take you as a social media sort of guy,' I say.

He doesn't blink. 'I like to stay informed.'

'Well, you'll see I only got into it recently. Strict parents.' I pull a face. 'I didn't get a phone until I had my first job, wasn't really into social media then. I'm still not that good at it.'

'And I love that about you,' Ford says, jumping in, and then looking at James. 'She's not glued to Instagram twenty-four/seven or obsessing over taking pictures of her food.'

I laugh, but James isn't smiling. He takes a sip of his tea and leans back in his chair, relaxed but distant. Ford pushes his food around his plate like an unhappy child trapped between recently divorced parents.

'Has Ford told you much about his job? It was so fortunate that I could get it for him,' James says, voice light. 'I try my best to throw him some extra work from time to time, when I'm busy. It's really the least I can do.'

'So you're a recruiter?' I ask sweetly.

James laughs, but it's more like a bark. 'Yes, you could say that. But my job is far too dull to explain. Definitely not as exciting as yours. All that stretching out on your back, which I suppose is still work, isn't it? In a way. Great exercise, I imagine.'

James takes another bite of his crumpet and wipes butter from his mouth with the back of his hand. He shares a mocking glance with Ford, who smiles weakly. Ford's face is pale, and he looks sick. He has to know that he's putting his relationship with me in jeopardy. I watch him expectantly, but he avoids my eye. I should keep quiet and let James goad me, I know that. But for some reason I think of my old job and all the crap I've been through to get to this point. I've had enough of putting up with shit from men. I'm not the woman I was a year ago.

I shrug. 'I know it's not much but I don't have a rich brother to give me a job.'

James chokes on his crumpet and coughs, turning red.

'Amelia!' Ford hisses.

Swallowing his mouthful with a harsh laugh, James wipes a tear from his eye. When he looks up, I can see that beneath the amused expression, his eyes are filled with loathing. Good. If he really is responsible for the disappearances and Bergdis's death, I need to make him angry. He might do something stupid.

James folds up his napkin and stands, yawning.

'I think that's enough food for now, don't you?' He taps his belly and looks at Ford. 'Well, she really is a lot of fun – but just as common as you said. It's a shame, Ford – you can do better.' With that, James lets out a sad sigh and departs, his movements stiff and clipped as if he's a clockwork soldier.

'What the hell was that?' Ford hisses once James is out of earshot. 'That's my cousin – the host's brother! Are you trying to get us sent home? Are you trying to get me out of a job?'

'He was being awful to me – and to you,' I say, opting for a wounded expression. 'You let him call me common.'

'What's got into you lately? I've never heard you talk like that.'

I exhale through my nose. 'He basically accused me of being after your money.'

'Well, you are wearing a lot of it,' Ford snaps.

'You bought me these things. I didn't ask you to.'

'You never had to ask.'

'So – what? I'm just a . . . a prostitute to you?' I say, pulling out the big guns in an attempt to shock him into an apology.

Ford mutters something.

'What did you say?' I ask, letting my voice crack.

'I said' – Ford huffs and gets to his feet. '. . . if the two-grand hat fits.'

He's clearly embarrassed that I heard him, but sticking to his anger. I need to try and douse this fire. Ford is my ticket into the party tonight. If he decides he doesn't want me here I will be on a plane home by the time the waitress clears the table.

I'm grasping for my next move when the sound of a phone notification interrupts us. Ford gets his phone out irritably and frowns at it. 'Not me.'

I know it's not me either. My phone is permanently silenced, just in case. I glance over the table, then reach for the black iPhone by the tea tray.

'It's James's,' I say.

Ford is already moving to leave the pagoda. 'He must've forgotten it – just leave it here, he can come look for it himself later,' he says. 'When he's calmed down,' he adds pointedly.

I nod, but as he moves away I quickly flip the phone over. The screen is still lit up with a new text message. An unknown number.

The message reads simply: *Fuck you. I won't do it.*

15

I HAVE NO CHOICE but to follow Ford back to our chalet like a scolded child. He's clearly fuming and doesn't want to get into it while guests are milling around. I have the awful feeling that James has scored a point against me. I lost my cool and let my mask slip, insulting him. Maybe that's what he wanted all along – something concrete to hold against me. Maybe Lawrence will send me home.

I've now been warned off by both Fowley brothers. I wonder suddenly if Sam's drowning story was also intended to scare me away.

I'm also turning the text on James's phone over and over in my mind, trying to fit it into what I already know about James. My first thought is that it was sent by a woman. He's propositioned someone, maybe even tried to manipulate her into his bed. He was having dinner with Ingrid the night Zak died. And he definitely seems to have a low opinion of women in general.

Maybe the text was from Lawrence himself, from a burner phone. Perhaps James has asked him for money or a favour of some kind. Something even Lawrence won't entertain. Then again it might be related to his accounting work. He could be into something shady – Cecile did say they'd had losses at Henley recently.

I wish I'd been able to take down the number. I could have called it to find out who was on the other end.

Ford and I reach the chalet and, as soon as the door is shut, he throws off his sunglasses and storms to the bar in the living room. I watch as he pours himself a triple measure of Scotch and downs half of it in one.

My spine is electric with tension. I've never seen Ford like this. He's normally pretty stable, predictable. I have no idea how to handle him at the moment and that scares me. It feels as if I'm one wrong move away from being asked to leave.

'Ford . . .' I begin, inching forwards over the plush rug. 'I'm so sorry.'

'You should be,' he snaps. 'Jesus, I mean, it was like watching a stranger, the way you laid into him . . . I hope you realize that James can permanently block me from working for one of the family businesses. You've just taken what chance I had and—' He waves his glass, at a loss for words.

I wince. Ford's end goal is to be part of the family empire, to prove he's worthy of a place as one of Lawrence's executives. He's talked about relocating to Norway before, of being close to the estate.

'I know, it was . . . rude of me. I just wanted to make a good impression and he was being so . . . abrupt,' I say. 'I was trying to keep it in but I just lost it. I couldn't handle him talking to you like that. I just made that one comment about how Lawrence is the reason he even has his job.'

Ford's expression darkens further and I realize minimizing

my actions isn't going to work. If anything I've just made things worse.

'Ford . . .'

'You can't speak to my family that way,' Ford says, his voice quiet. He turns his back to me and looks out of the window, shoulders drooping. 'I know James was being . . . difficult. But you are a guest here. We are both guests. James is only trying to look out for me, because that's what family does. We protect one another.'

Oh, I know that, I think bitterly. It's the reason I'm here. The reason Lawrence and James seem to think they're untouchable. Because they have each other and all that family money. If one of them is guilty, the other probably knows all about it. Likely helped to cover it up. Perhaps I've been naive in thinking I can pin this down to one person. Maybe it's bigger than that.

'He insulted you. He tried to make you look small, made fun of how you got your job,' I say, attempting to turn my actions into a gesture of love.

'You don't think I know that? It was just banter! That's how he is.' Ford sighs, aggravated. 'He wouldn't get at me if he didn't care.'

I can tell, though, that Ford doesn't believe this. He's embarrassed about what James said, and there's an undercurrent to his outburst that doesn't make sense to me. He begins to pace the room. There's something haunted about his expression, about the way he moves. Ford is . . . afraid. His eyes won't settle on anything and there's sweat at his hairline. His glasses are slightly foggy with it. I can hear a rough note of desperation in his voice.

A tingle passes over my skin. There's something here but

I'm not sure I can get Ford to talk about it right now. He necks the rest of his drink, refills the glass and then gulps that down too.

Ford's phone goes off and he swears under his breath, fumbling it out of his trouser pocket. He frowns at the screen, his expression dark and guarded.

'You're not going to the party tonight,' he tells me, without looking up.

I hold my breath, waiting for him to tell me that a car is waiting to take me to the airport. That this whole thing is over and they know who I really am. My mind goes into overdrive, throwing up plots and plans to sneak back on to the grounds, but I know none of them will work. I'd be spotted within moments of showing my face again. I can't look at him as a feeling of failure rises in my chest. This has all been for nothing.

'I am going to play cards with James,' Ford continues, his voice slightly strained. 'You are going to stay in the chalet and pray I can smooth things over with him. Hopefully you made a good enough impression on everyone else to out-weigh whatever James tells Lawrence.'

I want to fight this decision to essentially ground me. There are only two parties left, including tonight, and I can't afford to miss it. Ford's face is set. There will be no arguing. So I just nod, looking as cowed as possible, and take a seat on the sofa.

'I'm going for a shower.' Ford sighs and heads upstairs.

I wait until the soft rush of the rainfall shower filters down from upstairs, then I take out my phone, desperate to claw back some control. I might be in a timeout but I can still do research.

The first thing I look up is the school Sam told me James was sent to. There are a lot of 'St Jude's' schools. I scroll past primary and junior schools. Anything state-run is a safe bet to ignore. After adding in the Fowley name I eventually get a result for 'St Jude's Academy', whose media and arts centre is housed in the 'Fowley Building'. Perhaps it was a bribe for admitting James, or to make up for something he did.

I'd been imagining a sort of reform school – Borstal with boaters – but it looks like an entirely normal posh school. I scroll their web page and eventually land on class photographs. They don't go back far enough to show James and Tom, though. I head back to the browser and look through the results until I find some archived school newsletters. It's taking me a while, but Ford's shower is still running, so I put James's name into the search bar and wait. The screen loads and a picture appears – it's a younger, acne-speckled James with greasy blonde hair sitting at a chess board. The boy in the opposite chair, also glaring at the camera, is a similarly sullen adolescent. The caption reads 'Chess Tournament Hopefuls James Fowley and Thomas Slazenger'. My heart thuds in my chest. I study the picture itself and am about to move on when I notice what's going on under the table.

Presumably the photographer didn't spot it, but Tom has his foot on top of James's. I recognize the manoeuvre. When I was in my twenties, a friend of mine, Alison, had a boy-friend who did the same thing. We'd gone out to dinner and I was telling a story about work, when I felt pressure on my toes. It was Alison's boyfriend, Jake – pressing on my foot as though it was a brake pedal. I'd looked up, confused, as I'd never experienced this before. He'd looked me straight in the eye and taken advantage of my stunned pause to steer the conversation on to his job instead.

Since then it had happened to me a few times, mostly during work meetings. I've become much more adept at ignoring it. It is, unquestionably, a power play. An attempt at literally wrong-footing someone you consider to be inferior. So Sam was right: not only did they know each other, but from the looks of things they were rivals. At least in chess. But then, Bergdis only tried to make James tidy his room and he locked her in a freezer. He seems to have a tendency to overreact.

I listen for any change in the sounds from upstairs. Assuring myself that Ford is still in the shower, I google 'Tom Slazenger Norway Disappearance'.

There are a lot of results. I frown, wondering how I failed to find out about this during all my research on Lawrence. After clicking the top article, however, I begin to realize why. The piece outlines Tom's disappearance on a climbing trip in Norway, but doesn't mention anything about a party. Neither the Fowley name nor the estate itself is mentioned. I wonder if that's innocent or if someone paid the journalist off to keep part of the story out of the press.

After checking ten other articles and finding the same omissions and identical information, I finally find something more. It's a Reddit thread about mysterious disappearances in the wilderness. Lots of 'never seen again' hikers and mysteriously intact clothes found neatly folded by a shredded tent. Very *Blair Witch*.

The thread my search turned up is titled 'Missing Climbing Gear???'. I scroll through and find that whoever posted it was doing a climb in the same area that Tom supposedly disappeared in and heard his story from a fellow climber. That story basically being that there was a guy who did the climb solo but never came back, never called for help and was never found. The poster googled the story and came across one of the articles about Tom, which was where they'd found his name. They posted a link to the article and then a paragraph of their own.

I just don't get it. OK, so this guy supposedly goes on more or less the same climb as me and like a hundred other people this year. It's not a hard climb if you know what you're doing and he's meant to have climbed actual mountains with oxygen and shit so – not an amateur. He goes up and never calls for help, maybe he fell and died instantly, maybe he froze to death in his sleep. Whatever. But where's his stuff???? They sent out search parties, they looked for him and they didn't find his body – but also not even the rope he fell off or the tent he died in? His backpack? Not so much as a campsite – no sign of flattened grass or recent fires. Sounds crazy but either this guy didn't make it that far and left for some reason, or he was never there to begin with. Do you think he maybe faked his death???

Underneath the ranting and borderline conspiracy theories, he or she has a point. It was sort of weird that Tom had been pronounced missing – much like Rose – without leaving a shred of evidence behind.

The hairs on the back of my neck stand on end. This is too similar to Rose to be a coincidence. Two disappearances, both stemming from one of these parties. The death of the housekeeper also preyed on my mind – the way no one had admitted to driving her home. There was something there that I wasn't quite getting.

I hear the bathroom door thud against the wall upstairs, jolting me back to myself. I quickly open an app and start idly scrolling social media, acting the part of the sulky princess.

Ford is halfway down the stairs, hair wet and dressed casually in a clean shirt and chinos, when there's a knock on the chalet door. He looks down at me, his steps faltering. I look back, just as confused. A moment later I'm on my feet and obediently answering the door.

My stomach plunges. It's a man in a black suit, the Fowley crest embroidered on his jacket. My first thought is that he's here to take me away, that Lawrence has had enough. Will Ford step in to stop him from dragging me off to a waiting car? Doubtful. Whatever Lawrence wants is basically holy writ to Ford. Family is everything, after all.

'Good afternoon.' He nods to Ford, who has just arrived behind me. 'I have been sent by Mr Fowley with an invitation.'

'Oh . . . I'm sorry I already arranged to play cards with his brother tonight,' Ford says.

'It is for you, Miss Knox.' The man, who I now realize is likely a butler or personal assistant, ignores Ford and looks only at me. 'Mr Fowley would like to take you out this evening, on his speedboat.'

'He . . .' Ford stutters to a halt. I can see him in the corner of my eye, turning pink.

'I'm not sure I can,' I say. 'Ford and I—'

'You can go, of course,' Ford says, finding his tongue. 'If Lawrence wants you to. Where should she meet him?'

The man offers Ford and me a tight smile. 'I believe the

jetty furthest from the gardens. He doesn't wish to interrupt tonight's gathering.'

So, Lawrence isn't going to this party either. I think back over lunch with James and my conversation with Lawrence the night before. Is this a good thing or a bad thing? I'm starting to feel like the thin ice I'm walking on has cracks in it, and the cracks are getting bigger. What if James was acting on Lawrence's behalf and now the elder Fowley was ready to confront me? Perhaps some hole in my back-story has been found and he wants to pick me apart while we are alone, out there on the fjord? The thought makes my stomach churn. Is this what happened to my sister?

But there's no way I can pass up the opportunity to speak to him again.

'I'll be there,' I say, smiling. 'Thank you for coming to tell me.'

The man inclines his head and then turns, moving swiftly and quietly away through the trees. I shut the door, alone with Ford once more.

'What do you think that's about?' I ask, trying to sound innocently bemused.

Ford's mouth is a thin, hard line. 'It must be your perfor-mance at lunch. Be on your best behaviour for Lawrence, all right? And please don't do anything else to jeopardize my career.' He rubs a hand over his wet hair, stress pinching lines around his eyes. 'I can't handle any more embar-rassment.'

'I won't,' I say. 'And I'll wait up for you, so we can have some time . . . before bed.'

That seems to be the right thing to say, though Ford still looks conflicted. As we head upstairs to go through my luggage, I can see fear in his eyes. I wonder which of us will be in more danger tonight. Ford locked away somewhere with James, or me trapped alone on a boat with the man who may have abducted my sister.

16

THE PREPARATIONS FOR MY meeting with Lawrence are relentless. I have a shower, re-blow-dry and curl my hair, replace my slightly chipped nail polish and change into an evening, boat-appropriate look. One which I trust to Ford to choose for me. I think he ends up dressing me specifically to appear older than I am and very much with a view to domesticity instead of glamour. Perhaps he's worried about Lawrence's intentions? Or maybe he's trying to rehabilitate my image following lunch with James? I'm wearing tailored shorts, a striped jersey and a cashmere shawl with sensible sandals and, of course, a matching bag containing the usual essentials – phone, tissues and a knife.

At last, Ford has to leave for his evening of cards with James. Which is a good thing for a number of reasons, not least because I can't handle him being such an anxious wreck. He is acting cold and distant as he gives me instructions. It's unbearable and almost hurts, especially as we've been getting on so well recently. Even with the stress of travel hanging over us. I really screwed up at lunch. I beat myself up about it and wonder why I didn't keep my mouth shut, but there's nothing I can do about it now.

As soon as he's gone, I can relax slightly and get my phone

out to search for sites that can translate text from an image. I click the first non-sponsored link and upload the pictures of the police reports I found in Lawrence's safe. A small egg timer appears, rotating for a very long time, but eventually the translations start to pop up.

It's not perfect; the reports were largely handwritten, possibly because they were immediate reports which hadn't yet been typed up and filed. The website had some issues with the handwriting and smudges, but most of the text has been translated.

I start with Rose's report, but I'm immediately disappointed. It's just a record of my missing person's report and the fact that they spoke to Lawrence about her. There's the date and time she entered the country and what she was last seen in – green dress, gold necklace, and Lawrence's statement that he 'barely remembered seeing her' at the party.

Reluctantly, I move on to the Tom Slazenger report. It's also a missing person's case. The only odd thing is that he was reported missing by Lawrence Fowley, and there's a note that describes his relationship as 'employer'. So Tom wasn't missed by family or friends. Maybe Tom just didn't have much of a life outside of work. Maybe Lawrence had jumped the gun to keep attention away from himself as a suspect and direct the search elsewhere.

I turn to the final report on Bergdis Olsen. This one has more in it because the police obviously had her body. Her niece had insisted on the autopsy and a note stated that she considered the death 'too sudden', especially due to her aunt's 'active lifestyle'. I flip to the autopsy report and find the weights of all Bergdis's organs noted down, along with observations on their colour and condition. I wince. It's as if she's an animal being butchered for parts.

My eyes slide down to 'Cause of death'. Heart attack. Not out of the ordinary for someone of her age, even if she did love hiking. Then I glance back at the list of organs and the notes beside them. The section for her heart reads 'heart appears in good health, arteries clear and in excellent condition, surrounding fatty tissue minimal'. Yet her healthy heart had just stopped. There was a scribble with a question mark under that note but it was too messy for the website to translate. I couldn't even read it myself.

On the final page I find test results for levels of different minerals and vitamins – possibly looking for something that might have weakened her heart or made it start beating weirdly. Under that is a list of drugs she'd tested positive for. Ibuprofen and paracetamol, fairly standard for someone her age who'd been on her feet all day working. Fosamax, which a quick google tells me is used for postmenopausal osteoporosis, and a final drug called loprazolam. The amount was circled three times with a question mark beside it.

I go back to Google and find that loprazolam is a benzodiazepine, used as a sleeping pill. Powerful stuff and potentially habit-forming. I frown at my phone. Sleeping pills. Could those cause a heart attack? Apparently the person performing the autopsy hadn't thought so. Scribbled at the bottom of the report is a final note: 'Prescriptions on file – overdose probably accidental due to postmenopausal insomnia'. Apparently they'd decided poor Bergdis was just desperate for sleep and had taken more of her medication than she was meant to, but her death was unrelated.

But someone could have used the sleeping pills to subdue her and then she'd somehow had a heart attack – maybe brought on by the stress of being kidnapped. I could see her assailant might have panicked when she died and taken her home, to make it look as though she'd died in her sleep.

Were Tom and Rose taken using a similar method? It would be easy, I think, to slip a few benzos to someone at a party. Especially one like Lawrence's. Perhaps Tom or even Rose took them willingly, disguised as a party drug.

So, now I have an idea of how my sister was taken; I just don't know by whom, or why. Frustration makes my skin crawl and I close the tabs on my phone with a sigh. I'm out of time. My meeting with Lawrence looms ahead of me.

I let myself out of the chalet and creep around the edge of the party, down towards the beach. It's still fairly early in the evening and I vaguely notice that some small tents have been put up and that the guests seem to be louder than yesterday.

I hurry down a path in the woods adjoining the garden. Above the sound of my shoes against the flagstones, I think I hear something else. The tap of footsteps behind me. I stop and glance back, but the path is clear and quiet.

I start to walk again, slower, my skin crawling. Moments later, as I'm rounding a corner in the trees, I become aware of the footsteps again. I stop. My breath catches in my throat and I strain to hear anything over the gentle creaking of branches in the breeze. There's something damp and stagnant about this wood, as if the air has been trapped under the canopy of trees for thousands of years, and I'm sure it's much darker than any forest back home. Wilder and deeper. I stare through branches and over moss-covered rocks into the gloom. The hair prickles at the base of my neck as I catch a glimpse of movement. A dark shape flashing between trees, a twig snapping. It's probably nothing, just the light breeze stirring the pines.

I take a deep breath and begin to walk faster, picking up speed. I try to keep my eyes on the path, all the way down the slope, my feet thudding faster and faster until I finally leave the creeping limbs of the trees behind and step out on to the beach. My heart thuds and I suck in deep breaths of fresh air. The sky looms over me and the mountains that flank the fjord stretch away towards the sea. I stare back at the dark forest, crouched at the edge of the sand. There's no one here, nothing to worry about.

I've calmed myself down and fixed my hair by the time I reach the jetty. The speedboat is already there, white and pristine. I wonder if it's new or if Lawrence has a boat cleaner on staff. Lawrence is on board already, along with a hamper containing a bottle of champagne. There are no staff around. It's just the two of us, the sea air and the open water. I shiver, suddenly feeling very vulnerable. Knife notwithstanding, I'm about to go out on to the fjord in a small boat with a man I don't know. A man I suspect of at least one murder and two kidnappings. Still, there's no turning back now. I paste on a smile and take Lawrence's extended hand, stepping into the boat.

'I'm glad you came,' Lawrence says, sounding sincere.

'I was under the impression that it was an offer I couldn't refuse,' I reply, going for cheeky but fun. 'But I'm glad you didn't have me immediately run off on James's behalf.'

'Ah, yes, your lunch.' Lawrence directs me to a seat and takes up the controls. 'I wish I'd seen it first-hand, but James's apoplexy was just as entertaining after the event.'

I can't tell if his nonchalance is genuine. There's something unreadable about him, and I start to wonder if I should turn back. The boat departs from the shore with a lurch. Too late now. We move like an arrow out into the centre of the fjord. It's the second time today that I've been out on the water, so I'm less awed by its beauty. I also feel far more exposed than I did when Sam and Cecile were with me. It's dark now and the fjord feels wider and deeper. Less like a resort and more like the wilderness it truly is, underneath all the sparkling waters and white sand – this is the raw edge of nature, sharp teeth under a smile. It suits Lawrence. It suits me.

I think of the knife in my bag. If Lawrence has brought me out here to gloat, or to throw what he's done to my sister in my face before he does the same to me, I'll be ready for him. I have trained for this: self-defence lessons and hours in the gym. If pushed, I think I can physically match Lawrence, but I'm not sure I have it in me to kill. As angry as I am, as filled with hate and fear, the idea of taking a life, now that I'm so close to doing it, fills my throat with bile. My hands shake so much that I have to cling to my bag to hide the tremors. I am praying that I'm not pushed to it. Once I find Rose I can get us out of here, I know I can.

Lawrence takes us in a graceful arc until we're facing the shore we came from again. Then the boat engine abruptly cuts off. The boat rocks unsteadily. I can hear the sounds of the party: fast-paced club music thudding like a radio several rooms away, the raised voices reduced to a dull echo across the water. Lights swivel and flash, illuminating shapes twisting and dancing together on the shore.

Lawrence takes a seat beside me, too close. I can feel the hair on my arms prickle in alarm, but I manage not to move.

He follows my gaze to the house and grounds. I can feel his arm brushing against mine as he pours us both a glass of champagne. We're so close that if he wanted to, he could slit my throat without having to do more than move his arm. My skin burns at his touch, and I want to scream, to yell for someone to help. Yet all I do is sit and listen to his steady breathing, waiting.

'It almost looks manageable from out here, doesn't it?' he says finally. 'The manor, I mean. From here it could be just any old house.'

'It looks beautiful, but it must be hard to run, a lot to deal with. How has it been since Zak . . .' I let the sentence trail off.

'A very unpleasant accident. I obviously did my best to ensure his wife made it home to her family as soon as possible.' He sighs. 'I wish I could have done more. James and Sam were very helpful that night, as was Ford.'

I sip my drink and hum in agreement, not wanting to divert him from his thoughts.

'I think that's why I wanted to come out here,' Lawrence continues. 'Gives a sense of perspective that's hard to find in a . . . warren of ancestral history, even without the added tension since the accident. That place is all about building on to what came before, all those portraits, all the stories. It's like every room is packed with ghosts. This is where your third cousin threw a cocktail over the French ambassador, but it's also where your uncle proposed to his first wife. And, by the window, that's where your great-grandfather read that his brother had died in the war.' He heaves a sigh. 'All those moments, pushing you onwards, but also pulling you back. Making you so aware of your place in the family. Your role.'

He removes his cigarette case from a pocket and offers me one. I decline and he lights up, holding the tiny pinprick of light as far from me as possible, out over the water.

'I'd like you to help me gain that perspective, Amelia.'

'Me? That's . . . I'm not sure what you mean. What can I do?'

'I don't know,' he muses. 'What can you do?'

I let that one dangle, like the bait it is. Eventually Lawrence sighs.

'You left your necklace behind yesterday. I took it back to the house. Quite an impressive piece. Ford spent a lot of money on it, on you, considering his salary. I was surprised that you didn't notice it was missing.'

I had, obviously. Leaving it behind was a final gesture to show I didn't care about Ford's money. I'd hoped it would be the end of the suspicions and accusations. But apparently I was wrong.

'I already told you, money doesn't matter to me,' I say, back on firmer ground now. 'I've never asked him for anything. Anyone would think you and James don't want him to find someone. To be happy.'

'Oh, I'm quite satisfied that you're not here for my cousin's money.'

'Thank you,' I say, but the tension in my spine remains. I can almost hear the next words in his cut-glass voice: *You're here for your sister.*

'I don't necessarily mean it as a compliment,' Lawrence says. 'Or as an insult, come to that. You don't want his money, but you want something. That's obvious. James is rather good at digging things up about people and he's completely convinced that you don't smell right.'

I can't breathe. This might be his weird way of saying that he knows who I really am. Or perhaps James hasn't found any proof and they just suspect I'm after something more than Ford's money. That maybe I've come here to seduce Lawrence away from Cecile.

'You've gone very quiet. James said that you had a lot to say for yourself earlier,' Lawrence observes, not unkindly but not entirely light-heartedly either. He's tense, his shoulder rigid where it touches mine. He's waiting, but I feel power-less, frozen to the spot like a rabbit in the headlights. I neck the last of my champagne and put down the glass. Finally my mind seems to click back into motion. This isn't going to work if I play it safe – I need to push him and it seems like my best shot is poking at what's important to him – his family.

'I'm a bit tired, that's all. And Ford wouldn't want me to embarrass any more of his immediate family.'

'Ford . . .' Lawrence says, turning the name over. 'Yes . . . I feel as if I've done him a disservice, leaving him out in the cold since taking over as head of the household. I know he wants to work for me – he was very disappointed when I didn't reach out a few years ago – but . . . blood doesn't always guarantee trust.'

He's changed his tune from yesterday, when family was the most important thing.

'He's very loyal to the family,' I say. 'To a fault, given he got bumped off your invite list last year. And now, when he actu-ally does get to visit you, James just treats him like . . . trash.'

Lawrence is silent for a moment; then he sighs. 'James doesn't mince his words. It's something I admire about him. That and he has reliable instincts. But I'm glad you gave as good as you got at lunch . . . and with me, yesterday. For the most part, James is worried that Ford might get between him and success in the business. Ford certainly has more skill and he works harder.'

'You'd pass over your own brother?'

Lawrence pauses for a moment, measuring his words. 'James thinks I won't. But . . . even my loyalty to him has limits.'

'And he's tested them?' I say, reckless now. I've barely eaten today and champagne was probably a bad idea. The bubbles are going straight to my head. I should have just held it without drinking but it's too late now.

Lawrence is silent. I wait but it appears he doesn't feel like answering that question. Still, there's a feeling of secrets waiting to be shed. A weight hanging over us on a thread that's rapidly unravelling.

Finally, Lawrence speaks. 'Did you know, Cecile was the only person who could stop James bullying Sam? When we were children.'

I blink, unsure where this is going.

'He's always had a thing for her,' Lawrence continues. 'As long as I can remember. Though of course it's been common knowledge for our entire lives that our father and Cecile's wanted the pair of us to marry.'

'Sounds sort of old-fashioned.'

Lawrence laughs, a bitter huff. 'My father was old-fashioned. Never believed in "new-fangled" things like email, renewable energy or . . . relationships not befitting one's standing.'

My tongue runs away with me. 'That'd be me, would it? A "commoner".'

'He wouldn't have liked you at all – probably wouldn't have tolerated your presence here. Which would have been to his detriment. But yes, he was a very proud man, devoted to his legacy, to the Fowley name. He did everything he could to ensure his standards would be upheld, even after his death.' Lawrence finishes his cigarette and tucks the end into his case. 'I sometimes feel like a servant, more than an heir. I'm only here to carry out his wishes. To the letter.'

'Which includes marrying Cecile?' I say, bringing us back around to where we started. Something about his expression makes me press on. 'You . . . don't want to marry her?'

Lawrence sits up a little straighter and it's then that I catch the scent of vodka under the cigarette smoke and his cologne. He's had more than a drop. Liquid courage perhaps? Or a reaction to the stress of a guest dying on the first night?

'You and your questions. You seem to be into everything since you arrived – talking to my sister, my brother, fiancée . . . Cecile thinks you're lovely, by the way. She would know: I've never met anyone so perceptive and yet so deeply, truly kind.' Lawrence sighs. 'She deserves much better than me. Than this family.'

I have no idea what to say to that. It feels as if Lawrence is trying to lure me into something. Dangling a juicy hint right there, when previously he's been so studied and careful. Then again, maybe he's just drunk and being careless. But if he was, would he be able to pilot the boat so well?

We sit in silence for a long while, looking out across the dark water. My back is as tense as a wire. I don't want to give myself away, so I stay silent. Finally, Lawrence tips his drink over the side, stands and steps towards the controls.

'Thank you for accompanying me. It's been . . . illuminating,' he says. 'I do have to get back, though. I have to make an appearance at tonight's event.'

'You're welcome for the company – for what it was worth,' I say, wondering what I've given away in exchange for this trip. Perhaps this has all been a way to keep me away from the manor, the party and from Ford while something terrible is happening. Something like Zak yesterday, I think. Even so I feel my shoulders relax as I start to believe that he's not going to attack me now, not here.

'It was very worthwhile,' Lawrence assures me, starting the engine. 'I've been looking for answers and now, finally, I think I'm getting close to having them.'

17

ONCE WE REACH THE dock Lawrence disappears into the throng of the party. I follow behind, hindered by the guests who magically parted to allow him through, but closed ranks against me. I'm determined to see where he goes, but I quickly lose him in the crowd. Tonight the atmosphere feels more heated, less polite. I'm jostled as I try to walk towards the house. People are openly staring at me now, not bothering to hide it. I'm not paranoid, even if Ford couldn't see it. They're definitely watching me.

We've all been here for a full day and everyone appears to have shaken off the weariness of travel, as well as their inhibitions. People are dancing energetically to the pounding music, and the women who previously wore gowns are showing off their private-beach tans and personal-trainer-honed bodies. I catch a whiff of weed and spy at least five separate clusters of guests sniffing lines of powder from trays. One waiter pauses at my elbow, offering me a silver tray which holds a hundred pills, each one on a tiny china dish no bigger than a bottle cap. The pills are minutely stamped with the Fowley crest. I decline, politely. But I accept a glass of some unidentified cocktail with orange slices and frozen cranberries floating in it, just to look social.

The Perspex dance floor over the pool has gone, exposing the water, which is foaming and churning with jacuzzi jets and bodies, the water tinted with swirling mica, as if everyone is swimming in liquid gold. Very few people are in actual swimwear: most are in their party clothes; some have stripped down to exotic lingerie. They shriek and splash, Chanel mascara running over their cheeks. Nearby a woman in a drenched evening gown, ostrich feather skirt shrivelled to rattails, retches into an enormous stone planter.

A couple of guests catch me looking their way and glare back, as if they're offended that I'm even glancing at them. I feel unwelcome, as though I'm surrounded by a pack of animals. I can almost detect a feral quality to their expressions as they look my way – sensing an outsider. Sensing prey. I shake my head and push on, sipping my drink as my mouth turns suddenly dry.

The large dining tents from yesterday are gone, replaced by the smaller, more intimate bowers I noticed earlier. I pass a few empty tents and spy long couches and side tables mounded with fresh fruit, jugs of wine and towers of canapés. The luxurious fabrics and long, cushioned couches give the feel of a Roman bacchanal. The crowd is dense near them and for several minutes I have to shimmy sideways to get between people.

I stumble over someone's foot in the crush and grab hold of a random sleeve to keep myself from falling. I'm angrily shrugged off and yet I don't feel particularly annoyed or fazed by this. I feel mellow. I can hear the swimmers screaming over the music and the sound of glass breaking as someone fumbles a slippery champagne bottle.

The sounds seem to judder slightly, echoing on for a

moment longer than they should, like a CD scratching. I haven't eaten since lunch and my dizziness feels like plummeting blood sugar. I take a step and the world around me sort of twists. I'm left blinking and struggling to keep my balance. My vision blurs and then refocuses. Not blood sugar. What the hell? I glance down at the cocktail in my hand. I've only had a few sips. I can't be drunk. I hear laughter, bright and hard as diamonds.

Suddenly, as I look around for a way out of the party, the coloured spotlights hidden within the knot gardens turn white, swivelling their blinding lights upwards. I follow the beams and realize that the balcony over the garden is now illuminated – on it stands Lawrence, hand in hand with Cecile.

Up on the balcony, they look divine – literally – as if an Olympian god and goddess have deigned to look in on the festivities. Or maybe that's just my blurry eyes. Lawrence is still in his black suit, his long golden hair a halo in the light, and Cecile is wearing a dress with a corset designed to represent faceted crystal. She shines like a disco ball, and soon everyone is craning their necks and calling out to the couple, cheering and whooping.

'Good evening, my distinguished friends,' Lawrence says, his voice now devoid of any signs of drunkenness, sliding velvety-smooth from concealed speakers all around me. 'Thank you for your delightful company this evening.'

The crowd cheers. The noise is almost too much for me. Dimly I realize that I'm shaking, trembling, even though I feel weirdly relaxed. I notice waiters swiftly distributing glasses of champagne amongst everyone assembled in the gardens. No sign of James or Ford. They must still be at their card game. I feel a twinge of worry about Ford and what James is doing to him. But that worry soon vanishes into a feeling of warmth. Everything at the edges of my vision is going dark; the only bright point is at the centre. I whine in confusion like a child and try to blink the shadows away.

'I have but one announcement to make before you are free to return to your night of revelries,' Lawrence continues. 'My darling Cecile and I are happy to announce that our wedding will take place in six months – right here at the Fowley estate.'

Cheers and congratulations rise to deafening levels. I wince and set my drink down on a stone balustrade, unable to keep hold of it with my numb fingers. I shouldn't have any more, that much I know. I don't know what was in it but it's swimming in my veins now.

'And', Lawrence says, voice cutting through the chaos, 'you are all invited.'

The crowd reacts as if they've just been given front-row seats to a comeback tour featuring Elvis and the Beatles. I suppose it is quite exciting; Lawrence might not be a top-tier celebrity but that's part of the appeal. He's secretive, exclusive, and his wedding is likely to be massive and expensive, as hard to get into as a royal wedding, but without the paparazzi.

The spotlights swoop away from the balcony and I squint into the dark, trying to see where Lawrence and Cecile have gone. It's pointless, though. I can't see a thing. The gates to Olympus are closed and I'm still down here with the mortals. I wonder, though, if Lawrence might be on his way to his spot on the beach, for a bit of reflection. After all, the announcement of his wedding date came only a short time after he confessed that she deserved better than him. But that could have been an act for my benefit. He might be in denial, or just wilfully pressing on with his 'duty', but either way, I might find him in a fragile state. One in which he's more likely to make a mistake.

I keep thinking about what he said regarding James testing his family loyalties. If James is behind the disappearances of Tom and my sister, would Lawrence help him cover it up? He might be about to crack under the guilt and I need to be there when he does.

As I turn away I nearly trip over my feet, my vision flickering. I sit down on a bench and take a deep breath, closing my eyes. After a moment, I start to feel a bit better, and when I look up I spot a shape. Someone lingering in the shadows between two tents. I freeze at the sight of him. It's James and he looks furious, though he isn't looking at me. His intense, dark eyes are fixed on the unlit balcony. His thick fist is gripping a crystal tumbler so tightly I'm surprised it hasn't exploded.

Before I can consider getting out of his way in case he detonates, a laughing couple stagger between us. In the second he's out of view, he disappears. I look around but can't tell where he might have gone. Is his card game with Ford over, or was he just coming outside to see what all the fuss was about?

I remember what Lawrence said about James's crush on Cecile. He's an adult now, and it looked to me as if he was far too angry for this to be some childish fixation. He looked murderous. I'm willing to bet that James isn't just crushing on Cecile, he's obsessed with her. With everything Lawrence has that he doesn't. James looked as though he wanted to rip Lawrence apart. Out of the two of them, I know who I think is more capable of having harmed Rose.

I hurry the rest of the way to the beach, stumbling slightly even in my sensible shoes. Everything has its own aura of colour and my vision is tunnelling, making the world seem distant and strange. The shifting sand underfoot tilts my brain even further. Despite that, I'm still looking for him – but I can't think straight.

I spot a tiny pinprick of red light glowing near the furthest jetty and my heart leaps. Lawrence! Only when I get closer do I see that the silhouette is too short, too thin. The scent wafting towards me isn't some luxury mix of tobacco, it's a joint.

'Hello? Amelia, is that you?'

'Sam?' I get closer and find her leaning against the jetty rail, just as her stepbrother had done the night before. Like me she's not dressed for the party – she's wearing patchwork harem pants and a camisole, an oversized hoodie draped around her shoulders to keep off the evening chill. It looks so soft, I can't help but reach out and touch it.

'Are you not going to the party?' I ask.

'Hmm? Oh, no. I said I'd put in an appearance for Cecile but it's not really my scene. Besides, I've had enough of James today.'

'Same,' I say, without thinking, and Sam laughs.

'He has that effect on people.'

'He looked pretty pissed off about the wedding announcement,' I chance, fishing for a response. I clasp the rail of the jetty and try to power through my giddiness. I need to focus. It feels as if it might be working; that, or the cool breeze is grounding me.

'He would be. James has always had a thing for Cecile.' Sam lowers her voice. 'Mind you, I don't think Cecile does much to discourage it. Maybe she thinks it keeps Lawrence keen – having his little brother fawning over her. You want some of this?' She returns to her normal volume and offers me the joint. I shake my head.

'Ford doesn't like it – the smell—'

'Ah, and you don't do anything he doesn't like.' Sam interrupts me, exhaling and watching the smoke drift into the dark. 'A word of advice, Amelia. Getting involved with the Fowley family is like . . . walking into that bramble forest in *Sleeping Beauty*. You think it's just a matter of pushing on, getting through the worst of it, but those vines are closing in. Tighter and tighter, until you can barely move.' She examines the hand holding the joint, brushes at specks of ash which may or may not be there. 'Don't get trapped.'

'Is that how you feel?' I ask.

'Oh, you know. There are a lot of expectations, a lot of rules that Lawrence's daddy dearest left for us to follow. Less so for me. I mean, he barely acknowledged my existence, so I got some cash, a home and mostly no strings attached. Well, apart from having to come to this thing every year.' She gestures up at the party and the manor. 'I think it's so Lawrence can keep an eye on me. Make sure I'm not bringing the family name into disrepute. That's the other thing – gotta keep his name. Though that has advantages.'

'So . . . there are more restrictions on James, and Lawrence?' I ask. I feel as though I'm watching her from the wrong end of some binoculars but at least her words are making sense. Hopefully whatever this is will wear off as quickly as it kicked in.

'Oh yeah. I think I got off lightly. We were all there when the will was read. It was very theatrical. Mr Fowley Senior was so controlling I half expected him to leave a seating chart, maybe pick outfits for all of us. Make sure it all went exactly as he was imagining it. I think James got the worst of it, though. Lawrence just has to keep the business going and get married to Cecile before he's thirty-five. But James . . .' She whistles. 'I feel bad for him.'

'What rules does he have to follow?' I ask, my mouth dry.

Sam lets out a little stoned giggle. 'He has to live here, of course. Right under Big Brother's nose. Can you imagine? Can't move out until Lawrence gets married, then he has to live in one of the lodges in the grounds until he finds someone to marry him. That's when he gets his inheritance. Until then he has to ask Lawrence for sweetie money. Unless Lawrence doesn't get married in time . . . then James gets everything. That's a lot of uncertainty. Glad it's not on me.'

I absorb this, understanding now why James looked so furious at the party. He's caught in a trap, just as Sam said. On the one hand, he needs Lawrence to marry so that he can move out of the family house and have a shot at claiming his own inheritance. On the other, Lawrence has to marry Cecile, whom James has apparently always wanted for himself. He can't win, unless Lawrence doesn't or can't marry her.

'What if Cecile marries someone else? Or she . . . I don't know, dies in a skydiving accident?' I giggle at my own words, feeling heady and strange.

This ludicrous idea clearly tickles Sam, especially in her stoned state. 'Lawrence'd have to find someone "equitable". That's what the will said. Equitable. Like Cecile's a car or something . . . that can just be replaced with a similar model.'

She's very high, I realize. Well, we both are. If she'd been sober she would probably have noticed how unsteady I am. I look around, wondering if I'll need to walk her back to where she's staying. Then I realize I have no idea where that is and really I need walking home myself. I'm clinging to the jetty and unsure if I can trust my own feet.

Sam takes a long drag on what's left of her joint, then flicks it off into the darkness, slowly letting the smoke escape from her lips. She stops leaning on the jetty and nearly falls over into the sand.

'Sam . . . why don't I walk you to your room?' I ask, putting my hand on her arm to steady her and myself. It just feels like the right thing to do. Girls watching out for each other.

'Hmm? You don't have to. I can . . .' Sam trips over her own foot and staggers into me. I nearly fall over, but put my arm around her and get both of us steady. We start to walk up the beach. A forlorn three-legged race. Like two drunk girls hobbling home from a club. My stomach is churning and my skin feels clammy. Everything is swaying horribly in front of me.

'Here, we can cut through the rose garden,' Sam says.

The route takes us away from the main party, which is no bad thing. The noise and lights only make me feel worse. What little I glimpse through the hedges is fairly grotesque. The staff are still perfectly composed, doing the rounds with trays of champagne and pharmaceuticals, but the guests have deteriorated. The pool is full of people, wet clothes abandoned all over the patio, and there's a strong smell of piss which takes me back to the one and only festival I've ever been to, where people were just peeing in the woods all around us.

In the refreshing quiet of the rose garden I inhale the soft scent of fallen petals and try to get control of myself. I don't feel as though I'm going to pass out, I just feel . . . buzzed. Giddy. But that still makes me vulnerable. After I get Sam to her room – wherever that is – I'm going straight back to my chalet to lie down and try to sober up. I feel really weird. Not the kind of state I want to be in during the rich-person equivalent of feeding time at the zoo.

'Don't you dare touch me!'

I turn so fast that I nearly drop Sam on the dewy grass. She squeals and I shush her automatically. At the centre of the rose garden is a large lily pond, the walls about shin-high. There must be a few lights in the water because the area around it glows softly. Just enough that I can see Charlie, the cleaner from Lawrence's office, storming into the little clearing and pacing around the fountain.

I hear a man's voice, not Charlie, but just as far away as him. Whoever it is, they're clearly more worried about being overheard than he is. After some sharp murmuring, I see Charlie come back around to where he first appeared, arms up as if either threatening or entreating someone.

'I know what you said. But I'm telling you – no. I can't believe you had me sneaking around like . . . No. I'm done.'

Sam picks that moment to lose her footing, swaying into part of a nearby box hedge. The sound of twigs snapping and branches rustling makes me wince.

'Who's that?' Charlie calls, but I'm already dragging Sam away, stumbling.

On the other side of the rose garden she staggers to a stop, peering at the path in front of us. It's white gravel, luminous as stardust in the dark. The path goes three ways, back through the rose garden, towards the house and off into the orchard.

'I can get myself to bed,' Sam announces, swinging me into a hug. 'Thank you, Amelia. You're one of the good ones. Don't let the bastards get you down.'

I feel sick to my stomach, because I know she's wrong. I'm awful. I'm an intruder, probing at all her family's most private business and using her against her brothers. I hope she never finds out what I really am.

'G'night!' Sam calls, stumbling over the gravel path towards the house.

I turn and start to retrace my steps. My pulse pounds behind my eyes. I can feel my body crawling with cold sweat. What have I been given and why?

Was it slipped into the cocktail as I squeezed through the crowd or . . . did Lawrence put something in the champagne? Maybe all the drinks are drugged for this party. I need to get somewhere safe. I think of Bergdis's autopsy report, the sleeping pills, and wonder if I'm about to experience what she did in her final moments.

Suddenly aware of how isolated I am, alone in the dark, I quickly take the path back through the rose garden. There's no sign of Charlie or his mystery man. They must've gone somewhere more private. I'm freaking out too much to wonder what they were up to or how it related to what he was doing in Lawrence's office yesterday. Perhaps tomorrow I can ask him . . . I just need to survive tonight.

I avoid the party by staying close to the manor house,

skirting the mayhem in its shadow. Despite the darkness outside, my world is full of colours; every light is a prism full of rainbows. They trail after people in strange shapes. I consider trying to stop someone, ask them for help, but there's no point. Those people watched Zak crack his skull open on the patio and didn't care. I am under no illusions that they'll help me if I pass out in front of them. My vision swims and I stagger onwards, desperate to reach the chalet.

The path to the guest chalets is again lined in candles, but by now most of them have burnt out, leaving the way in darkness. The distant sounds of the party – the screaming and the music, disjointed and weird at this distance – are muffled as I enter the trees. I shiver at the memory of earlier, at the sensation of being followed. I can't let that thought return now, not when I'm like this. Yet as I walk I can't shake the sense that there's another sound, close by. The soft, stealthy movements of something or someone in the treeline. Voices and shouts reach me occasionally like bits of old memories. I almost lose my footing and stray off the path but manage to keep myself moving in the right direction.

I pause a few times, listening and looking around me. There could be someone there. Is that a figure, standing still? My mind is awash. My pulse is racing. I'm not sure if it's fear or the drugs.

I reach the chalet door and fumble for the key in my bag. It slips through my sweating fingers and I swear, struggling to focus. Expecting someone to grab me at any moment. The light touch of fingers on my spine. Eventually I snag the key but as I slide it into the lock, the door opens – it was unlocked. The room beyond it is dark.

'Ford?' I call out, slowly opening the door and stepping inside. The silence that greets me is eerie and strange. 'Are you back?'

No answer. I can't see a thing, but still I take a step forward, holding my breath.

My foot crunches on broken glass.

18

I REACH FOR THE light switch, struggling to find it in the unfamiliar room. I catch it without warning and light floods the chalet, making my brain scream in protest. I gasp at the sight before me.

The place has been completely turned over. Every ornament thrown, every piece of furniture stripped. Several tables are on their sides. Bits of smashed crockery litter the floor.

I slip one hand into my bag, gripping the handle of the ceramic knife inside.

'Ford?' I call again, moving slowly towards the stairs, vision speckled with dark spots, my knees going weak. I begin to climb, pulling myself up by the banister, my ears straining for any sounds. A tense silence is the only thing that greets me.

A quick glance into the bathroom tells me that it too has been ransacked, the contents of my real cosmetics case mingling with Ford's toiletries on the floor. Things have rolled across the counter. A bottle of red nail polish has exploded, spattering the tiles and drying like a haunted-house bloodstain.

The last place to search is the bedroom. I step along the corridor towards it, my heart thudding in my chest. I try to control my breathing as I stand at the door and listen. Silence. I push the door open tensed for an attack and am relieved to find no one there. Not even Ford. By this time I'm clutching the doorframe to stay upright. All our suitcases have been emptied out and some have the lining cut away. A thorough search, but for what? I blink and rub my eyes. Is this all because of the drugs I've been given? I have no idea. My knees buckle and I struggle for the bed, finding my other cosmetics case on the floor beside it. My limbs feel like lead, my eyelids fighting to stay open. I'm losing the battle.

I sprawl out on the bed to reach the bottle of water on the night stand. My mouth is so dry that my tongue is sticking to the roof of it. I can't quite reach the water but I force myself to inch closer, my fingers eventually catching on the edge of the drawer. My vision begins to darken and fade and my hand falls to the bed.

I wake up, freezing cold and with a throbbing headache. For a moment I can't remember why I feel so terrible, why my mouth tastes as if I've licked the beach. Then it comes back to me: the panic in my syrupy veins, the realization that I'd been drugged. The ransacked chalet.

I sit up and whimper. It feels as though my brain is sloshing around in my skull, bruised and raw. Through eyes like slits I squint around me and realize quickly that it's early in the morning, practically still night, and that Ford isn't beside me.

Slowly I drag myself to the side of the bed and get my feet on the floor. I reach for the bottle of water and glance at the open drawer of the bedside table. I freeze. I yank the drawer the rest of the way open just in case, but there's no denying it.

My passport is gone.

The passport which has my real last name in it. The same surname as Rose. Feeling panicky I lunge for the cosmetics case and check the contents, only to feel shards of ice trickle through my veins. The photo of Rose and her invitation to Lawrence's party are both gone. The only evidence I physically had in my possession. To top it off, without my passport, I'm stuck here in Norway.

Whoever tore the chalet apart either found what they were looking for or chanced upon my secret by accident. Either way, they know. They can connect the dots now, if they didn't know already.

All I can manage to do is get my phone out with a shaking hand that leaves smudges of sweat on the screen and text Ford about the break-in. I check my messages but there's nothing from Ford, or from Elena. A prickle of worry runs down my spine. Elena hasn't contacted me since I left her that message. I fall back on the bed and drift off again, hoping she made it home in one piece and is just ignoring me. Whatever I was drugged with has left me weak and tired. I don't wake up again until gone seven in the morning.

The sun is up and I feel better, if still shaken and a bit panicked. Ford hasn't yet returned. I check my phone. No texts or calls.

With nothing else to do but get up, I change out of last night's clothes and dress in jeans, boots and a crisp white shirt. I tie my hair up in a ponytail and apply my makeup, sipping water and trying to get back to normal. I can't go around looking weakened or worried. Whoever did this needs to see that I'm not afraid. I feel about as close to my old self as I have in months. The no-nonsense get-up might be designer and not in shades of black and grey, but it's nearly there. I don't feel like being 'gym bunny Amelia' today. I need a little bit of edge. A bit of grit to ward off my enemies.

Downstairs, in the ruined living area, I make an espresso to try and get myself to a functional level of wakefulness and wait for Ford to come in. As the time wears on I start to wonder if maybe he's the one who's found me out. Maybe he looked at my passport for some reason, then realized what I had done and tore the chalet apart in a rage? Ford would have called me though, sent me a message. He would have wanted to talk things through. No, this was someone else, maybe Lawrence or James. They were out of my sight for long enough. Equally, they have any number of staff they could have ordered to go through my things. I'll have to see what they are like this morning. They might tip their hand a little, try to get more information from me.

Finally, the chalet door opens and Ford spills in through it.

'Ford,' I begin, ready to launch into an account of the burglary. I think I might be able to summon tears for it – I certainly feel crappy enough – but one look at his pale, slightly grey face and my throat dries up. Something's wrong.

'What is it?' I ask, terrified of what he's about to tell me.

He stumbles into the room, his clothes wrinkled, the stale waft of cigars and booze rolling off him, a sheen of unwashed grease on his face. He looks worse than I feel and I was drugged yesterday.

'There's . . . They've found a body,' he says, looking at me as if he can't believe the words coming out of his mouth. 'On the beach.'

'Body?' I stand, one hand flying to my throat. Elena's face flashes across my mind. 'Who? How?'

Ford reaches the sofa and, apparently not noticing the destruction all around, collapses on to it. He rests his elbows on his knees, hands clasped together, as if he's about to pray.

'I was walking back, trying to get some fresh air down by the water. There were staff there, pulling it out of the fjord. I ran over and . . .' He shakes his head. 'They said it was one of them – a staff member. A new cleaner. Archie?'

'Charlie?' I say, so softly that I'm surprised to see Ford's head jerk up. My mind is whirling, thinking of the argument I overheard last night. The rose garden wasn't that far from the beach.

'Yeah, that's what they . . . Do you know him?'

'I, uh, met him. Just around, the other day. Young guy, sandy hair?'

'No idea. But sounds like the person they . . . I mean you could see he was dead. Someone said it looked like he'd maybe gone for a swim. There were clothes on the beach, and an empty bottle of vodka.'

I feel cold all over. How much time had there been after the argument for him to get rip-roaring drunk and then decide to go for a swim? He was a cleaner, surely he knew that he'd have his work cut out for him today? It was a weird choice, to drink a bottle of vodka only hours before a long shift mopping up the vomit of the rich and fabulous. No, something about this feels . . . wrong.

'What happened here?' Ford asks, apparently just noticing the ransacked living room. He reaches for my hands. 'Jesus . . . are you OK?'

'I think so . . . It was like this when I got back. Lawrence dropped me off at the beach, then I hung out with Sam for a bit before I walked her to the manor. It was late when I got in and found this,' I say, deciding not to mention the drugs someone slipped me. Ford might not even believe me.

'You should have called me, texted, something!' Ford fumbles his phone out and groans. 'You did. I'm sorry, Aimes. James told us to turn our phones off – for the game, you know? I was going to come back last night but we were all so drunk . . .'

'It's fine,' I assure him. 'I mean, I was a bit freaked out and too scared to go back up to the house to look for help, but the chalet was empty by then. I missed whoever it was that did this. I don't even know why they'd do something like this.'

'Did they take anything?' Ford leaps to his feet, energized by this new worry. 'Fuck, your jewellery! My iPad, my watches!'

'There isn't anything missing,' I say. 'Not that I can see. Nothing like that, I mean.'

'What does that mean?'

'Well . . .' I try and laugh it off. 'I can't find my passport. But that's probably just me being disorganized. It'll turn up.'

I had thought, as I waited for him to come home, of lying to him. But if my passport doesn't show up I won't be able to keep that from him. I'm stuck in Norway, on the Fowley estate. I've no car and no ID. My licence – also with my real name on it – was hidden inside my passport case. I couldn't risk Ford looking through my bag and finding it. Now it's gone too.

'Jesus Christ!' Ford accidently kicks a half-shattered earthenware vase across the floor as he paces. 'What the hell were they doing in here?'

'Maybe it was guests? They might have come into the

wrong chalet by accident. Or they decided it would be funny to wreck shit in here. Things were getting quite out of hand last night. I saw a lot more than I wanted to on the way back.'

Ford pinches the bridge of his nose, pushing his glasses up his face. 'We'll have to sort you out an emergency passport or something if you can't find yours. I'll tell Lawrence or James about the mess and have a cleaner come over.'

At the mention of cleaners, Ford turns pale again, clearly remembering the body he'd seen being pulled from the fjord. I wondered whether whoever had turned over our chalet had decided to cap their night off with a murder. I shudder. The second party of three and the second death.

'Uh . . . I need to get showered, get dressed,' Ford says, moving towards the stairs. As he hurries up he calls back to me, 'We're invited to breakfast with the rest of the family – in the orchard. I'm not sure if it'll go ahead now but . . . as no one has said it's cancelled I suppose we should go.'

'Might be a good idea – to find out what's going on,' I say.

But Ford has already shut the bathroom door.

A body on the beach and breakfast in the orchard. Not what I expected for my final day at the Fowley estate. My skin prickles with nerves; I might be about to have breakfast with the person who drugged me and tore my room apart last night, then killed someone on the beach. I only have one more day to get to the bottom of things. Even if I am without a passport, I doubt I'll be able to stay on. Ford will likely book us into a hotel. He won't want to impose.

Ford emerges from the bathroom sometime later, dressed in a beige suit and blue shirt combo which reminds me of the beach. This only makes me think of poor Charlie's final resting place, but I paste on a polite smile and accompany him out of the door for breakfast.

The morning is crisp but not cold – the kind that promises a sizzling afternoon. The early autumn heatwave shows no signs of leaving and the air is sweet with the scent of fallen apples and grass baked into hay. A long table draped in white has been set up between the apple trees in the orchard. As Ford and I approach I can see that Sam, James and Cecile are already there. Lawrence is conspicuously absent from the head of the table. James has taken the other end.

The table itself is laden with food, from smoked salmon with lemon and dill to crisp croissants with seashell-shaped butter and silver dishes of jam. Everything about it looks so clean and fresh that for a moment the excesses of the night before feel like a dream. Then, out of the corner of my eye, I spot a staff member in elbow-length Marigolds carrying a bundle of mops and a bucket towards the pool.

'Morning,' Cecile says, her usual bright voice slightly tarnished by the morning's grim discovery. 'I assume Ford has told you about . . . what's happened?'

'Yes,' I say, taking a seat. 'It's awful.'

I risk a glance at Sam, wondering if she remembers seeing Charlie the night before. She isn't looking at me, or at anyone else. Her bloodshot eyes are fixed on a point in the middle distance as she drains a glass of orange juice and pours herself another. She might well not remember anything.

Sam looks so awful that, by comparison, James is almost fresh-faced. His clothes are apparently the ones he was wearing last night, if the amount of creases and the slight smell of cigarettes are anything to go by, and he's unshaven, but he's at least awake and alert. It's odd, I think, that he's chosen not to change. Perhaps it's a protest for Lawrence's benefit, or he just can't be bothered.

Cecile is the only one who appears truly well rested, her skin peachy and her eyes bright as a puppy's. She smooths a napkin into her lap and looks up, catching my eye and smiling. Then her gaze slips behind me and her expression crumples.

'Oh, Lawrence,' she says softly.

I turn in my seat and spot him. His long hair is limp and, though he's wearing a fresh shirt and tailored trousers, there's something rumpled and worn about his posture. Something haunted about the way his eyes dart around the table, settling on Cecile.

'You're all aware then,' he says, his voice a hollow version of itself. 'Of the death that has occurred.'

'Yes, it's awful! Come and sit down.' Cecile beckons him over. When he takes his seat at the table, she pours him a cup of tea from a silver pot and places a slice of lemon in it. Her hand finds his arm and squeezes as she sets the cup down. 'I can't imagine how such a thing happened.'

'The police have been made aware. They seem fairly certain already that it was some kind of drunken accident.' Lawrence looks down the table. 'They did say they'd need to do some tests, to be sure, but . . . in the meantime it's not being treated as suspicious.'

I watch Lawrence carefully. There's something stilted and steely about him today, as if he's struggling to control himself. I can't tell if it's a reaction to the shocking death or something darker. Something like guilt. I wonder why the police were brought in this time, when they weren't for Zak. Unless Ford was mistaken and they were. Perhaps one of the staff members raised the alarm before the family could hush it up.

'How awful,' Cecile says. 'I can't imagine what he was thinking, trying to swim in the dark.'

'It's been unseasonably warm, but at night – well, I wouldn't want to do it,' James says with a wrinkled nose.

'Might seem like a fun idea after a bottle of vodka, though,' Ford says, still sounding a bit numb. 'Jesus, to think it was probably happening during the party . . .'

Sam shakes her head. 'We were at the beach, weren't we, Amelia? We didn't see him and it was already really late by then.'

I look at her. 'Do you remember me walking you back to the house?'

Sam's eyebrows shoot up. 'Did you? Fuck, I don't remember. Did you walk back along the beach afterwards?'

I shake my head. 'No. I went around the back of the house, straight to the chalet.'

'Weird,' Cecile says. 'That you didn't see him.'

I don't want to come out and say *actually I did and he was arguing with someone*, not with my two main suspects sitting at either end of the table. Thankfully the mention of the chalet prompts Ford into action.

'Oh yes, you'll never guess what Amelia found when she got back last night – our whole chalet turned over and pawed through. Like we'd been burgled.'

'Really?' Cecile looks aghast. 'Who could have done that?'

I catch Sam levelling a hard look at James, who's studiously ignoring her.

'We've no idea,' Ford says. 'Amelia thought perhaps it was another guest – drunk, I suppose.'

'Was anything missing?' James asks me, the words pointed, but Ford answers before I have a chance to.

'No, which is the weirdest thing. Though you couldn't find your passport, could you, Aimes?'

'It'll probably turn up,' I say, summoning a careless smile. 'I can't imagine why anyone would want to steal that.'

'Maybe someone's trying to steal your identity,' Cecile says. 'You never know these days.'

'Excuse me, Mr Fowley?'

We all turn to look at a maid, who is blushing furiously and twisting her hands into her apron. Behind her a trail of footprints in the dewy grass lead straight to the back door, where several other staff members are clustered around. They disappear as soon as they realize they're being watched.

'Yes?' Lawrence asks.

'The police are here. They've just passed the main gate.'

I watch as Lawrence swallows, then stands up, discarding his napkin on to the table. It lands in the untouched tea Cecile poured for him, the heavy linen soaking up the liquid. He departs without a backward glance or a word of excuse, and I see Cecile's lips twist downwards. She looks upset and maybe scared, though I can't tell if she's worried for him or because of him.

I do, however, spot a chance to get some answers and quickly excuse myself to go and find a bathroom. Lawrence went into the door at the back of the house, but the maid went around the side, possibly to continue the clean-up operation in the garden. I catch up with her on the driveway.

'Excuse me?' I call, only a few feet from her.

The maid jumps, apparently shocked to see me. Then she schools her expression back to professional blankness. 'How can I help you?'

'I was wondering, the man who died – Charlie . . . he was new, right?'

She blinks at me, caught between answering my question politely and being appalled that I would even ask.

'It's just, I thought I knew him from back home – I'm sure he worked for a friend of mine before. She'll want to know, you see, so she can send flowers to his family.'

It's a massive crock, but Charlie was British and I'd noticed how new his uniform was when we met. So I'm hoping I can sell her the story. It seems to work, as the maid's expression softens slightly.

'He was new. This was his first year working with us.'

'Had he only just been hired by Black Diamond?' I ask, remembering the name of the company Elena had told me she worked for.

'No, he wasn't from there,' the maid says.

'I thought all the event staff came through them?' I say. What I do not add is that he was wearing a uniform with their logo on it.

She frowns slightly. 'I'm not sure I'm meant to . . .'

'Sorry, I don't want to pry, it's just – my friend will need to know who to contact for his most recent address.'

It's a paper-thin excuse, but the poor girl is obviously still in shock. Her eyes dart from left to right and her face is pale.

'Right . . . Well, Charlie never said he wasn't with Black Diamond, but a few of us noticed that he never got a payslip when we did. It's this big thing; they come in a pile to the beach house where we're staying. He never got one. One of the kitchen guys said he was probably a "direct hire". Not from the agency. But he was wearing agency uniform, which I thought was weird.'

Me too. 'Do you know who hired him?'

She shrugs. 'No idea. I'm not sure anyone knew.'

Frustrated that her information has run dry, I thank the maid and head back to the breakfast table, my mind whirling. It seems odd that someone hired a non-agency cleaner just for the hell of it. The security is incredibly tight and using the agency is probably a part of that.

Perhaps someone hired him to pose as agency staff – James or a journalist wanting access to the inner workings of Lawrence's household. Zak Bakshi might have been desperate enough to do it, if he wanted an advance look at those redundancy notes. But it isn't as if I can ask him now. Perhaps he was killed for the same reason as Charlie – to keep whatever they'd discovered from getting out. What could Charlie have found and why did it get him murdered?

19

FOLLOWING THE VERY TENSE breakfast in the orchard, Ford takes my elbow and tells me he's going to the sauna to try and 'sweat out' his hangover. He asks what I'm planning to do and I tell him I'll probably go for a walk. James has already said he would have some staff sent over to the chalet to put things right, so I can't go there. Not if I want to make the call I'm planning to.

'See you later,' Ford says, giving me a hug, which is a bit unusual for him. I wonder if the death of Charlie has affected him more than I thought. 'Don't go too far from the house, OK? I worry about you.'

I head back towards the chalet, but instead of going straight on towards it, or right to the manor itself, I take a trail to the left. It's marked with whitewashed stones, winding on through the mossy forest and occasionally crossing the stream that runs behind our chalet. I walk for a while, hopping over stepping stones and pausing on a log bridge to take in the view. After so much stress and a night spent being drugged and freaked out, the last place I want to be is the woods. But at least out here I'm away from anyone who might overhear me, or potential bugs in the chalet. Still, the dark trees loom over me and even though I'm in the great outdoors, I feel just as trapped and panicky as when I was in the stone basement of the manor. Once I've looked around and made sure no one's hiding behind the nearby trees, I take out my phone and call Elena.

I haven't heard back from her since I left a voicemail message the day before. Not even a text or a missed call. I need to get hold of her now more than ever, to ask about Charlie and where he might have come from. She must have arrived home by now. Perhaps she's reconsidered our deal and resents me for talking her out of a lucrative job. Maybe she was dodging my calls, hoping I'd get the message and go away. She'd had her money, after all.

I hold my breath as the phone rings. I'm starting to tense up, waiting for the message to play, telling me that Elena isn't able to pick up, but then the call gets cut off. So she is ignoring me. I feel a flash of relief that she's home and keeping her head down. Probably wise if she's looking to avoid further trouble with the Fowleys. Still, it's not ideal. I don't have many sources of information left.

I walk on, trying to work out what to do. If she's screening I could try calling from another number. I don't have another phone but I could maybe use a landline or borrow Ford's – but that would come with risk. Ford might go through his calls, see the unknown number and try to ring it. What if Lawrence is recording calls from the landlines on the estate? I couldn't risk it.

I suddenly remember the number Elena gave me for her friend, Sara. The person who signed the NDA over her assault. I've been so fixated on Tom's disappearance and the intricacies of the Fowley family's history that I haven't phoned her to confirm her story. She'll be able to tell me about Elena – maybe give me a home number I can try and reach her on. I find the number, which I entered into my phone, and dial.

Someone answers on the fifth ring.

'Hello?' The voice is low-pitched and raspy, as if they've just woken up.

'Hi, is this Sara?' I ask, pacing along the path to control my nervous energy.

'Yes . . . who is this?' Sara's voice is sharper now, more alert.

'I'm sorry for the sudden call. Elena said she'd contact you – tell you she'd passed on your number? I'm Amelia, the journalist?' The lie makes me feel bad but it's what I told Elena so I have to stick with it.

'Oh . . . yes, she told me.' She sounds uncomfortable now, distant. 'Look, I don't know what Elena said but I can't talk about what happened. She knows that.'

'Because of the NDA?' I say.

Silence.

I sigh. 'I'm calling because I haven't heard from Elena in almost two days and I need to get in contact with her – she's not taking my calls on her mobile and I wanted to see if you could help.'

'I can do that,' Sara says slowly, as if reluctant to give an inch in my favour. 'I'll send her a message.'

'Thank you.' I can feel her pulling back, ready to end the call. 'I know you can't tell me about what happened, and Elena said you couldn't tell who it was who . . . attacked you, but can you answer one question for me? One question that's not about that night at all.'

Silence again, but weighted differently. A silence of consideration. At least, I hope it is.

'Just one question?' Sara finally asks.

'Yes. I promise.'

'OK . . . let me hear it.'

I inhale, clenching one fist in victory. 'When what happened that night happened—'

'You said it wasn't about that,' she cuts in.

'It isn't – it's about after. Afterwards, who was it who offered to pay you off? The person who gave you the money and the NDA?'

Sara tuts uncomfortably. 'I'm not sure I can say. I haven't read it in a long time . . . It might get me in trouble to tell you.'

'Sara, I promise you, it will stay between you and me.'

'But you said you're a journalist. You're going to print this.'

I inwardly curse myself for coming up with that story. It helped me with Elena but it's definitely hurting me now. I consider whether to tell the truth and sabotage what little trust I have with Sara, or lie again to try and convince her. I'm not proud of it, but the choice is easy.

'The story that I'm working on isn't about what happened to you. I don't need to publish anything you say – it'll just help point me in the right direction on another matter I'm looking into.'

'Which is?' Sara asks.

I take a breath. 'A missing girl. Who might have been attacked at the party last year. I think that perhaps the same person might be responsible.'

Sara's silence is deafening. Then, just as my heart is sinking and I'm waiting for her to hang up on me, she lets out a long sigh.

'I wasn't expecting him to come himself. I left the beach house and caught a lift with a delivery driver into the city the day after the party. I didn't have another job to go to but I couldn't stay there. I booked into a backpacking hostel for a few days, tried to work out what to do. That's when he found me – he must have bribed someone to look at my card statements. I can't think of another way he could have found me.' She sniffs. 'Lawrence Fowley came to my room at the hostel. I wasn't even sure it had been him until he turned up. That mask . . .' She trails off, as if trying to find the words. 'It was all I could see in my nightmares for months. That blank face looking at me while he was . . .'

'It's OK, you don't have to talk about that,' I say as gently as I can.

Sara clears her throat. 'When he came to see me, it was at night and he had the paperwork for the NDA and some cheques.'

'Cheques, plural?' I ask, frowning.

'Lots of them. One for each of his companies, in kroner. Altogether it was roughly a million euro. I suppose it was to help him hide what he was doing. He told me to open an account in the name of the business he'd written the cheques to – SJ Enterprise – my initials. Then I could do whatever I wanted with the money.' Sara takes a deep breath and lets it out in one long, shaky exhale. 'I knew I couldn't fight him. He has friends in government, in the law. I know what you probably think of me, but taking that money was the only thing I could do to survive.'

'I know,' I say, and mean it. 'I've met him. He seems like someone who can get away with anything.'

'But you're going to get him? For this girl?' Sara asks, a painful kind of hope in her voice. 'You'll stop him?'

'I'm going to try,' I say. 'I don't have anything left to lose.'

Sara is quiet for a moment, then sniffs. It sounds as though she's trying not to cry. 'Be careful. And I'll message Elena now – tell her to be careful too.'

'Thank you, Sara.'

'Please, don't call me again. The next time I think about him, I want to be seeing his name in the papers.' She hangs up before I can say anything else and I slowly take the phone from my ear and look down at the blank screen.

The woods around me seem so still and quiet after that conversation. Frighteningly still, as if every bird and animal has been warned off by the presence of someone else in the forest. Someone other than myself. I'm so tense I can feel my teeth aching in my skull. I blink away tears, forcing myself to carry on along the wooded path. There will be time for tears when I have dealt with Lawrence Fowley. Not before.

All the doubts and suspicions about James, about Zak. I was wrong to second-guess myself. How could I have allowed Lawrence to worm his way into my head? I thought of how unhinged he looked at breakfast this morning, as if he could barely contain himself: how could I have been stupid enough to believe his lies?

It's only a few minutes later that the phone in my hand lights up. It's a text from Elena. My insides unclench.

Sara just texted me. I'm sorry for worrying you. What's going on at the house?

I quickly type out a response. *Sorry for bombarding you, I just wanted to know you're OK. There's been a death here – Charlie the cleaner washed up on the beach.*

Elena's response takes some time, the icon indicating that she's typing flicks on and off. *That's awful! Was it an accident or . . . something else?*

I type back: *I'm not sure. I also haven't been able to get inside the house again to look around. I think maybe Charlie was up to something.*

Elena's response is immediate. *Today is the last day of the party – you have to get inside. Mr Fowley will be busy because of what's happened – I just remembered, there's a way to get the code to his suite on the top floor.*

I am immediately on edge, my heart thudding. This is it – the opportunity I've been waiting for.

Elena texts again. *He changes the code every week, but his new housekeeper can never remember it. She writes it down on a piece of paper hidden on a console table in the second-floor corridor – under the clock. She can't risk being caught with it, that's an immediate dismissal.*

Thank you, I text back. *I promise I'll get to the bottom of this.*

A moment later Elena replies: *Be careful.*

I make much better time on the way back to the manor. I'm no longer wandering without purpose; I have a mission to accomplish. I'm glad I've kept my bag stocked and on me at all times. It means I don't have to return to the chalet to fetch anything.

Once I'm back in the woods near the guest chalets I pick my way through the undergrowth until I reach the ice house. I open the door and look down the long, chilly tunnel. The shadows in there are even more menacing than they were before. Perhaps because I now know more about the dangers lurking inside. Zak and Charlie both went creeping around in Lawrence's house, and now they're dead. I cannot be next.

20

THE TUNNEL IS THANKFULLY just as empty as it was on my first time using it. Apparently the staff are too busy for cigarette breaks today. I reach the basement storeroom without incident and turn off my phone's torch. At the door out of the basement I stop to listen and hear voices right outside. A pair of female staff members talking in hushed tones.

'Mr Fowley took them out to the beach, to see the . . . you know.'

'The body, Clementine. It's not a dirty word.'

'Shhh! Don't be so crass.'

'It's not crass. You're just worried Mrs Holm will hear.'

'You should be worried, if she even thinks you're . . . '

Their voices grow fainter as their footsteps recede, echoing as they climb. I slip into the stairwell on the other side of the door and head up, towards the key-card door I had to bypass before. I move cautiously, careful to stay out of sight around the corner. I get to the door just as it's swinging closed behind them. I let it shut, knowing that the pair of them have just stepped into the foyer. One more flight of stairs and I'll be at the offices. I need to go one floor higher after that, right into the heart of Lawrence's home.

I can only hope my supposition that Lawrence wouldn't

leave even Cecile alone in his private rooms proves accurate. If there is someone in there when I arrive, then the game will be up. But there is not enough time to be cautious now.

I don't come across anyone else on my way up the stairs, though I do have to wait while two servants carry a chair on to the office floor. After they've gone, I go up past the study and finally reach the top of the servants' stairs. The highest point of the house – Lawrence's private apartments, where his enormous balcony is located.

The door at the top of the stairs has the same kind of key-card lock as the one below, though I suspect most of the staff key cards, if not all, wouldn't work on it. This is the most secure part of the manor, after all. I check for cameras but can't see any. They might be hidden, but I don't have any choice other than to carry on and hope that no one checks the recordings until I'm long gone.

I take out my credit card and attempt to open the door as I did the one downstairs two days ago. It's a struggle and I'm impatient, knowing how little time I have. After three tries I accidently apply too much pressure and the card snaps. Fuck. I nearly curse out loud. There goes option one.

My hands are shaking as I take two kirby grips from my bag and try to use those in the same way as the card. One at the top of the card reader and one at the bottom. I apply pressure and attempt to slide them with equal force at the same time. I'm sweating, the thin grips sliding around in my fingers. This is when I really regret losing my RFID encoder. With it and my tablet I could have stolen a card days ago and made myself an all-access pass to Lawrence Fowley's secrets.

My mind strays, wondering where my things ended up. Maybe they were handed to Lawrence days ago and he's just been playing with me. Maybe James has them or they got carried away in the stream. I wipe sweat from my forehead and listen, dreading the sound of footsteps coming up behind me. I can hear staff moving around at the bottom of the stairs, but no one nearby.

I force my focus back to the lock. This method is trickier than the card, requiring a defter touch and pinpoint timing. Panic isn't the best friend to either of those things. I struggle, jamming the grips in at the wrong angle a few times in my rush to get them in. After taking a deep breath and forcing myself to slow down a little, I finally manage to get the card reader to accept my trickery. The door clunks softly and I let out a sigh of relief.

I pass through the door and close it behind me, taking a deep breath. I'm in a foreshortened corridor. The floor is highly polished wood and the walls are covered in antique silk wallpaper – even the air smells expensive, like beeswax and oak. The heavy security door ahead of me slightly ruins the feel of the place – gunmetal grey with a keypad. Through a pane of reinforced security glass in the door, I can see a more decorative internal door. Lawrence's rooms. The tiny area I'm in holds only one piece of furniture: a green marble-topped console table sporting a vase of lilies and roses plus a few ornaments. One of these is a gold carriage clock.

In no time at all I've lifted the carriage clock and found the tiny piece of paper Elena told me would be there. Thank God for human error. No security system in the world could account for it. I read the note and replace it, then type 'elskede' into the keypad. The passcode registers and the lock disengages.

I close the door behind me as quietly as possible and let myself into Lawrence's private rooms. Holding my breath, I listen for any sounds and then tiptoe along the corridor.

The first space I enter is a library. All four walls completely stacked with bookshelves, every one of them full to the brim with leather- and cloth-bound volumes. Set after set with gilded titles and decorated spines. A ladder on rollers, something I've only seen in films, stands halfway down the room, a pile of books beside it. Hard to tell if that's a sign of use, or a design choice. The only other furniture is a pair of leather sofas arranged on either side of a fireplace and a couple of side tables with green glass lamps. No desk to search and no sign of anything personal. There's a reassuring sense of stillness, though. It feels like coming home to an empty house – no one appears to be here at the moment.

I move on, taking the door on the other side into a sitting room with a well-hidden TV, stereo system and a wall-length library of vinyl records. There's also a full bar and, through an open set of folding doors, I spot a snooker table large enough to sleep a family of six. The ultimate gentleman's bachelor pad. All that's missing is a set of swords on the wall, I think, as I turn and see just that. A pair of sabres crossed above the Fowley crest.

Both the sitting room and the library are so large I could ride a bike around them and never worry about running into anything. Lawrence, or one of his predecessors, must have had some walls removed, turning the apartments into a more open-plan penthouse. I'm beginning to understand how Lawrence can spend so much time away from all of his guests. Everything he needs is either up here or a phone call away. This place is his own private fortress. I shudder and wonder if Rose is here somewhere, if he's been keeping her locked up behind all these doors, afraid and alone.

To the left of me a set of glass doors reveals the balcony. It's even larger up close than it appeared from below. A table for four takes up one end and the other is home to an aviary, full of red cardinals. On the edge of the balcony I spot a heavy cut-glass ashtray, spotlessly clean.

Finally, through the doors opposite the ones leading to the library, I enter Lawrence's bedroom. The bed itself is enormous, easily half as big again as a king-size. It's a four-poster to boot, all carved wood and embroidered hangings. At its foot is a huge wooden chest. The rest of the space is full of dark wood furniture: a dressing table, armoire, desk and some bookcases. Two doors lead off the room. I assume one is for a bathroom – perhaps the other is for a second office, or a prison cell for his captives.

For a moment I just stand there, unable to believe that after all my planning, all my waiting, I'm finally in the belly of the beast. Then I go to work.

I check the doors first of all, disappointed to find that the second is a personal gym and not Rose's holding cell. Turning back to the main room I start with the chest by the bed, finding nothing but blankets and bedspreads. The bedside tables yield nothing more interesting than condoms, painkillers and a phone charger. On the dressing table I find Lawrence's gold cigarette case; presumably he was in a hurry earlier and forgot it. There's also one of those coffee-table lighters, the size and weight of a brick, made out of onyx.

213

The dressing table has several locked drawers but they have the keys in them. Just a design choice. I'm only slightly disappointed to find nothing inside but velvet boxes, each one containing cufflinks or watches. If I were a thief I'd be ecstatic, but as it is I keep looking.

I check the two side rooms – the bathroom and the gym – but find nothing. Finally, I get to the desk. I know I should have started searching it immediately, but in the moment I wanted to be thorough, starting from one end of the room and working my way around. Maybe I just wanted to prolong my hope of finding something, anything.

I start opening the desk drawers and shuffling through racks of suspended files and trays of pens. It's all private stuff, nothing company related: Lawrence's personal insurance documents; surveys and invoices relating to the house; his passport. All perfectly legitimate.

I sit back on my heels, finding no locked drawers in the desk to pick. Whatever Lawrence is hiding, it's not here. I check the dressing table and find hundreds of thousands of pounds' worth of jewellery just sitting there with the key in the lock. Perhaps that's the point. In this place, Lawrence doesn't need to hide anything. He's behind so many levels of security – security that he must believe to be impenetrable. I'm going about this all wrong.

I stand up and look at the surface of the desk. The green leather blotter holds a laptop, closed, several gold and onyx ornaments – inkwells, paperweights and a pair of brass bookends shaped like sphynxes. In between them is a row of notebooks, small, dark green and monogrammed in gold – LAF – Lawrence Anthony Fowley.

The first notebook is all lists: family and executives'

birthdays, anniversaries and crib sheets on the names of their partners and children. Addresses and phone numbers – nothing so useful as computer passwords. I pick up the next book and find that the first page bears an embossed card.

'The diary of Lawrence Fowley: 2016–17'.

The next book is 2018 to 2019 and so on. My elation is tempered with the painful knowledge that these would have been so much more useful to me days ago. Perhaps if I'd found them then, Zak or Charlie would still be alive.

I find the journal for the year of Rose's disappearance but it's packed with undated entries, just like the rest. Dense black handwriting crawls between the margins – it's in shorthand and barely readable. I let out a sigh of frustration, then stuff it into an inside pocket of my bag to take with me. I've no time to try and read through it all right now. My shorthand skills are poor. I barely bothered trying to learn it and I'm surprised Lawrence did. Maybe he picked it up just for the sake of keeping his diaries brief, but more likely his old-fashioned father pressed the skill on him.

I pick up the final notebook. It's a palm-sized Moleskine, like all the rest, but it's mostly blank. Not a diary. I frown. The initial blank pages give way to a single page with writing on it – not much writing either, though what's there is in plain English and it makes my skin prickle.

Tom Slazenger
Bergdis Olsen
Rose Spencer

Each followed by the date of the party corresponding to their death or disappearance. Then a series of letters and numbers, some of which have been crossed out. Some look like car registrations, others as if they might be ID numbers – I recognize the configuration of a UK DVLA number – Rose's. Personal information then. Maybe it's how he stalked them prior to their attendance at the parties.

I feel furious tears welling in my eyes as I think of the opportunities I'd had to make him give me answers. Opportunities I'd talked myself out of or passed up because I wasn't sure. Because even after months of research that told me who Lawrence Fowley was, I'd been taken in by his charm and his good looks just like everyone else. I'd allowed myself to transfer my suspicions on to James simply because he was so off-putting, so rude. He had an association with two of the victims, but not Rose. I should have seen that sooner. I should have stayed true to my mission. I had wasted time and, somewhere, Rose was paying for it.

I flick through the rest of the notebook and a piece of paper falls out. It's a printed-out scan of a police report, exactly like the ones I found in his safe. But this one isn't for Rose or either of the other two. It's Zak's autopsy report. I suppose Lawrence brought it up here to look over. He must have bought it from the police like the others, maybe even hurried it along for his own benefit. It's all in Norwegian but I recognize something that needs no translation: loprazolam.

The same drug that Bergdis was incapacitated with.

Zak Bakshi was on drugs when he fell to his death. I'm not sure what the proper dose of the drug is, but I'm pretty sure it's not measured in grams. Milligrams is more usual. Which means that if he was on over a gram of sleeping tablets, as the report says, he'd taken an overdose on purpose or been deliberately poisoned. And it's a pretty big coincidence if he just happened to take a load of the same drugs as Bergdis. Besides, who would break into a house just to OD?

I tear the page with the names out of the notebook and fold it with the police report. I'm not sure how much good it'll do me. I had all the evidence available to me and I'd still fallen for Lawrence's lies. For his sorrowful, wealthy-recluse routine. It was likely that no one would ever believe me, but I could still confront him with it, use it to get the truth about Rose. I'm desperate now. Forget the police and the courts: I just want to know where she is, what happened to her. I can get that out of him with this as leverage. I'm sure of it. I just want her back.

I think I hear a noise and freeze, listening hard. It could have been a door shutting on my floor, or outside. I can't tell. After a moment, I let out a breath, as quietly as possible. There's nothing, just the gentle sounds of an empty house. I'm getting jumpy, like Lawrence. I can tell he's unravelling, taking more risks. He might make a mistake soon, but I can't rely on it. He might even cancel the party tonight.

I'm pacing the room, chewing my thumb. What I need is a way to get him alone, away from the manor. There are too many people here, guests and staff. I need quiet and darkness to catch him unawares and subdue him for long enough to get him to confess. Perhaps I can convince him to walk down to the beach with me, or up into the forest. Much as I'm loath to head out there, into the dark woods. I'll record what he says, even if I never get to show it to anyone – as long as my sister and I are safe.

The longer I think about it, the more my doubts start to return. Can I really use a knife to extract a confession?

What would I be willing to do? Even just the thought of the struggle, of trying to hurt him and hearing him yell in pain, makes me feel almost physically sick.

But I have to. I've promised myself. I've promised Rose.

There's a sound behind me: the tread of a shoe. The exhale of a breath. The click of the latch.

I turn, my heart thumping, and find myself looking straight into the eyes of my sister's abductor.

Lawrence lets the bedroom door swing closed behind him.

'Well, now . . . what might you be doing in here?'

21

Numb with shock, my fury feels as if it might cook me from within. I'm torn between my emotions, but it's anger which finally loosens my tongue.

'You know why I'm here.'

Lawrence's shoulders are set, straight and tense, but his tone remains artificially light. 'I imagine you came up here to look for something, knowing that I'd be away. Did you have any luck?'

'Yes.' The word slips out between my teeth. I realize I'm trembling. Lawrence's hands are empty and he's all the way across the room, but still there's a threat in the air. His eyes are bloodshot and wild, his face gaunt. I know only a little of what he's capable of, but he's made at least two people disappear like it was nothing. I don't plan on being next.

He narrows his eyes. 'What it is you think you've found?'

I say nothing, but jump as he takes a half-step towards me. He freezes, watching me with an expression of interest which appears to be genuine. My hand clutches at my bag. It's hanging off my shoulder, slightly behind me. If I can just get my fingers inside, I stand a chance of reaching the knife.

'I wonder if what you have is worth it, worth everything you've done to get close to my family, to get into my house,'

Lawrence says conversationally. He looks at me warily. I say nothing, inching my hand closer to the knife.

'I have been racking my brain since I realized there was something wrong with you – trying to work out who you are and why you've come here. It must have taken a lot of time and effort. I can understand how committed you must be, to come in here, as you have, today of all days.'

Lawrence shakes his head, turning away from me. I watch, on edge, as he grips the post of his bed and seems to sag against it. When he twists to look at me, I'm stunned to see that his face is pale, despairing. He looks worse than he did at breakfast, the careful veneer of politeness having fallen away to reveal a broken man.

Uncertainty roils in my gut and I hesitate, my fingertips now on the ceramic knife in my bag. I'm no longer certain of Lawrence's intentions. He looks torn between anger and sorrow, and though his posture isn't threatening, his words and his tone are. I realize he could do anything right now. Anything at all, and I'm all alone with him.

'Is it not enough', Lawrence says, voice growing louder as he tries to keep it steady, 'that I have spent hours standing over Charlie's body? And now, finally, I have the opportunity to return here and I find you – digging into my life. Looking for what? This?'

He shoves a hand into his pocket and withdraws an old-fashioned-looking mobile. A flip phone like the one Rose begged for when she was thirteen. It's not hers – at least I don't think it is. I've never seen it before.

'I thought you were a lot of things – a liar, a con artist, a gold digger – but I never thought you were without conscience. That you were dangerous. You seemed so tense, so desperate. I told myself this can't just be about money.' Lawrence sighs. 'That maybe it was you who . . . but why would you want Charlie dead?'

'I didn't kill him!' I'm aghast. 'I only just met him here.'

Lawrence's eye muscle ticks. 'So it is about money. Of course, it's always about money. My father taught me better than this . . . He would have had you thrown out the moment security found those things in the water behind your chalet.'

So, they had found them, but then why am I still here?

'If you hadn't been with Ford . . . Well, I would have followed my father's example but . . . Ford made things difficult. I didn't want him to storm off with you.'

'I don't understand,' I say, before I can think better of it. 'I'm not after a phone. I don't even know who's that is. And I don't care about your money.'

Lawrence's eyes bore into me, as if he's searching the inside of my skull for secrets. Then he sinks down until he's sitting on the end of the enormous bed. The phone hangs limply in his hand.

'Who is it that you work for?' Lawrence finally says, all the fight having left him. 'Hmm? I know it's not Ford. It's not James either. I did think it was – and he's certainly blood-less enough to have you carry on with the plan while I deal with—' He breaks off, shakes his head. 'But it's not him. Everything he has comes from me and I've combed his finances, can't find a whiff of any payment to you. Besides which, even he couldn't fake the anger your lunchtime row caused. So – it must be an outsider. A professional rival, a paper or more likely some grubby gossip website looking for scraps.'

There's a creeping note of mania in Lawrence's tone and I slip my hand down into my bag, fully gripping the knife now. If he makes any sudden movements, I can't afford to hesitate.

'I don't know what you're talking about,' I say cautiously. 'No one hired me; no one is paying me to be here. You're not making any sense at all.'

'If you're not being paid, why are you snooping around my apartments and my office?' Lawrence seethes. 'You've been looking for something.'

'Charlie told you he saw me,' I say slowly, trying to catch up, and Lawrence nods, though it wasn't a question. 'Did he tell you he was also going through your things?'

'Charlie—' Lawrence's voice breaks and he closes his eyes for a second. 'Charlie was there, looking for something for me. He wanted you gone from that moment. He told me you couldn't be allowed to remain on the estate, that you were here to spy on me. To leak information. But I told him . . .' He sniffs. 'I told him no. I wanted to meet you, to see if I could crack you – because I knew it didn't stop with you, someone put you up to it. Ford, James . . . Sam. Any of them. All of them. It seems I can't trust anyone these days.'

'Is that why you hired Charlie? To keep an eye on your family?' I ask. 'Or was he in charge of covering up your mess?'

'My . . . mess?' Lawrence frowns at me.

I'm sick of dancing around the subject. 'I know about it, about the disappearances. Tom Slazenger, Bergdis Olsen . . . I know she was drugged, that he probably never made it to his trip. You've been covering up what happens to people at your parties.'

Lawrence's expression is agonized. 'No! I . . . That is nothing to do with me. How do you . . .' He gapes at me. 'I thought you were here about Charlie.'

'Charlie? What the hell does he have to do with this?'

I jump when Lawrence stands up. I flinch back but he doesn't come towards me. Instead he's looking at me as though he's simply surprised to find me in his room, uninvited. As if I've appeared out of thin air. Whatever it was he thought of me before, I can see that he's abandoned those notions. He's just as confounded as I am. He also looks tired. Exhausted, even. As if he doesn't have the energy to carry on.

'The awful thing is . . . it doesn't matter any more.' Lawrence sighs. 'Even if you did come here to expose us . . . It's done. He's gone.'

I wait, and after a moment Lawrence takes a shaky breath and lets his shoulders slump.

'Charlie and I – we were in love.'

22

A HUNDRED THINGS SLIP gently into place in my mind. The way Lawrence talked about his impending marriage to Cecile, his old-fashioned father, the will and its specifications, the accusations of spying, Lawrence's demeanour ever since the news of Charlie's death had broken. I realize that, all day, he has been grieving the death of his secret lover, and when he came to his room, expecting to finally be alone, he found me.

'That's why I "hired" him,' Lawrence says, finally, into the silence his declaration leaves hanging in the air. 'So he'd have a reason to be here. No matter how much I pay the staff, or how well vetted they are, I couldn't trust them. That' – he gestures with the phone –'was what I thought you wanted. My secret. This is the phone I use . . . used to talk to him. I keep it hidden in here, usually. He was meant to come to see me last night . . . When he didn't I kept the phone on me, trying to get hold of him. Of course that was . . . pointless. Without him it's all pointless.'

Ever since I got here and he realized something was off about me, he must have assumed I was here to expose him. To get evidence that he was not only in a relationship with another man, but in danger of losing his inheritance. James would probably cut off a hand just to have access to information that would make him the only heir to the Fowley fortune. Which he would be, if Lawrence were forced to come out and Cecile refused to marry him; either because she wanted a real marriage, her father's input or due to the fact that Lawrence's fame would mean she'd be a figure of ridicule – at best a naive fool and at worst a gold-digging opportunist.

'Oh my God . . . I'm not here to get information about you and Charlie,' I say, trying to sort through my emotions as shock gives way to doubt and confusion. 'I came here on my own. No one hired me to spy on you. This is . . . it's nothing to do with any of that. I don't care who you're in love with!'

'Then why are you here?' Lawrence asks, despairing. 'Why do all this? Is it Ford, is he—'

'I'm here because of Rose,' I say, desperation and grief entering the maelstrom of doubt inside me. 'My sister. Rose Spencer.'

I wait for a flare of understanding or horror to cross Lawrence's face. For his eyes to harden or for his mouth to open, a lie spilling out to try and claw back some control. What I'm not expecting is . . . nothing. He frowns at me, completely nonplussed but wanting so badly to understand. Nothing about his expression indicates that he's unnerved or impacted at all by the mention of her name. He looks right at me and says, 'Why?'

'What the hell do you mean, why?' I demand. I only realize that I've drawn the knife when Lawrence throws up his hands and backs away slightly. 'My sister – Rose. You invited her to your party last year, and she's been missing ever since. Missing for a year!'

Lawrence wets his lips, clearly still unnerved by the knife. 'I can assure you, I didn't invite her. I told the police everything I know – I saw her here and I just . . . assumed she came with someone else. Until they showed me her picture I had no idea who she was.'

'Bullshit!' I say, so close to an answer that my patience, stretched as it has been for months, has finally snapped. 'I saw her invitation – "My dearest Rose, Please forgive me for allowing so many years to pass us by. I was a fool to ever let you go. Can we begin again?"' I quote angrily.

'I don't—'

'"Perhaps we can find some way to return to those days at Cambridge, before I committed the unforgivable sin of taking you for granted? Yours always, if you'll have me, Lawrence,"' I say, spitting his name. 'It was the last thing I had to lead me to my sister. You might have stolen it from the chalet, but I have read it a hundred times.'

Lawrence is looking at me as if he's trying to translate my words into another language. 'Cambridge?'

'Yes! My little sister, Rose. You remember? She was in love with you, and you two kissed at some ball or other. I still have the picture! You invited her here, and she never came home!'

Lawrence shakes his head slowly. 'I didn't invite your sister, and I certainly never kissed her.'

Furious, half blinded by tears, I pull out my phone, knife still held tightly in my other hand. I open the picture I downloaded from Rose's old phone. Her and Lawrence kissing at the ball under the flashing coloured lights.

'Lie to me again,' I say, gripping the knife so tightly that my fingers ache. 'I dare you.'

Lawrence stares at me, squinting at the phone in confusion.

I step forward slightly, holding the phone out towards him. My hand holding the knife shakes. 'That's my sister, kissing you. And this' – I scroll, knowing that the next picture in the folder is the one I snapped of Rose at the party, the one hanging upstairs in his office bathroom – 'is my sister, at your party, talking to you.'

Lawrence swallows, looking at the second picture. His eyes are roving over it, absorbing every detail. 'That's just an arm in a suit jacket. It could be anyone.'

'But you're the one who invited her. And he's wearing your father's gold cufflinks. Yours now, I guess.'

'I told you, I didn't . . .' Lawrence says, but there's a new tension to his voice. His jaw is ticking, a frighteningly intense expression settling over his features. I can tell, almost at once, that he is hiding something. Whereas before he'd been cloaked in outrage, in grief, now there's a careful emptiness to his eyes. Whatever he knows, it's making him anxious, desperate. Ready to do the unthinkable.

I realize this all at once, but my body is slow to react. Something flashes across his face and, before I can blink, he jumps forward and knocks the knife from my hand.

23

'No!' It bursts out of me as I try and snatch back the knife, but it's too late. It clatters on to the floor a few feet away. Lawrence grasps hold of my arm and tries to drag me across the room. My shoulder bag slips off and I trip over it as he pulls me, kicking and screaming.

'Don't!' Lawrence shouts. 'Just . . . listen to me!'

All of my training flies out of my head and I revert to an age-old impulse in women everywhere – I claw at Lawrence's face.

He bellows as my fingers gouge his forehead and cheeks, missing his eyes by sheer chance. I'm already pulling away from him as his grip on my arm loosens. I drive my elbow back into his side, winding him enough for me to get out of arms' reach.

I'm halfway across the enormous sitting room when Lawrence catches up to me. His stride is longer than mine and I'm at a disadvantage in heeled boots.

'Amelia, wait!' he calls behind me, one arm flying over my shoulder as he makes a grab for me. He latches on to me, holding me back.

This time I remember to use his weight against him, executing a throw which brings him over my shoulder, crashing to the floor. Once he's down I deliver a kick to his nose, hoping to disorientate him and blind him with tears. I just need to get away, to get out of this prison and out into the open where there are places to hide and witnesses around.

As Lawrence yells after me, I sprint through the library, shoulder the door open and fumble for the inner release on the keypad lock. I can hear him behind me, his shoes slipping on the well-polished wood. His injury gives me the edge I need. I get the door open and slam it shut behind me. I have just enough time to grab hold of the marble-topped console table and bring it down in front of the door before Lawrence reaches it.

He collides with the door, fumbling as I did for the release. His face at the reinforced window is sweaty and his nose is bleeding. As I dive for the servants' stairs I hear the door hitting the marble-topped table again and again, trying to drive it out of the way so he can get free. It won't hold him for long.

I make it down one flight of stairs, to the office floor. As I set foot on the next flight of stairs I hear a colossal bang from behind me. The table must have given way.

Half running, half sliding, I reach the foyer door and, by some miracle, it's open. Someone's rammed a chunk of card under it to hold it that way. Perhaps it was the men I'd seen carrying the chair up to the office, coming back for more furniture? I snag the improvised doorstop and close the door as quickly and quietly as possible, then sidestep, looking for a place to hide. A door to my left is open, revealing an airy sitting room with a piano and plush cream sofas. I dart inside, boots sinking into the soft carpet.

A moment later I hear Lawrence clattering down the servants' stairs, straight towards the kitchen.

I'm not safe yet, not by a long shot. I'm still stuck on Lawrence's estate, with no passport and no driving licence. None of the guests would help me, nor would the staff. But I am at least out of immediate danger. I just need to find somewhere safe. I can feel everything spinning out of control. If it was ever in my control to start with. I've been deluding myself into thinking I'm anything but a mouse in a trap.

Thankfully, the sitting room has large sash windows looking out over James's Japanese garden. It only takes a moment for me to unlock one of the windows and slide it open – it's virtually silent. I climb over the sill and drop down, gently easing the window closed behind me. From there I cut through the garden and into the orchard. It's very exposed, so I race towards the forest, where I'm more likely to find cover in its wild gloom. If Lawrence chases me all the way downstairs and finds the passage out to the ice house, that'll bring him out on the opposite side of the house, well away from me.

The orchard is thankfully deserted. I half run to the first sauna, just to get something between myself and the house. I duck behind it and rest my back against the wooden structure, catching my breath. I briefly wonder if Ford might help me but his loyalty has always been to his family. He'll also be crushed if I have to come clean about who I really am and why I've manufactured our life together. As soon as Lawrence tells him the truth, I'll have lost him anyway. No, I need something else, a weapon or a vehicle. I need outside help.

My hand immediately goes to my bag for my phone, but then I remember losing my bag and my phone in Lawrence's room. I have no way of contacting Elena or the authorities. I'm on my own and the only thing I know is that I need a way to survive long enough to find Rose and pay her kidnapper back for what he did to her.

'Amelia?'

I flinch, half crouching automatically. I look up and find Sam looking at me in confusion. She's halfway along the path behind the orchard, wearing loose shorts and a sports bra, her skin slightly sweaty. She's holding one AirPod and removes another as she wanders over to me.

'What's happened? You look really freaked out. Is everything OK?'

I'm so shocked by her appearance, still running on adrenaline from fleeing for my life, that I just spit out the truth. 'I need to hide.'

Sam's eyes widen and she glances back at the house. She frowns but looks unsure. I need her on my side. Her loyalty is less ingrained than Ford's. I can convince her, I know I can.

'Please, Sam,' I stress. 'It's life and death.'

She stares at me for a moment longer. Then, to my surprise, she nods.

'This way.'

With Sam just ahead of me we cross the orchard to a denser patch of trees at the edge of the forest. There are stacks of cut logs and several bell-shaped metal tanks from which a heat shimmer rises. Hot metal and smoke scent the air.

'They're charcoal kilns,' Sam says, seeing my look. 'To make the fuel for the sauna. No one comes over here until a batch is ready. We should be all right.'

'Thank you,' I say, suddenly feeling a weight of exhaustion hit me. I lean against a stack of logs and try to get my thoughts to stop racing so the rest of me can catch up. Sam comes towards me and sits down on a chopping block.

'What's going on? Is it Ford? Has he done something to upset you?'

I shake my head, still trying to calm my racing pulse, my breath coming in shallow sips. Everything has gone so wrong so quickly. What if Lawrence is out there somewhere trying to get rid of Rose before she can talk? I might have just signed her death warrant.

'Was it James?' Sam asks. 'Did he try something?' She lets out a sigh. 'James is one of those people, thinks he deserves whatever he can get his grubby hands on just because he was born rich. I mean, Lawrence already had to pay off one woman for him. One of the staff.'

That slices through the hopeless fog in my mind. I suck in a painful gasp of air and stare at her. 'Sara? One of the Black Diamond workers?'

'I think that was her name, not that anyone told me about it directly. I just heard it – staff chat, you know?' She shrugs. 'One of the benefits of not being a "real Fowley": people aren't so careful what they say around you. I also sometimes buy weed from them, if I'm stuck out here for a while.'

Lawrence didn't assault Sara then. He might have delivered the cheques and the NDA, so she'd assumed he was the one who'd done it, but he'd been covering for his brother. Alarms start to ring inside my head. Lawrence had been adamant that he hadn't invited Rose to his party. Hadn't kissed her at the university ball. Was that the truth? I wasn't sure any more but when he'd tried to get my phone he'd definitely been spooked by something. Maybe one of the pictures?

I think back over the mad rush of events since he discovered me in his room. Had Lawrence been trying to attack me, or stop me from rushing off and making accusations? Was he protecting himself or someone else?

'What is it?' Sam asks, her hand resting lightly on my knee. 'If James did something to you, there's no way I'm letting him get away with it. No matter what Lawrence says. Ford won't either.'

'Sam . . . do you remember the party, two years ago, when your housekeeper died?'

'Bergdis?' She frowns. 'What has that got to do with . . . Yes, she had a heart attack. How is that anything to do with James?'

'Do you remember who drove her home that night?' I ask, my lips so dry I can feel them cracking. It hadn't been in any of the articles I read, or the police report – that one little detail. How she got from the party to her house, presumably already drugged. Now I'm wondering if Lawrence suppressed it, just as he suppressed any mention of the party in the news reports about Tom Slazenger. Or perhaps nobody knew or cared to know. She was just staff, after all – to most people at the party, she would have been invisible.

'Oh.' Sam's eyes go wide, her cheeks pallid even with her natural tan. 'Oh my God. You don't think James had something to do with that? I mean, I know he hated her but she was a little old lady . . .'

'Did James drive her home?' I ask.

She nods slowly. 'I think so. I remember she wasn't feeling well. I thought . . . Well, I think we all thought it was the start of the attack that killed her. I just assumed Lawrence had told James to take her home. I was smoking by the drive and I saw him go. But you're saying he was involved in her death? Like . . . murder?'

'I think . . . maybe yes.' I take a deep breath and tell myself that it's pointless keeping my cards to myself now. Lawrence knows; soon everyone else will too. I need to use everything I have to convince her to help me. 'The truth is . . . I'm not here because I just happened to be seeing Ford. I started seeing him to get here.'

'You mean, you've been lying to everyone? Why?' Sam asks, shocked. She recoils from me as if I've threatened her. 'Who the fuck are you?'

I suck in air, knowing I'll only have one chance to explain myself. To keep her on side. 'My sister, Rose, was invited to this party last year and she never came back,' I say. 'I came here to find out what happened to her.' I tell her what happened when I confronted Lawrence.

'And you think . . . James somehow forged an invitation and then cornered her at the party?' Sam is clearly sceptical. 'Why would he do that? How would he even know your sister?'

'He might not have known her at all. As for why . . . to try and lure Lawrence away from Cecile? To cause a scene? I don't know. But I think . . . if Lawrence already covered up for him once – with Sara – and maybe other times with other people, he could do it again. I think he's doing what his dad would do in this situation: protecting the family. I think James killed Tom as well, the year before Bergdis died. Or at least made him disappear – maybe took him somewhere. The same place he's now keeping my sister.'

'Tom . . . Slazenger?' Sam's face contorts in confusion. 'Why?'

'Because Tom was involved in Lawrence's business and James saw him as a threat. I don't know all the details . . . but I just . . . I know it's him. Please believe me,' I beg. 'I'm not safe. I just want my sister back and to go home.'

Sam stands up, pacing away from me, putting the chopping block between us. Shaking her head as she pads over the ground.

'Hang on – this is crazy . . . I mean, I know James is a creep. Cruel, yeah. Twisted? Completely. But a murderer?'

I'm losing her, and it makes me desperate.

'I'm sorry, I know this is a lot. I never meant to involve anyone else in this . . . but I'm in trouble,' I say, going to her and taking her hand in mine. 'Lawrence has all the evidence. By now he's probably ditched the lot in the fjord. All that's left is my word and I already know that's not enough. Please. I need to know: is there anywhere James might keep . . . trophies, or somewhere he might have taken Rose or Tom to keep them hidden? Somewhere I can find evidence to prove he did this. If you can help me find her, you'll be saving her life, and mine.'

Sam is trembling, chewing a hangnail as her doe eyes search my face. 'I can't think. I . . . This is insane . . . They're my brothers.'

'I need to know. Now. I'm sorry but there's no time. It has to be now or . . . it might be too late.'

Sam pauses for a long moment. 'I don't want to believe you but . . . something about this . . . I don't think you're lying.' She lets out a long breath, her eyes watching the woods. Eventually her expression resolves itself into one of clarity. 'There's only one place it could be – but . . . I don't know if we should . . .'

'Please,' I say at once. 'I have to find her. There's no time. I'll go alone – just . . . please tell me where he's keeping her.'

Sam looks torn, but I can see her relenting. 'The only place he could make it work is the lodge.'

I remember her telling me about James's future home. 'The one in the woods?'

She nods. 'It's James's – or it will be once Lawrence marries and James is allowed to move out of the manor. He uses it as a sort of unofficial bolthole, whenever he and Lawrence fight. He doesn't like anyone else going up there. Not even staff . . . If he's keeping someone captive, that's where he'd do it. There's nowhere else he could go without someone asking questions. Even renting a place would have to go through Lawrence.'

My stomach swirls with nausea, even as hope makes my blood sing. That's where she is. That's where he took my little sister. I can feel it. I'm going to save her, at long last. But the thought of climbing the steep slope into the heart of the woods gives me chills. Anything could be out there: lynxes, wolves, a murderer. My sister.

'I need to go there, now,' I say. 'You don't have to come with me. I can go alone if you don't want to risk it. Just tell me how to get there. I'll get Rose and we'll be gone – straight to the police.'

'No . . . not if he did something to Tom. I want to know,' she says. 'I want to . . . If he's still alive I need to help him. Besides, you won't be able to find it. It's easy to spot from a distance but the woods are tricky – there's no marked path.'

'OK,' I say, still worrying if allowing Sam to come with me is the right decision. She's probably not ready to see what her brothers are capable of. But there's no other choice. 'Let's go.'

24

'ONE THING I STILL don't get,' Sam says as we walk uphill through the towering pines, 'is what your sister had to do with all this.'

'I have no idea.' I'm only focused on reaching Rose now. Nothing else matters. I don't care why, or how, she got here. There will be time to make sure James is held accountable later. Even thinking of his hands on my sister makes me want to scream until I throw up.

'She had to want to see Lawrence, right? For the invitation to be the least bit effective?'

'She did,' I confirm. 'I think she had a bit of a thing for him and he . . . Well, I have a picture of them kissing at her university ball but he swears that wasn't him. He might have forgotten her while she held a torch for him all this time.'

'Maybe that's why James wanted to get her here?' Sam starts walking again, mulling this over. 'James thought getting your sister to fancy him instead of Lawrence would be . . . consolation . . . for Cecile,' she says. 'Or else Rose had proof that Lawrence was gay and James wanted it.'

I stumble to a stop. 'You know?'

Sam shrugs. 'Sure. It doesn't bother me, but yeah, I've picked up on a certain . . . vibe. His dad was a complete dinosaur when it came to that stuff so I don't blame him for hiding it.'

'Does James know?' I ask, thinking of the will.

Sam raises her eyebrows. 'I'm sure he suspects. He just can't prove it.'

The thought stirs something in my mind. James would do anything for dirt on Lawrence? If that was true, then did that involve the text somehow? The one I saw on James's phone after he stormed out of lunch. *Fuck you. I won't do it.*

'Amelia?' Sam has carried on but has realized I'm not following. 'What is it?'

'I think James was trying to prove it,' I say slowly. 'Maybe you're right. Maybe he thought Rose knew something and that's why he brought her here. Only it didn't work . . . You don't remember the night of the second party, not after we met on the beach, right?'

'No, sorry.' Sam pulls a face. 'I hate the whole thing, to be honest. It's best to just be out of it.'

'Well, on our way back through the rose garden, we heard a noise. Charlie was there, arguing with someone. A man.'

'The dead cleaner from the beach?' Sam asks, brow furrowed. 'What does that have to do with James trying to prove that Lawrence . . . Oh!' Her eyes widen. 'Was James bribing Charlie to spy on Lawrence?'

I shake my head. 'Lawrence and Charlie were . . . involved.'

'Involved . . . Oh my God.' Sam covers her mouth, her many silver and gemstone rings clacking together. 'That's why he looked so cut up about what happened. Oh, poor Lawrence. Jesus, he had to pretend like it was just some random cleaner . . .' She looks at me. 'I know if you're right he's been covering for James but still . . . no one deserves to go through that.'

'Whatever Lawrence has done, I do believe he really cared about Charlie. But what if James was trying to get to Charlie – to use him to out Lawrence and disinherit him? Which would mean, if he was arguing with Charlie in the garden, that James was the last person to see Charlie alive.'

We continue to walk in silence, both deep in thought. This far out in the woods it's as if we're a million miles from the rest of the world. I know it's only an illusion, but still it makes the back of my neck prickle. Anything could happen to us. Anyone from the house could catch up to us at any time and it's gradually getting dark. If we're not careful we'll be stumbling around the woods completely blind. Even now, Lawrence might be chasing after us, or making plans to smuggle James out of the country.

We crest a slope and I look down it, spying the end wall of the lodge through the trees. A shiver runs along my spine. Who would want to spend time out here? The whole place feels watchful, as if it's waiting for something. The trees sigh in the wind and twigs snap and fall, interrupting the stillness.

'Do we know for sure that James isn't here right now?' I ask.

Sam nods. 'I saw him earlier, heading towards the guest chalets, and he's going to the party tonight. He never bothers coming out here unless it's for the entire day – too long a walk for him.'

I think of James's plump frame and nod. It makes sense. I wonder if he's even looking forward to living all the way out here, instead of in the manor.

'Come on,' Sam says, already hurrying down the slope towards the lodge. 'I'll be missed if I'm not back in time for the party.'

'You're sure it's still going ahead?' I ask, following her.

'Lawrence can't afford to let everyone down; besides, cancelling the party would mean coming clean about him and Charlie.' She laughs bitterly. 'As far as any of his guests are concerned, Charlie was staff – the world doesn't stop for them. And the party doesn't stop for anyone.'

I think of poor Zak and realize she's right.

We've reached the lodge now, its log walls patterned with moss and a single wind chime hanging from the corner of the porch roof, clunking in the breeze. It looks abandoned, creepy even. Though I suppose James wouldn't value it much, this insulting little shack. Perhaps he liked the idea of it being a blight on Lawrence's land. Or else he was so determined to replace Lawrence as the head of the Fowley family that he thought he'd never seriously need to worry about living in this place.

'Men like my brother never end up in prison,' Sam says, interrupting my thoughts as she folds her arms around herself, chilled by the breeze stirring in the air.

I know she's right; that's why I'm here, after all. I know as well as Sam does that the Fowleys of the world never get what's coming to them. They hire the best solicitors, the best barristers; they pay forensic experts to dispute even the most incriminating evidence. James could bribe anyone, get private investigators to dig up every crumb of dirt on Rose and my family. By the end of the trial it would be James Fowley, upstanding, well-educated heir to a major Norwegian energy conglomerate, verses Rose Spencer, a wild child raised in poverty who has pursued a string of wealthy men.

Sam leads me along the porch to the front door. It doesn't have the same level of security as the main house. I'd been expecting at least a camera, a mortice lock or something. Instead, the weathered-looking wooden door is held shut with a chain as thick as my arm threaded through the iron door handle, a thick hoop bolted to the wall and a heavy padlock. I climb the steps to the porch and heft the rusty lock in my hand. I'm not sure if it's pickable, but that's beside the point. I lost my bag at the house and the only tool at my disposal is the kirby grip in my hair. That's not going to cut it.

'How do we get in?' I ask, glancing at the small, shuttered windows.

'James was never any good with keys – his dad had to pay his school about a million times to replace the ones for his room, his locker. Everything. He probably has one hidden nearby.' She gestures to an assortment of glazed pots on the porch, all holding very dead plants. 'Check over there.'

While Sam checks the wood pile on the other side, I start lifting the pots and sweeping aside leaf litter with my boots. No sign of a key. I'm not really sure what type I'm looking for, given the padlock's unlikely to be a standard Yale, more likely a hefty bit of metal. Not the kind of thing that could fit under a plant pot.

I turn around to tell Sam this and find her kneeling on one knee, her hand in the woodpile. She's side on to me and clearly struggling to reach something..

'I think it's in here, but it's stuck on something.'

'Let me see.' I kneel down beside her, glancing down at the sight of what I initially think is a spider on her leg. But

243

it's not a spider, it's a tattoo on the spot where she'd had a sticking plaster over some scratch or other before. But there's no scratch now. Just the faded, slightly blown-out tattoo – crossed oars under a red lion.

In her running shorts I can see the writing arching blurrily over the lion – which looks more like a dragon in its poor condition – 'Cambridge University Women's Squad 2018'.

The same university as my sister. Not just that but one of the years she was there. My mouth is half open to ask Sam if she knew Rose, when she rears up and cracks me over the head with a pine log.

I hit the plank floor of the porch, my vision shrinking down to a point as blackness takes over. The last thing I see is Sam taking a large iron key from her pocket and stepping over me towards the lodge's front door.

25

I WAKE UP IN near total darkness. The only light is coming from a gas lamp on a table to my right. Even that tiny glow makes my eyes water. There's a headache rampaging through my skull, throbbing from one side of my head to the other, a heavy metal concert of pain coursing along my facial bones, echoing in my eye sockets. My teeth still feel as if they're vibrating. My mouth is crusted with what could be blood or drool.

As my eyes adjust to the light I take in my surroundings. It becomes immediately obvious that no one has called this lodge home in a long time. The room I'm in looks like a lounge, but the few bits of furniture are covered in dust-sheets, which are themselves grey with dust. The floor is littered with leaves and twigs and there are cobwebs matted up in the corners. It smells of damp, of human dwellings being reclaimed by nature. Mingled with the clinical tang of bleach. Lots of bleach.

I flinch as memories of what happened hit me, one after the other. Followed by the realization that I'm tied to a chair, thick ropes pulled so tightly that my arms and legs have gone numb. Yet I'm not gagged. A moment later I remember that we're all the way out in the woods. I could scream for hours and not be heard by anyone.

Anyone might include Sam herself, because she's not in the room with me. I strain my ears but can't hear her nearby. Not that there's much more of the lodge that she could be hiding in. Across from me there's a doorway – minus the door, which has fallen off its hinges – beyond which is a bathroom suite so old and rotten I'm surprised it's still standing.

As my mind clears I start to struggle, moving my hands and shoulders. I can't be here when Sam returns.

I look down at the ropes binding my arms to the chair. They're not that old and look as though they're made of nylon or some other synthetic material. They're patterned in tiny diamonds of colour, almost like the scales on a snake. Not the kind of rope that might just be lying around this old cabin, or the rough blue type used in construction and shipping. These, I realize with a shiver, are climbing ropes.

Tom Slazenger's missing climbing ropes. Spattered and stained with dried blood.

My breath comes in short, sharp sips. I look around the cabin with new eyes and finally spot – by the table with the gas camping lamp on it – a dusty backpack with half its contents spilling across the floor: tent pegs, a water bottle, silver foil packets of dehydrated food. This is where Tom's things have been for the last three years.

Why on earth would Sam keep them? Looking around me though, it seems like this was the safest place for them. No one has been here for a long time. My thoughts stray to my missing passport and I shiver. Maybe Sam just likes to keep trophies?

I'm just shaking from side to side in the chair, trying to gauge its durability, when the door to the cabin swings open. I freeze as Sam comes in, out of breath, with a wheel-barrow full of logs. She kicks the door closed behind her and, without ceremony, dumps the logs out on to the floor. The noise makes me wince and the logs roll every which way, but she doesn't seem concerned. She just kicks several of them out of the way and comes to a stop in front of me.

'Sorry, that took longer than I remembered,' she says. 'I wanted to be back before you woke up but what can you do?'

Sam slips a backpack off and roots around in it before bringing out a bottle of water. She unscrews the lid and offers it to me. I look between it and her, not sure what the best move is here. For the first time since arriving at the estate, I'm completely helpless.

'It's not poison – see.' Sam takes a swig herself and lets out an exaggerated sigh of refreshment. 'No drugs either. I mean, you're already tied up so . . . not much point, right?'

'You drugged me, before – didn't you?' I say. 'At the party.'

She smiles at me. 'You're really bad at this, aren't you, Amelia? No, I didn't drug you. But you should have known better than to gulp down a random drink at a party like that one.'

She's right. I should have kept up my guard, and now it's too late.

When she offers the bottle again I gulp down some water, glad to wash the taste of blood and dust from my mouth. Once she's satisfied I've had enough, Sam takes the bottle away and sets it on the table, beside the lamp.

Then she takes a seat on the dustsheet-shrouded sofa, legs folded lotus-style. She watches me, either waiting for me to act or considering her next move. She looks eager, like a school kid ready to take a test they've been practising for. As if she can't wait for what comes next.

In the end, I'm the one to break the silence. One thing I know is that if you get someone talking, it's easy to keep them talking. Right now, it's the only thing I can do to delay whatever it is that's going to happen to me.

'I'm guessing this isn't James's cabin then,' I say, as if we're still sipping cocktails on her brother's yacht.

Sam laughs, a big generous 'dinner party' laugh. 'No, it's mine. Though I've never lived in it. You see, my mother insisted that her husband leave me a home in his will. This' – she indicates the walls around us – 'was his little joke. I guess she never cared enough to ask to see it before she died.'

'And how long have you been planning to bring me out here?'

'Oh, only since you arrived.' Sam shrugs. 'I knew who you were as soon as I saw you. You have the same eyes. Couldn't change those, could you?'

So she had known Rose. My stomach turns over. My mind is racing, trying to get ahead of whatever Sam's plan is here. Wondering what she knows and what she had to do with Rose's disappearance. Sam smiles at me.

'You want to know about her, don't you?' she says. 'Go on, ask.'

'Where is she?' My voice cracks. I suck in a long, shuddery breath. 'Why did you kidnap my sister? What have you done with her? Tell me, right now!'

Sam's face shuts down abruptly. It's as if she's switched a light off behind her eyes.

'No,' she says coldly. 'Not like that. You don't get to jump ahead. That's what everyone always does. They never want to hear my side. Never want to know about me. It's always about someone else – Rose. Lawrence. My stepfather.' She spits the word out as if it's poisoned. 'No one is ever interested in me for the sake of me. Just as a way to get at them.'

She settles herself against the sofa and glares at me. 'You have to start from the beginning. You have to ask me the right question.'

I stare at her, seeing the spark of madness in her for the first time. What I thought was a stoned indifference I now see as something more twisted. Desperation bubbles through me, making me queasy. What does she mean, the right question? What could that possibly be? I shift in the chair, the ropes pinching at my skin. Looking down at them, I feel a flicker of understanding. All my careful research, all my discoveries since coming here. They fall into order in my mind, page after page of articles and photographs flicking back and back, to the earliest event. The first domino in this insane series of deaths, disappearances and deceit.

'What', I ask slowly, 'happened three years ago? To Tom Slazenger? What started this?'

Sam's face breaks into a broad smile. 'Now that . . . is the right question.'

She scrambles up off the sofa and heads to the ruined bathroom, returning with a laptop, which she sets primly on a dustsheet-shrouded table in front of me. A 'play' symbol appears on a black screen and she clicks it, returning to the sofa. On her way I see her grab a video camera from her backpack and she retakes her seat, pointing it at me.

'Watch,' she instructs me as the laptop screen comes

to life, revealing a familiar room. In the centre, on a sofa amongst the leaves and the twigs and the dust, is the unmistakeable figure of Tom Slazenger.

26

'Here? Really?' Tom looks around the room, disgust clear even in the dark footage.

'What's the matter, afraid of a few cobwebs?' Sam laughs. She cosies up to him, looking into Tom's face with wide eyes. 'Remember when we used to sneak out here that summer?'

Tom's laugh joins her flirtatious giggling. 'Yeah, well, we were both younger then.'

'Mmm . . . but I was a little younger than you,' she singsongs.

Tom noticeably stiffens. 'You weren't complaining at the time.'

'Of course not . . .' Sam wraps her arms around him and smiles. 'How about a drink?'

She disappears for a moment and Tom looks around the cabin. It's about as decrepit as it is now but someone had obviously planned to use it that night. There's a nice throw over the dustsheet on the sofa, candles stuck to a plate on the table. And of course the camera hidden away. How Tom doesn't see it I don't know.

On screen, Sam returns with two glasses of amber-coloured liquor. Tom downs his and Sam smiles at him, sipping hers carefully. After a few moments Tom takes her glass away and impatiently ushers her to the sofa, pressing her down on it and climbing on top of her.

'Who was that girl you brought with you?' Sam asks while Tom pulls at her dress.

'What? Oh . . . no one, just a date for this. You know how it is.'

'Mmmhmm . . . I bet she's really impressed with you, landing such a good job from my brother.'

Tom pauses and looks down at her. 'Are we doing this or not?'

'Sorry, just felt like reconnecting,' Sam says softly. 'We haven't really spent much time together since the summer we were . . . involved.'

Tom huffs. 'Involved is stretching it, isn't it? But we had fun – bet we can have some more tonight.'

Sam smirks at him and he dives at her neck, kissing loudly. My mouth screws up in an involuntary expression of disgust. He does seem like someone who would have hit on poor Ingrid. He's too slimy for words.

'And she doesn't mind?' Sam continues, absently running her hands over Tom's back.

'Who?'

'Your date, silly.' Sam laughs. 'She doesn't mind that you're out here with someone else?'

Tom sighs, apparently getting irritated. 'She's a fucking escort, Sam, OK? She doesn't care – and if I'd have known you were going to be all over me, I wouldn't have bothered to bring her.'

He kisses Sam in a clear attempt to forestall further con-versation, and starts to paw insistently at her dress, pulling

252

the straps off her shoulders and tugging the top down to reveal the bra underneath.

'Probably a good thing she's not your girlfriend or something,' Sam says, looking up at the dark beams of the ceiling. 'Though it would have been fun to see her face when I told her how you used to bring me up here when I was fifteen, to screw me.'

Tom pulls back, recoiling to the end of the sofa. His face flickers between horror and anger while Sam looks at him with the same playful coyness as before. My stomach twists. Tom's the same age as James. Two years older than Sam. Making what he did to her statutory rape. She was his school enemy's little sister. Was that why he'd sought her out?

I glance up at Sam and find her watching me, stone-faced.

'Keep watching,' she says. 'It's getting to the good part.'

Feeling sick, I look back at the screen in time to catch Sam speaking again.

'I suppose I'll just have to content myself with telling Lawrence all about how you fucked his little sister – and then pretended I didn't exist,' she muses.

'He won't believe you,' Tom says in a low, dangerous voice. 'Or care, if he does. Like you said, James didn't. You're not even really his sister.'

'You're probably right.' Sam sighs. 'Guess you win.'

'I'm out of here. You're still the same crazy bitch you were back then.' Tom levers himself off the sofa, and then sags back on to it as his knees give way. He blinks, tries to get up again and fails, turning to Sam in horror.

'I am, yeah,' she says. 'Still crazy, still a bitch . . . but I'm not stupid any more.'

'What did you . . .' Tom slurs, head dipping.

I know he must be on the same drugs as Bergdis, as Zak. Sam lured him out here for sex and gave him a drink spiked with sleeping pills. What happens to him now though, that's the part I don't know. All I've really worked out for myself is that he went missing.

Sam watches, expectant and gleeful, as Tom slumps over and collapses on the sofa.

The screen goes black for a second before a new image appears. Clearly some time has passed and been edited out, because the scene has changed. Tom is tied to a chair with his own climbing ropes, apparently still unconscious. The same chair and ropes I'm currently trapped in. Sam must have brought them from the house to use on him and somehow moved his body to the chair.

'Toooom,' Sam says in a sing songy voice. She wanders towards him, and my eyes are immediately on the knife in her hand. 'Wake up . . .' She frowns and looks towards the camera. Then she picks up Tom's hand by the middle finger and holds the knife against it, as if she's about to start peeling a carrot.

She sighs. 'Well, you'll have to wake up eventually.'

I gag and turn my head. My eyes are clamped shut as screams burst from the laptop's tinny speakers. I can hear Sam mocking him, taunting him. The sound of his finger hitting the floor is loud in the silence as he presumably passes out again. Then she laughs.

I flinch as Sam slams the laptop shut, still with the camera trained on me. For a moment I forgot she was there with me. I was so focused on the appalling video.

'The rest's private,' Sam says, as if she's apologizing to me. 'Just for the two of us. But I think you get the picture.'

'Why are you showing me this?' I croak, throat dry and dusty.

Sam smiles softly, her voice a gentle, patronizing whisper. 'Don't you want to know what I did with his body?'

'What did you do?' I ask, thinking of Rose.

'Not so fast.' Sam laughs, pacing away from me and aiming a kick at Tom's backpack. 'It was good, though. Very clever, I thought, to hide his stuff up here so after a while everyone thought he'd died on one of his stupid macho adventure trips. Everything was back to normal . . . but that night? That was the happiest I'd been in years. Not just because Tom got what was coming to him, but because—' She cuts herself off with a dreamy look.

What is she thinking about? I wonder. What was it about that night that meant so much?

'So obviously I had to do it again. But then the next party came around and . . . things went a bit wrong.'

She smiles and gestures in a 'What was I to do?' sort of way, but I'm the one to actually say it aloud.

'Bergdis. Your housekeeper.'

'That fucking bitch,' Sam says, still smiling. 'She was the worst of the worst. None of the staff cared about me, but they were at least professional. She thought she was more a part of the Fowley family than I was. To her, my mother was a vile parasite – which we were in agreement on, to be fair – but she couldn't do anything to my mother. So she did it to me.'

Sam strokes the closed lid of the laptop. 'She always found a way to get to me. The radiator in my room was always broken in winter, my sheets always washed with the soap I was allergic to. Once, I saw her actually spit in my tea.

No idea if that was the only time.' Sam shrugs. 'Sometimes I think the only reason James went apeshit on her when she took all his comics was because he couldn't stand being treated like me. It was the ultimate insult. Yet even after he locked her in a fucking freezer, she still had more respect for him than me. Because he was a Fowley, and I was . . . nothing.'

'So you drugged her and, let me guess, she had a heart attack before you could torture her?' I say.

Sam smiles. 'She deserved worse than being tucked up at home, but it was kind of perfect. No one suspected a thing.'

'Except that you left her car on the estate,' I say, hating the smugness in her voice.

'Hardly worth bothering with. Do you think Lawrence knows what his housekeeper's car looks like? No one cared and no one noticed until the police looked into it. No one saw who drove her home, or if they did, they didn't remember. That's the thing about this place: no one notices you unless you're one of the shiny people. We can just do whatever we want. Waiting for someone to find her body was the real nail-biter. She served three generations of Fowleys and not one of them thought to check up on her when she missed a week of work. Sad.' Sam pulls a mocking pout.

'And last year,' I interject, desperate to know but fearing the answers I've been pursuing for so long, 'that was when you decided to kidnap my sister?'

'No,' Sam says. 'Last year was when your sister got what she deserved.'

27

My head throbs from where Sam hit me, waves of pain radiating from what feels like a hole at the back of my skull. I know it can't possibly be that bad, but it feels as though my brain is being stirred with a sharp knife. My skin is slick with sweat, prickling as dust settles on me. My lungs feel raw with the amount I've inhaled – it tastes of secrets and death. Sam opens the laptop, eager to finish her story.

I thought it would be worth dying to find out what happened to Rose. I'm about to find out if that's true, or just a lie I told myself so I could be strong.

'Are you ready?' Sam asks. 'You're actually quite lucky I recorded it. It would really lose something in the telling.'

My sister is dead. That knowledge settles in my chest and begins to rot. Did I suspect it? Yes, occasionally. But now . . . here in this cabin . . . I know it to be true.

If it's anything like what happened to Tom then I'm better off not knowing. Not having those images in my head. But there's nothing I can do.

'After Bergdis,' Sam says, fingers hovering over the keyboard, 'I thought, next year is going to have to make up for it. I needed to do something that would really keep the spark going, you know? I mean, look at you – you know what it's like. You and me, we're the same. We're just trying to keep things interesting.'

She's delusional, insane.

'The invitation was the easiest part,' Sam breezes. 'I got into Lawrence's room – using the code that old hag's replacement always hid under that clock – and I wrote her an invitation and slipped it in with the rest. Did you know you can find out someone's address from their online wish-lists? It's not even that hard.'

So, Lawrence had been right to assume the invitation the police showed him was forged. He just blamed Rose, having no idea his stepsister had done it to lure her here. I just don't know why.

Something else she said strikes me, turning my skin tight and cold. Sam must have spotted it because her grin widens. She watches me, waiting.

'The code under the clock,' I say weakly.

'The one *Elena* told you about.' She doesn't break eye contact but reaches into the pocket of her shorts and withdraws a mobile phone. '*Hola.*'

'What have you done with her?' I pull uselessly at the ropes, guilt pressing down on me like a thousand tonnes of steel. If anything has happened to Elena it's my fault. 'Let her go!'

Sam sidles closer and unlocks the phone screen, show-ing me the text thread between me and Elena. 'By now she's probably halfway home' – she leans closer and whispers into my ear – 'floating down the fjord.'

I let out a scream and Sam steps back, laughing at me as hot tears run down my face.

'You think that stupid bitch and the staff are the only

people who know about that tunnel?' Sam says. 'How do you think I got your sister out of the party once I'd drugged her? That day in the woods, when you were chatting away with Elena? I was following the pair of you. I heard everything. Wasn't too hard to intercept her on her way out of the beach house with her stuff – I told her she looked scared and I was worried and she let me drive her to the airport.' Sam smiles. 'We may have stopped off on a cliff, but for a while she was so grateful. Kind of heart breaking actually.'

I can't keep from sobbing now. Elena's family in Seville are probably wondering if she's ever coming home. An agony I know well. I wonder if Sam has been messaging them, stringing them along as she has me. The idea makes me want to vomit.

'Don't cry,' Sam says, patting me on the head. 'I thought you wanted to know what happened to your sister? I'm just getting to the best part. The part where she was sitting where you're sitting, crying like you're crying . . . only I had a knife in my hand and there was plastic on the floor. I've never liked cleaning, you see, and I learned a lot from Tom.'

Fresh sobs burst out of me and I sag against the ropes as Sam hits play on the laptop.

I can't look away. There she is, my sister. Rose is tied to the same chair as me, with Tom's climbing ropes. She's in the outfit from the police report, a green dress, though it has bits of leaf and stick stuck in the netting skirt underneath. She looks dazed, just coming round from the drugs.

'Wh . . . Where'm I?' I hear her voice, for the first time in over a year, and heave a sob. Despite everything, I can't help but hope for a different outcome for her. As though maybe, if I keep watching, Rose will escape. She'll be spared.

'Hey, Rose . . .' Sam ambles into frame from near the camera, having apparently just turned it on. 'Did you enjoy the party?'

'What? Who're you? What . . .' Rose tries to move and notices the bloodstained ropes for the first time, struggling in earnest as the fog of the drug recedes. 'Let me go!'

'Sorry, can't do that. Actually, that's a lie . . . I'm not sorry. You should be, for trying to worm your way into my brother's life again after all this time. I bet you were so excited when that invitation arrived, weren't you? Dollar signs just flashing in your eyes.'

'Lawrence?' Rose asks blearily. 'I just wanted to . . . get away for a while I . . . I haven't even seen him since I got here . . .' Her head dips and it looks as if she's being sucked back into unconsciousness.

I jump as Sam slaps her across the face. 'Stay awake.'

Rose whimpers, shaking her head.

'You really thought that one kiss, years ago, meant so much to him that he'd invite you? You certainly think a lot of yourself, don't you? For some little council-house scrubber.'

My skin crawls with rage. Rose looks at Sam as if realizing for the first time how insane she is.

'I just wanted you to know, before we get started,' Sam says, taking a familiar knife from behind her back, 'that you never had Lawrence. Never. You delusional slut. You never knew what you had, right, sweetie?' Sam looks directly at the camera, as if she was always planning on showing this to me, and wanted to meet my eye, then she sinks her knife into my sister's thigh.

I yell, as if it'll do anything, and struggle against the ropes. Rose's screams go straight through me, right to the bone, making their home in my soul. Blinded by tears, I turn away, but I can't stop the sounds. The awful shrieks and agonized begging. The last, gurgling breaths of my sister as Sam finally, blessedly, kills her.

I look up just in time to see Sam's blood-covered hands reaching for the camera. She blows a kiss to the lens before turning it off and the laptop screen goes blank. In front of me, the real Sam takes the camera she's holding and props it up on the table, beside the laptop. Filming me.

'Afterwards,' Sam says, finally, though I can hardly hear her over my own sobbing, 'I did the same with her that I did with Tom. You see this?' She gestures at the wheel-barrow. 'I put her in the bath back there, cut what was left of her up and wheeled her down to the orchard under a pile of logs. It was dark; the party was in full swing. No one saw me load her into the charcoal kiln – those things get really hot if you open all the oxygen valves. Ruins the charcoal but' – she shrugs – 'like I care, right?'

I'm bent over, looking down at my knees, sobbing so hard I can't breathe. Sam leans on the back of the chair I'm tied to. When I open my teary eyes, I see the knife in her hand – a tarnished carving knife she must have stolen from the manor, its blackened handle embossed with the Fowley crest.

'It was so hard to keep a straight face earlier,' she whispers, just above my head. 'There you were, terrified of my brothers, hiding in a wood pile . . . inches away from where I incinerated your sister. Where I already knew I was going to burn you up too.'

I close my eyes. Tears run off the end of my nose, dripping into my lap. I feel completely broken. Death, at this point, would be a kindness.

But not without a tiny bit of revenge.

With a cry of despair and rage I bring my head up, battering it right into Sam's downturned face. I feel the crunch of bone breaking against my skull, hear her scream of pain.

That was for Rose, I think, as my chair tips sideways and I land on the floor, eyes still firmly shut against my impending death.

Now do your worst.

28

The worst, however, never comes.

As Sam continues to shriek, staggering to regain her footing and nursing her broken nose, I hear the sound of splintering wood. I open my eyes and look up just in time to witness the cabin door crashing from its hinges. A flash of terror bolts through me. I scream. Out of the rectangle of pitch black, Lawrence rushes in.

'Help!' I yell.

Sam sees him but stays motionless, hunched on the floor. She groans, her hand still covering her face.

Within moments Lawrence is across the room. He grabs Sam's wrist and tries to drag her away. 'Sam! Stop it, now!'

I can't do anything but watch as Sam goes with him, moaning in pain. Blood spatters from her nose on to the floor. For a moment it's hard to believe she's dangerous, that she's a murderer.

'It's OK, Sam. It's over. Just come with me.' He leads her to the door, his expression calm and assured, the big brother coming to sort everything out. But Sam's spine is stiffening, like a cat about to swipe with its claws extended.

'Lawrence, watch out!' I shout.

But it's too late. Quick as a flash, she twists out of his grip so easily that he can't have been holding her too tightly. Wouldn't have wanted to hurt her, I realize. I see the glint of the knife in the dim light. An expression of surprise crosses Lawrence's face.

'Don't touch me! You're not my brother – you're nothing!' Sam screams, and then the only sound is all the air rushing out of Lawrence's lungs in one ragged sigh. Followed by Sam's footsteps as she backs away across the floor, looking at Lawrence as he clutches his side. A hysterical little laugh bubbles out of Sam's throat and she glances between the two of us before she flees the cabin, vanishing into the night.

Sideways, still bound to my overturned chair, I watch Lawrence crumple to the floor, holding his wound. He's in the same suit he was wearing earlier in the day and blood blooms across the white shirt like ink in water. It drips between his fingers and patters on to the wooden floor. The knife is gone – I assume Sam ripped it out of him as she fled. He's already ashen, wincing as he moves.

'Untie me!' I scream, knowing that he's my only chance at getting out of this chair. Anger rages in my stomach. The images from those videos are burnt into my mind. I can hear my sister screaming, hear Tom's fingers hitting the floor. Sam doesn't get to run away from that. From me.

Lawrence half crawls, half drags himself across the floor and starts pulling at the rope on my left wrist with bloody fingers. Once he's worked it loose I slip my hand out and make quick work of the rest of my bindings. I scramble upright and am halfway to the door when the red fog in my brain parts for a second, and I start thinking clearly again. Rage and hurt giving way to frustration.

Lawrence is injured, and he's innocent. He also just saved my life.

'Fuck,' I growl through gritted teeth, forcing myself to return to Lawrence. 'Let me see.'

'Sam,' Lawrence pants. 'She's . . . getting away.'

'I know.' I pull his shirt up, away from the stab wound, and grimace. It's bleeding a lot but it looks like it's gone through his side. I'm no doctor but I've done enough research to know that Sam missed Lawrence's vital organs. That doesn't mean he's in the clear, though.

'Help me get your shirt off,' I say, pulling at it. 'You need to put pressure on it.'

Between the two of us we get off his suit jacket and shirt. I scrunch the shirt into a ball and press it down on the wound. Lawrence groans, but I ignore him and force him to hold the shirt steady while I roll his jacket diagonally into a makeshift bandage and tie it around his waist, securing the shirt bundle in place.

As I fumble with the jacket Lawrence's burner phone shoots out and slides across the floor. I grab it and flip it open, but one look at the screen confirms my fears. Not a single bar of signal. I'm not going to be able to call for help; neither can I leave Lawrence here. I pocket the phone and make a snap decision.

'We need to get you back to the manor – call an ambulance or a doctor,' I say, hauling him to his feet and jamming my shoulder under his armpit to keep him upright. I'm already panting from the effort. Our only hope is if adrenaline keeps me going. If exhaustion gets its claws into me we're both screwed. He's not getting back to the manor alone, and without him to vouch for me, I'm not getting away from his estate.

'Sam – she might come back.' Lawrence gasps as I manoeuvre him out of the door and try to remember which way Sam and I came from.

'I know.' Together we start limping towards the slope, which I think takes us back to the vague path we followed. 'How long have I been out here?'

'I was looking . . . hours, before I . . . realized you were here.' He grunts.

'Fuck.'

In the silence that follows, aside from our shuffling footsteps and Lawrence's laboured breathing, I pick up the odd snatch of music floating on the night air. The party. It must have gone ahead after all. It sounds as if it's in full swing, and judging from the blasting music it's a wild one. The climax of the three days of celebrations. Will any of the guests be in a fit state to help us? Will they even care when I haul their bleeding host into their midst?

'I went after James,' Lawrence says as we crest the slope. 'He . . . I suspected him . . . for a while now.'

'Don't talk – just focus on walking,' I say, for once not leaping on the information he has to offer. Right now, survival is more important. With every step it feels as if the guilt and rage that's haunted me for the last year is falling from my shoulders, replaced by grief, pure and simple.

'I need you to know,' Lawrence insists, panting for breath. 'In case . . . I didn't mean to scare you off, I was panicking – that picture – his . . . cufflinks. I thought it was the proof I needed that he'd killed Tom and Mrs Olsen too. I was so stupid – I never guessed it was Sam all along.'

'But you were going to cover it all up for James?' I hiss. 'Again.'

'No . . .' Lawrence groans as we stumble over a hole in the ground. 'I've made that mistake before. Paying off that waitress. There were others too. I just . . . It was my job to protect him, to protect the family. But I've only made things worse. I'm to blame for Sam . . . I think, God, I think she killed Charlie. Maybe Zak. He was drugged. Maybe they both were.'

I stumble to a stop, causing Lawrence to grunt in pain.

'She was with me the night he died. We saw Charlie arguing with someone else. Then I took her to the house but . . . she was out of it, could hardly walk. Unless that was all a show and she circled back after I went to bed, it couldn't have been her.'

I'm aware that we can't afford to be standing still, so I urge Lawrence to walk again with a nudge. As we go, he continues to speak, despite my attempts to shush him. Perhaps he thinks this will be his last chance to unburden himself to someone. It seems best to keep him talking, if only to try and make sure he remains conscious.

'After I lost you, I went to confront James about all of it . . . the photos of your sister. He denied it, which I didn't believe . . . for a moment – until Ford provided an alibi. They were playing cards the night of Charlie's death . . .' Lawrence coughs and splutters.

'You should stop talking. You can tell the police everything when we get back,' I say, struggling to half carry him over the uneven ground.

But Lawrence won't be silenced. 'Today, when I checked the security cameras to try and find you – I saw you running into Sam, heading into the woods.' He pants, struggling. 'After that I knew she'd probably brought you to the cabin my father left her in his will. Nothing else out here. Didn't know *why* though. I just wanted to talk to you – and then I heard her, and I realized . . .'

We're shuffling through the trees, heading downhill now. The faint music becomes louder as we crest the last slope. Lawrence stops talking and I can hear shrieks and screams and laughter. The sounds of total abandon. Not good. It means our odds of stumbling across help are diminishing. There might still be staff about who're at least sober, but then again, they might be busy looking for their boss, who's currently bleeding in my arms. I'm hoping that the flash of light I just spotted in the trees ahead isn't just wishful thinking, but a sign we've reached civilization. I summon the last of my strength and barrel ahead into the darkness, carrying him with me.

I nearly start crying when we pass through a line of trees and the fleeting flash of light resolves into a garden lantern. We've deviated from the path Sam led me on and come out of the woods closer to the guest chalets than to the orchard. At the sound of voices ahead I start to call out, dragging Lawrence with me along the path.

'Help! Help us! He's been stabbed!' My voice is ragged, torn by exhaustion.

I can hardly make out the answering cries: it's all just noise. My blood is drumming in my ears and I'm starting to feel as if I might faint. The back of my head is still throbbing, a painful reminder that I was recently bludgeoned unconscious.

The bacchanalian tents have been moved from the gardens. I see them under the trees, slivers of flickering lights through the closed draperies. The thick, dark fabric of these tents obscures anything going on inside, but does little to block out sound. Grunting and moaning add to the chorus of noise outside. No one in there is coming to help us. They probably don't even realize we're here. Even if I threw the drapes back, would anyone inside notice?

'Help!' I yell again, as the path winds past a hefty tree trunk. 'Help us!'

Suddenly, there are people in front of me. A trio of guests stumbling along the path. Two men and a woman – all three of them in masquerade masks, body paint and nothing else. It looks as if they've been slinging coloured paint at each other, slathering it with their bare hands, and they're all clearly high or drunk, blundering into each other and giggling.

'Help us!' I yell again, not so much to them as to the darkened trees, trying to attract the attention of anyone sober. The giggling guests stop to gape at us but don't move to help.

I struggle on towards the house, passing the patio, which is streaked with colour. Guests rush around in between guttering tiki torches, mostly nude and covered in paint. A few are holding torches pulled out of the ground, and a ring of naked women are dancing around a marble garden statue that's been smeared with pink and green paint. Two men pass by carrying a laughing woman between them like a hunting prize. The formal gardens are filled with hooting and inhuman screeching. Several dogs are chasing each other, barking. Statues have been pushed over, tables smashed to pieces. There's a dress floating in the swimming pool and one of the bar structures has been tipped over and set ablaze. A long buffet table that clearly once held a roasted pig and piles of pastries, towers of side dishes, looks as though it's been ransacked by a thousand hungry hands. The meat torn apart and platters smashed on the ground, bones chewed and scattered. A man wearing a sinister pig mask runs past us. Was this Lawrence's idea or have things spiralled in the hours he's been away?

'Over there!'

I look up to find several figures rushing towards us from the manor. Clothed figures, thank goodness. As they get closer I realize that James is one of them, accompanied by Cecile and two policemen in slightly unfamiliar uniforms who seem to be wishing they were anywhere else. In the utter chaos of the gardens and surrounding area they look as if they've drastically misunderstood the brief for costume party.

'We've been looking everywhere for you,' Cecile says to Lawrence, not to me, as she catches hold of him, supporting his weight. I look at James and catch something flash across his face as he stares at Lawrence. It's the same expression he had when he watched him with Cecile on the balcony – pure hatred – but this time it only lasts for a second and then it's gone. But it's not replaced by concern or horror, he's just carefully blank.

'Oh my God, you're bleeding!' Cecile says.

'Sam tried to kill us,' I pant. My knees are shaking, seconds from giving way.

'What?' James bursts out. 'Sam did this?'

'You're OK,' Cecile is whispering to Lawrence. 'You're safe now.'

'I . . .' Lawrence gasps, clinging to her shoulder, before pulling away, reaching for the nearest police officer. 'I want . . . Sam found . . . arrested.'

'She's in the woods,' I add, staggering a little as Lawrence's weight is lifted off me. 'She has a knife and she's . . . insane.'

'You need an ambulance, Lawrence – can someone phone for an ambulance?' Cecile cries, looking around us for further help or staff members in the vicinity.

Lawrence turns his pale face towards Cecile as he collapses into the grasp of a policeman. 'Cecile . . . I'm sorry.'

Lawrence passes out and, to my horror, I find all eyes are on me.

29

THE POLICEMEN RUN OFF to call an ambulance and get the doctor – apparently they have one on staff, living in a house on the estate. Between us, James, Cecile and I manage to carry Lawrence to the main house. James swipes us in through the front door and even in the chaos of that moment I can appreciate the irony in being given easy access to the manor now.

I finally know the truth, or at least most of it, terrible as it is. I saw what happened to my sister, even if I have no idea why. Why Sam chose her out of everyone Lawrence might have kissed once. I just hope the police officers, who are even now calling in more units to search the woods, find Sam before she gets away, and recover her laptop and the other evidence at the cabin.

After laying Lawrence's unconscious body out on a sofa in the same sitting room I escaped through earlier, Cecile sends James to find help.

He returns with several exhausted-looking waiters and waitresses. Cecile tells them to fetch first-aid kits from the kitchen and they rush off obediently. Even in a crisis Cecile somehow manages to remain both polite and gracious. She thanks the waitress who brings her the first-aid box and tells her to dismiss the remaining house staff for the night while those outside work to calm things down alongside the police.

'OK, let's see . . . gauze, bandages. Here, take this.' Cecile hands me a sterile packet of wound dressings. 'We should try and stop the bleeding while we wait.'

'Do you know what you're doing?' I ask, watching as she snaps the end off of an ampoule of disinfectant.

'I have a medical degree,' she says absently, totally focused. 'And I'm fully qualified in my specialty. I'm just not registered. My father didn't see the point of me working once I was fully trained. It wasn't as if he wanted me to have a career. He just wanted bragging rights.'

I watch as she carefully dresses Lawrence's wound.

'OK, that's about all I can do with no sutures. The doctor should have some, and pain relief. But at least it's clean. Looks like the bleeding is slowing down.' Cecile takes Lawrence's pulse and seems satisfied that he's stable.

James passes me by, carrying a glass of something amber-coloured. He takes a seat on the nearby piano stool and sips his drink. After several seconds of disbelieving silence, Cecile raises her eyebrows.

'Well? Aren't you going to help? Is the doctor coming? Did they call for an ambulance?' she asks pointedly.

James holds up a finger, swallows the last bit of liquor, and then nods. His eyes are dark, empty of emotion. Yet for the first time since I arrived at the estate, I think James looks genuinely happy. I suddenly wish the policemen were here.

'On their way.' James gestures in Lawrence's direction. 'He's looking less deathly pale now. For a moment there I thought he was going to drop dead before I had a chance to share my good news.'

'What "good news"?' I ask, cutting off whatever Cecile was about to say.

James smirks and from inside his suit jacket he produces a thick bundle of paperwork, folded neatly into an envelope.

'I'm going to inherit my father's estate.'

I glance at Cecile but she's looking at James, completely baffled.

'You're . . . what?' she says. 'Lawrence isn't dead. Thank God! So, I don't know what on earth you're talking about . . .' She trails off as James tosses the envelope at her. It scythes through the air and drops into her lap.

'I have copies, don't worry,' James says, getting up and crossing to a decanter by the fireplace to refill his glass. 'The original is also quite safe.'

Cecile is still watching him, but her hands are slowly working the envelope open. She extracts the papers and rifles through them, freezing when she reads something on the third page.

'This is . . .'

'A statement provided as testimony by one Charles Braithwaite – former employee and lover of my brother, Lawrence Fowley,' James says, relishing each word. 'Which shows unequivocally that my brother has violated the stipulations laid out in my father's will – leaving me as his only heir.'

'Cecile,' I say, unable to keep silent in the face of her heart-wrenching expression. 'I'm so sorry, he wouldn't have wanted you to find out like this . . .'

'You knew?' Her eyes meet mine and her voice catches. 'Oh my God – you knew! Who else knows? Why didn't he tell me?' She covers her mouth with her hand and looks down at Lawrence. An expression I can't quite read passes over her features. She takes his limp hand in hers and squeezes it, then she gets to her feet and strides towards James.

He doesn't flinch when Cecile tosses the papers at him, but he's nearly knocked over by the force with which she slaps him. He drops his glass and the tumbler bounces and rolls across the floor, whisky spilling after it. I wince, afraid that she's forgotten herself in her fury. Forgotten the risk that James poses. If he attacks her now, it'll be me that has to intervene. James steadies himself against the mantel and glares at her, but Cecile glares back, unflinching.

'You vile little snake,' she says. 'To do this to your own brother . . . after everything he's done for you. You disgust me.' She spits at his feet.

'I disgust you?' James says, his eyes narrowing. 'He's the one who lied to you. Led you on this whole time. I'm the one who gets all of this . . .' He gestures to encompass the grand room around us. 'He gets nothing.'

'No, James,' Cecile says, her voice soft but lethal. 'You get nothing. Just an empty house, with no one to care if you live or die. Lawrence will always have me – maybe not as his wife, but as his friend. I will always be his friend.'

Out of the corner of my eye I see Lawrence stir. When I turn, I see that he's awake, looking at Cecile's back as she tears James to shreds. He looks simultaneously sad and proud.

I, on the other hand, am thinking about the papers that Cecile threw aside. While James sputters insults at Cecile, I step forward and stand between him and the door.

'How exactly did you get Charlie to give you that statement?' I ask.

James turns to me, so slowly I can almost hear the gears shift in his head. He's sweating, his jaw tight with rage. This moment is not all he hoped it would be. Clearly.

'He offered to write it, for money,' he spits the words, disdainfully.

'Liar.'

We all turn to look at Lawrence, who's propping himself up on one elbow, wincing in pain. Cecile snaps out of her shock and goes to him, helping him to sit up.

'Charlie wouldn't sell me out. Sell us out. That's something you'll never understand.'

'Or you didn't know him as well as you thought,' James counters.

'There's an easy way to know,' I say, drawing everyone's attention. 'James got a text yesterday, the afternoon before Charlie died. It said, "Fuck you, I won't do it."'

The room is so quiet that I can hear James's nervous swallow.

'The police can check to see if that text was from Charlie. Maybe even recover any deleted messages between the two of them. I'm sure they'll find evidence of you and him coming through the rose garden last night, down to the beach?'

James's eyes narrow behind his glasses. 'I have no idea what you're talking about.'

I continue, my certainty growing as the pieces fit together snugly in my mind. Sam may be a killer, but she isn't the only killer here. I can see it in James's eyes.

'Were you hoping he wouldn't be found? That he'd float away into the fjord, leaving just the clothes and the bottle to explain it all?' I ask.

'This is insane,' James blusters, turning on Lawrence. 'I

277

didn't do anything to your precious Charlie. Sam's the one who stabbed you. She must have killed him, obviously, unless you've lost all your sense as well as your money. You can't prove I had anything to do with it.' He gestures dismissively at Lawrence. 'Now it's convenient for you, you want to pretend I'm a murderer? You never did like to lose.'

'Sam might have killed Tom and Bergdis and Rose,' I say, pronouncing my sister's name loudly and clearly. 'Maybe even Zak. But I'd bet anything that when the police find her, she'll tell them she had nothing to do with Charlie. And she was awfully keen to tell me every horrible thing she'd done. Yet she never mentioned him. She has no reason to try and wriggle out of that when she's killed others and bragged about it. So, to me it looks very much like someone else is responsible for Charlie.'

As James speaks his face goes from red to beetroot. 'She won't say anything like that, and if she does it'll be a damn lie. Told by a crazy woman. That's if they catch her, by the way,' he hisses. 'You let her run off, remember? Sam's got money of her own; they'll never catch up with her.' James's face is shiny with sweat, his hand trembling slightly as he wipes the palm on his trousers. 'Besides which, I think you're all forgetting that I have an alibi for last night. I was playing cards, all night – with your boyfriend. Who, by the way, you've been lying to since the day you met. And Lawrence won't keep me from spilling your secrets any more. I can't wait to see his face when he finds out.'

Behind me I can hear Cecile asking Lawrence what he means, but all I can focus on is James's flushed face. Why has Lawrence been keeping him from telling Ford about me?

'Lying about what?'

I turn, slowly, already knowing what I'm going to find. My head throbs and I let out a sigh. It's Ford. He's still got his hand on the French door to the garden, the night breeze coming in behind him and a look of shock and hurt on his face.

30

'Go on, tell him,' James urges, clearly loving this awful moment. 'Tell him how you lied and schemed and screwed him just to get into this house. How long have you been—'

'Shut up, James,' Cecile says, looking between me and Ford. She might not know what's going on, but she's still on my side more than his. At least for now.

Ford lets the door swing shut behind him and takes a few hesitant steps into the room. He's dressed for the party, or he was. At some point he clearly realized the party was over and ditched some of his outfit. Like the rest of the family he's probably been busy looking for Lawrence instead of joining the madness outside. Looking for me. Guilt hits me like a wall. I notice that he's missing the jacket for his suit and he's rolled his shirt sleeves up, the way he always does when he's stressed. The shirt is also untucked, which is practically a first for Ford. I've never seen him so dishevelled. A blotch of green paint apparently soaked through his jacket into his shirt, because there's a muted patch of colour on his shoulder.

My heart immediately breaks for him. He's been so worried about me, clearly searching since I failed to return from my 'walk', yet I've hardly spared him a thought.

'Ford, I . . .' I start, but then flounder.

'What does he mean, Amelia?' Ford asks. He doesn't even sound angry. That's the worst thing. He just sounds hurt.

The only way to do this, I realize, is to get it all out in one go. Like purging an infection. All my lies need to be laid bare. I glance quickly at James, then I steel myself. I'm not going to give him the satisfaction. I'm not letting him turn everyone against me so that he can get away. I just have to get Ford to believe me, now, and hope for forgiveness.

'When we met,' I say, giving Ford my full attention, as he deserves, 'I lied to you and I've been lying ever since. I made sure we'd run into each other, so that I could use you to get an invitation to this party.'

Ford's mouth hangs open, just slightly, as if he's not sure if he wants to ask a question or yell at me. I catch sight of Cecile, who looks as aghast.

'I told you!' James says gleefully. 'I told you, she's a gold digger.'

'I am not!' I snap. 'Ford, I used you – yes. But I did it because my sister, Rose, disappeared from last year's party and no one has seen her since. No one would believe me when I told them something had happened to her. So I had to get myself here and try to find out for myself.'

'And you found . . . Sam?' Cecile says.

'What about Sam?' Ford looks at me in utter disbelief. 'You think Sam did something to your sister?'

'Sam killed my sister. I know she did. She told me so,' I say. 'She . . . she showed me a video of her torturing my sister to death. Just like she tortured Tom Slazenger. She showed me that too. After she hit me over the head and tied me up.' I swallow, suppressed tears burning my sinuses. 'She told me how she dismembered my baby sister and burnt her in the charcoal kiln. Told me she did the same to Tom and she would have done the same to Bergdis, if she hadn't had a heart attack.'

Cecile's gasp is ragged and loud. I see Lawrence put a protective arm around her as if to shield her from the unpleasantness. Ford looks ill, but he takes a few steps towards me.

'So, the entire time we were together . . . you were lying to me. Why didn't you just tell me that you needed help?' he says, as though it's the simplest thing in the world. Who knows, maybe to him it is just that easy.

The idea is so surprising I nearly laugh. 'Ford, you love your family. You never would have believed me.'

'Maybe not,' he allows. 'But . . . God, I feel like . . . it's been nearly a year, Amelia – if that's even your name.'

'It is,' I say, knowing that it changes absolutely nothing.

'A year,' he repeats. 'To think that all this time you didn't want me, that you were just pretending? I feel sick, remembering all the times I've kissed you, been with you, and you were just . . . tolerating me.' His cheeks are pinkening and he looks like he might cry.

I take a step towards him, but Cecile gets there first. She walks past me, pressing lightly on my arm to tell me to stay where I am, then she puts her arms around Ford.

'I know, believe me,' she says, 'that it hurts to realize you've been living a lie. But you need to know none of this was your fault, and it doesn't make your feelings any less valid.'

I glance at Lawrence and find he's already looking at me. In a weird way this is something we share: keeping a heavy secret from someone who only wanted to love us and be loved in return. Someone who was better than we deserved.

'I'm sorry, Ford. I really am,' I say. The air in the room is so tense that it's almost hard to breathe. Outside I hear a whoop and something shattering. The party is raging on, but in here we're all frozen together. Trapped in this moment. 'By the time I knew you enough to feel bad about it, it was already too late to stop. I couldn't go back. Please believe me, I never wanted to be involved in any of this, but because of what happened to Rose, I didn't have a choice.'

Ford sniffs; he's holding Cecile's hand tightly in his. 'Yes, you did.'

I look at the floor, ashamed but knowing that he's wrong. No one else was looking for Rose. No one thought she was even missing. It had to be me.

'You chose to do what you felt was right, no matter the cost, for the good of your family,' Ford continues, finally turning from me and glaring at James. 'Which makes you braver than me.'

I look at James, whose eyes are boring into Ford's. He doesn't speak but his lip trembles as if he wants to. The balmy evening has turned to frigid night and a cold breeze flutters the curtain of a nearby window. I shiver. I'm on the wrong side of midnight and I'm desperate for sleep. But even as I think it, I know that as soon as I close my eyes it'll be Rose I see.

Ford takes a deep breath and runs a hand through his hair. 'James invited me to play cards last night,' he says.

'Don't you dare,' James says.

Ford glares at him. 'But he wasn't there for most of the game. He left. When he came back he told me that if I didn't back him up and say he was there all night, he'd ruin me, get me fired, and that I'd never work for any of the family businesses . . . once he inherited everything.'

There's a stunned silence.

'You . . . ungrateful fucking bastard,' James whispers. 'You'd be nothing without me.'

'He came back,' Ford says, voice gaining volume, blocking James out, 'stinking of vodka, with sand all over his shoes. This morning, when I saw the body on the beach, saw the empty bottle . . . I had suspicions – no, not suspicions, I knew! – I knew and I kept quiet because I was afraid. Then I saw how hard Lawrence was taking it and now . . . Well, I can't stay quiet. No matter what it costs me.'

'I'm proud of you, Ford,' Cecile whispers.

'Maybe she'll lend you some cash when you're fucking bankrupt,' James snaps. 'I'm going to make sure you never get another job in the City.'

'You won't be calling in any favours from prison,' Cecile replies coldly. 'And if Ford's company even thinks of firing him on your say-so, I will gladly hire him a solicitor and sue them into the ground.'

'I'm not going to prison.' James glares at all of us in turn. 'You've got no proof. Some sand? A text? That's it?' He looks at Lawrence and that expression is back on his face: uncontrolled rage. 'All right, maybe your little boyfriend tried to welch on our deal, so I had to get creative, threaten to have his mother deported – did you know he's half-Polish?' James sneers. 'Maybe he tried to get the papers off me once he'd signed them and I had to take him out to the rose garden, remind him what was at stake. Maybe I lost it a bit, hit him over the head, poured vodka down his neck, dumped him in the water. You just try and prove that. It's your word against mine. And *you*' – he points at Lawrence – 'just lost your inheritance to me. You' – he moves on to Cecile – 'just lost your golden-ticket fiancé. Ford owes me for getting him a job, loaning him money, so there's his motive to lie and this *fraudster*' – he turns to me – 'she's hardly reliable. Any decent solicitor would have that case thrown out before lunch.'

There's a long silence as everyone digests his words. James isn't bluffing and he has a good point. We might all know he's guilty as sin but who's going to believe us? There are too many personal motives and secrets between us all for a case to be made based only on our word.

Fortunately, I'm a forward thinker.

'A decent barrister, however,' I say, digging Lawrence's burner phone out of my pocket, 'would have been record- ing this conversation from the start.'

James blinks, pauses. He looks at me, his eyes so wide I can see the white all the way around his iris, magnified by his glasses. He's torn between rushing me and fleeing the room. After a few seconds he collapses into a nearby arm- chair, puts his face in his hands and lets out a sound that's half sob, half scream.

Through the front windows, flashing blue lights illumin- ate the room and the sound of raised voices and crunching gravel fills the air. Cecile is across the room in moments, rushing to let the paramedics in. They come barrelling inside the charged room, treading dirt into the plush rugs, oblivious to the revelations that have been spilled.

Ford and I share a glance, and then we both look at James. Cecile returns and hovers as Lawrence is manoeuvred on to a trolley and swept away towards the ambulance. As he's wheeled out he points a damning finger at his brother.

'You'll get nothing from me for your defence, you hear? Nothing. I'll see you rot for what you did to Charlie.'

'It's my money!' James bellows, as red-faced and clammy as a toddler in a tantrum. 'You're disinherited!'

Lawrence chuckles darkly as he's wheeled away. In that moment he is every inch the murderous sociopath I first took him for when I began my search for Rose's abductor.

'That document is worthless. Just like you.'

With that, the paramedics spirit him away, Cecile following them out into the dark. The Fowleys' doctor, a rumpled man clutching a medical bag, appears in the front doorway. As the vehicle accelerates over the gravel, James jumps up and hurls his empty glass across the room. The doctor flinches but doesn't otherwise react, apparently used to James's temper.

'You. Bitch!' James yells.

He hasn't taken two steps towards me before Cecile returns from outside, a senior-looking police officer in tow. She points at James with an imperious finger.

'Please remove this man and arrest him for the murder of Charlie Braithwaite.'

James snarls, 'It's got nothing to do with me. Get your hands off me!'

Several other officers have entered the room and together they restrain James as he rages, cries and spits obscenities. I sit still and feel the doctor probing the wound on my head, watching as James is dragged from the room in handcuffs.

'Two Fowleys arrested for murder,' Ford says numbly. 'I can't believe it. They have both completely ruined the family name.'

'It's Lawrence's name too, and yours,' Cecile reminds him. 'You should be proud of your loyalty. I am.'

Ford smiles down at her and despite myself I feel a flicker of loss. He's looking at her the way he used to look at me, or at the woman I was pretending to be. A woman I can now leave behind.

But what's left of who I used to be? No Rose. No mission. Just . . . me.

'I'm sorry,' one of the police officers cuts in, more heavily accented than any of his younger colleagues. 'I'm afraid we haven't yet been able to locate Miss Fowley in the grounds. More units are incoming from Stockholm. We'll be using dogs as well to try and catch her trail. She can't hide forever, not now we know what she's done. We recovered a laptop from the cabin. She will be brought to justice.'

I am standing in the heart of the Fowley manor, a place I once would have given anything to get into and I've just heard the words I've been desperate to hear for nearly a year now. My sister's killer will be brought to justice. It's done.

31

'I'LL DRIVE YOU TO the hospital,' Ford says to Cecile, once the police have split up to secure the house and guest chalets. 'So you can see Lawrence.'

'Do you have any experience, driving on the right?' Cecile asks hesitantly.

'No,' Ford admits. 'But, well, I'll come with you then. You shouldn't be alone.'

Cecile gives him a grateful smile. 'Thank you. I'll just grab my bag.'

She goes into the entrance hall and I hear the flap of her putting on a coat, the jangle of a bag strap. The doctor sticks a dressing to my head, over some closure strips, and tells me what to watch out for, in case I'm concussed. I thank him and he heads into the hall. I hear him telling Cecile that he's also going to the hospital and will meet her there.

Ford looks at me with a mix of pain and worry in his eyes. It hurts to see that expression on his face, to know that I'm the reason it's there. Ford has his faults but he trusted me, cared about me for the months we were together. If he knew just how much I'd resented him during most of our relationship I have no doubt that he'd be crushed.

'You should stay in the manor for tonight,' he says halt-ingly, as if he's not sure any more if we have the kind of relationship where he can offer advice. I feel it too, the weird sense that we're strangers again, or exes who haven't seen one another in years.

I want to tell him that it wasn't all a lie. That I didn't just tolerate his touch, and that in another world, one where he isn't part of this family, we might have been a good match. But there's no way to do so without it coming out all weird, and right now he probably doesn't need me confusing his feelings any more than they already are.

I nod. 'Thank you. I will, in case Sam comes back. Though there's a secret passage into the kitchen . . . I should tell the police that.'

'How do you . . . Oh.' Ford blinks. 'I suppose that makes sense, but God I feel like I've missed a lot these past few days. Months even.'

I wince. 'I owe you a proper apology. Not that it could ever make up for the past year, but . . .'

Ford holds up a hand. 'Look, this entire situation is insane and I can't exactly fault your reason for doing what you did. I just wish that it hadn't been me – you know?' He looks broken, but also somehow relieved, as if a weight has been taken away from him. Maybe I wasn't as convincing as I thought and he always knew something was a bit off about me.

I nod. 'I get that. I really am sorry.'

'But . . . once we get home, we'll sort things out at the flat and, I guess, go our separate ways. Don't worry about anything, OK?'

'Ford? I'm ready,' Cecile calls from the foyer. Her voice is gentle; I suspect she's been listening, giving us space.

Ford lights up at the summons and gives me an awkward half-smile as he flees the room. The front door opens and thuds close, then I'm alone. All the staff have been dismissed to their accommodation and the police are outside, setting up a perimeter in case Sam attempts to return. I don't think she will. Granted I only just met her, the real her, but she had the desperation and viciousness of a trapped animal. If I were to lay bets, it would be that she'd avoid people at all costs, retreat into the woods that were once her safe space. Her killing ground.

I shudder at the thought of those leaning trees, the endless rows of pines, their moss-covered trunks. The secretive whispering of their branches and the things hidden in the undergrowth beneath them. No wonder Sam felt so at home there, a predator in the wild woods. I feel sick as I remember the things she did to Tom and to Rose. Things I will never be able to unhear. Images I will never be able to unsee. She will be put away for a long time once those videos are shown to a jury.

A while later one of the police officers returns with an update on the search. He seems uncomfortable to find only me at the house. All the Fowleys are injured, arrested or elsewhere.

'We've stationed officers at the door to every guest chalet, just in case,' he finally tells me. 'There's also now a perimeter around the manor house.'

'There's a tunnel in the old ice house,' I say. 'I can show you where it is if you need me to?' It feels like years since I entered that dark passage on my way to uncover Lawrence's secrets.

'We're aware,' he states. 'We were actually called in earlier today to determine the whereabouts of a missing staff member, Elena Silveira? In the course of interviewing staff we were informed about the tunnel, that Elena often used it to leave the house to smoke. We were just wrapping up our interviews when Ford Fowley made us aware that his cousin was missing and hadn't been heard from in hours. We'd only just begun to organize ourselves when you arrived.'

Elena. In all the chaos and accusations I had allowed her to slip from my mind. Shame made my skin prickle unpleasantly. 'I know what happened to Elena . . . She was killed several days ago, by Sam Fowley.'

The police officer goes very still. 'You're sure of this?'

I nod. 'She told me – Sam. She confessed to killing Elena and dumping her body into the fjord from a cliff, near the roadside. She'd been using Elena's phone to text me and she still had it on her. It'll be recorded on that camera she was using.'

The officer's face seems to age five years on hearing this. He looks like someone who has tried to give up on hope but nevertheless continues to be afflicted with it. Clearly he was holding on to the idea that Elena might still be alive.

'If that's the case, we will have to search the fjord for her body. The phone we might be able to trace if Miss Fowley attempts to use it. I will inform Mrs Silveira's husband . . . he's the one who contacted us. He hadn't heard from her and they usually speak every day.'

'I know she has family in Seville,' I say. 'I . . . I gave her money so she could leave this job and go home earlier than planned, but Sam got her first.'

'She will answer for her actions,' the police officer says stiffly. 'I can try and see to it that Elena's family is aware of the money, so they know to withdraw it from her accounts.'

'Thank you,' I say, my voice coming out so small I'm afraid he won't hear. I clear my throat. 'Can I write down my details for you? I . . . uh . . . I can't leave the country for a while – no passport – but I don't think I'll be welcome here for much longer.'

He looks as if he wants to ask, but he probably has other concerns right now. He passes me his notebook and I scribble down my details.

After he leaves I sit down on the sofa, my head in my hands. I keep imagining Elena's family receiving the news about her murder. Of all the people I've hurt to get my answers, she is the one I regret the most. The guilt is like acid in my blood, eating its way along my veins. I will never, ever forget her. I will never forgive myself.

Sunrise comes eventually, turning the room grey and then pale yellow. There's a light rain in the air and it's cooler than it's been since we arrived. The autumnal heatwave has broken and I can almost feel winter approaching. I'm still in the dirty, bloodstained clothes I was wearing yesterday when Ford returns to the manor. He opens the door and peers in at me.

'Cecile wants to stay with Lawrence,' he says by way of hello. 'I said I'd come back here and pack some things for them.'

'How is he?'

'Stable.' Ford's nervous energy is obvious; he's clearly hesitant to enter the room fully. It's as if this is my ancestral home instead of his. 'They gave him a blood transfusion, antibiotics . . . He should be OK. Sam missed all the major organs. He'll need a tetanus injection too. They weren't sure what he was stabbed with but they're being cautious.'

'Good, that's good,' I say, getting up from the sofa. The world tips and I stagger a little. When I recover, Ford is half-way across the room towards me, frozen in the act of coming to my rescue. We share embarrassed looks.

'Sorry, I'm not sure if it's the head injury or the lack of sleep,' I say.

'Yeah . . . you do look like shit.'

A surprised laugh bursts out of me. Ford blushes and smiles, shoulders dropping in relief that I've taken the joke well.

'Thanks. I feel like shit,' I say.

This time, he laughs too. I think we're both slightly punch-drunk from the events of last night. Nothing feels real, until it does. I'm experiencing waves of unreality followed by moments of crushing guilt and it's exhausting.

'We're meant to fly home today,' Ford says. 'I'm not sure what to do.'

'Stay.'

He looks at me, surprised. 'Here?'

I nod. 'You should be here – there's no other Fowley to take responsibility. Keep things running, for the sake of Lawrence, the staff and for Cecile. It's what you've always wanted.'

Ford's cheeks pinken just a tad. There's a flicker of a smile on his lips. 'Maybe. There's probably a lot that needs taking care of – what with the police search and Charlie's death to consider. Would you' – he seems to wrestle with something internally – 'like to stay here, too?'

I'm shaking my head before I can even think. Last night I felt the distance growing between Ford and me. More than that, I no longer feel tied to this place. To this family.

'That's very kind of you to offer,' I say, wincing at the

formality in my voice. 'But . . . I think I've done enough damage here. I've given my information to the police; they've cleared me to leave the estate.'

Ford doesn't try to argue. 'I suppose you got the answers you were looking for?'

'Not exactly the ones I came here to find but, yeah, I got them. I'll, um . . . I'll go to a hotel near the airport and stay there while my new passport comes through. I suppose we should meet up later so I can get my stuff from the flat – just my stuff, not anything you bought.'

Ford shrugs. 'What am I going to do with it? Take anything you want from the clothes. The jewellery I can sell but the rest would just go to waste.'

'You should really keep all of it,' I say firmly. 'It's not me anyway.'

I wish I hadn't said that last bit when I see Ford's eyes dip to the floor. There's a part of me that can't believe I'm getting off this lightly. I'd been expecting Ford to threaten all kinds of legal action over my deception. Which probably meant I didn't know him as well as I'd convinced myself I did.

I sigh. 'OK . . . let me know when you're back in the UK then.'

'Right . . . and good luck with whatever it is you do next,' Ford says. 'I hope you can be happy, after everything. I can't imagine how hard it'll be but you deserve it.'

'You too,' I say, a lump rising in my throat. 'You deserve to be happy.'

'Do you need me to walk you to the chalet?' Ford asks. 'Most of the guests are leaving this morning, there'll be plenty of people about but they're in all kinds of a mess so, to be on the safe side . . .'

'I just need to grab the essentials,' I say, shaking my head. 'Shouldn't take too long. But thanks.'

'I nearly forgot – Lawrence left this here when he went to check the security footage,' Ford says, retrieving my bag from where it's fallen off the back of a sofa. My heart lifts – I was worried how I'd manage without a phone or cards. I could have done it, but this is definitely a lot easier.

Ford passes me the bag and I shoulder it, beyond ready to change into fresh clothes, shower off last night and get some distance between me and the Fowley estate. I take a breath and nod, telling myself and Ford that I'm ready to go.

'Take care of yourself, Aimes,' Ford says softly.

'Right back at you, Mr Fowley,' I say, shoving open the door to the bright light of day. 'Right back at you.'

32

It isn't until I'm in the chalet, getting changed, that I remember the notebook stuffed into my bag's inner pocket. I'd forgotten all about it and had honestly thought Lawrence would have taken it back when he took my bag. Maybe he hadn't thought to search it fully. He'd been too busy trying to find me.

Call it morbid curiosity, but I'm going to keep it. I also keep the police report on Zak's death, which Lawrence must have gathered up with the rest of my things and had returned to me with my bag. I have no idea if he intended for me to end up with it, but I have it now.

Ford has arranged a car to take me anywhere I want to go and I google hotels near the airport to get an address. I'm not too worried about the cost. I have more than enough in my accounts to stay out here for months. It's just the idea of waiting that's getting to me. Sitting in limbo.

Getting back to the UK proves to be even more annoying and time-consuming than I imagined, but it at least gives me plenty of time to think. Shut up in my hotel room and waiting for my new passport, I spend the days coming to terms with what I've learned about my sister's final moments. As much as I will ever come to terms with that. I cry, I stare at the ceiling and I curse myself for being too late.

I get updates from the police. They're still looking for Sam but there's been no sign of her. James still isn't talking except to denounce his brother to anyone who'll listen. The police officer sounds particularly done with him; it must be tough dealing with James Fowley all day. I sometimes feel a prickle of fear as I look out of the window of my hotel room at the trees nearby and wonder if Sam's out there somewhere, hunting me down. I don't think I'll feel fully safe until she's been found.

I just wish they'd find her so it would all be over. So I would know why. Why Sam picked my sister. Why she lured her here just to kill her. All over a kiss with Lawrence? It still makes no sense to me.

That's what takes me back to the diary, to the police report. The urge to understand. Neither Sam nor James had mentioned Zak. So which one of them had killed him? The report doesn't really have much of any use that I haven't already seen. Only one little detail that I overlooked. Apparently they hadn't just tested Zak's blood for drugs and alcohol. The police hadn't been called to the scene of the accident, but they had been escorted on to the estate the next day. Probably to avoid speculation from the guests. They'd found no evidence in the room that he'd been pushed, or that anyone had helped him up to the window. But they had collected the glass Zak was drinking from, along with an empty decanter. Both were heavily contaminated with the same drugs in his system. Loprazolam.

I'd assumed he'd been drugged but it was odd to me that it was in the decanter. I'd assumed whoever it was – likely

James – had slipped something into his glass. But if it was in the decanter that sort of made it seem like someone had just drugged the alcohol and left it lying around. In James's room, where they couldn't have known Zak was going to drink it. Unless James invited him up and just declined to drink with him?

I turn to the diary instead. Now I have all the time in the world to turn the squiggles of shorthand into actual words. Without any dates I'm left going from back to front – the events closest to the party where Rose was killed obviously being of the most interest to me. I work page by page, backwards, in case I miss anything. It's slow going and I'm still translating when I finally get my passport and can return home.

On the plane I settle in with my own notebook and re-read the translated entries, checking to make sure I haven't missed anything.

Meeting set up for Monday to go over options re: financial inconsistencies at Henley Ltd. Don't want to confront James without evidence. ZB convinced it's someone embezzling but hasn't brought me any proof yet. I need to be sure – it's bad enough having James as a brother, I don't want him as an enemy.

So, even a year ago Lawrence was looking at James and suspecting he was the reason his company was in financial difficulty. No wonder James had it in for Zak Bakshi. He was blowing the whistle on his scheme.

Preparing for this year's party. Wish it didn't have to go ahead but it's all part of Father's wishes. At least once I'm married, Cecile will be able to take most of this on — she relishes anything to do with organization and her taste is unparalleled. Except when it comes to me, I suppose. Checking RSVPs, realized Ford not coming. Need to do more to include him, he's our only close relative remaining and Father always spoke well of his mother — he'd have wanted him to feel welcome here.

Nothing too surprising there. Lawrence hated the parties and was conflicted about Cecile. I already knew Ford hadn't been invited to the party that year too. The next entry, however, proves more interesting.

Sam excited for the party for once. Not sure why, put this down to her missing last year's and being fresh out of another stint in rehab. Worried it'll be too tempting for her. Of course the idea of a sober one of these things is laughable. Not the reputation I've cultivated and the investors will be furious if they're denied the chance to let loose. Considering offering her a holiday or hiring someone to keep her away from temptation. Will talk it through with her, see how she feels. If she'll tell me. I can't really do much without her input and agreement.

I sit back in my seat and look down the length of the plane. I check the dates again, to make sure. My pulse flutters painfully. Sam lied to me. Lied when she didn't have to lie. She had me tied to a chair and had just shown me a video of her torturing Tom Slazenger to death. So why did she feel the need to lie and tell me she was involved in Bergdis Olsen's death when she couldn't have been? She wasn't even there that year.

I try and work my way around the problem. Maybe she

snuck in just like I had. But she was meant to be in rehab – they didn't just let you out for a long weekend without telling anyone. If Lawrence put her there he'd have wanted to be made aware if she was acting out or had gone missing. No. Sam wasn't at that party. Which meant she was just pretending she helped abduct Bergdis and then staged her death. The only reason I could see was that she'd been lying, and the only reason to do that would be to protect the person who'd actually killed Bergdis.

I think of Sam, blowing a kiss at the camera as if she knew one day she'd show me the video. As if she was taunting me. But what if that kiss was meant for someone else – a partner. Someone who was also involved.

What had she said? 'I needed to do something that would really keep the spark going, you know? I mean, look at you – you know what it's like. You and me, we're the same. We're just trying to keep things interesting.' I'd thought she meant for herself, but looking back it sounded more like she was talking about keeping a relationship fresh. Comparing whatever bond she had with her partner to my efforts to keep Ford happy.

Sam had a partner. Could it be James? Had they conspired to kill Zak together when he threatened to reveal his embezzlement? James and Sam, together. I feel ill just thinking about it.

I flick back through the diary, page after page, looking for information about Sam's absence the year Bergdis died. It's a while before I come across anything of note. The rest is just Lawrence's dark mood and complaints about the 'rigmarole' of throwing the yearly party. It's just a line but it gives me pause.

Offered B time off in view of Sam's return, but B assured me Sam had no idea it was B who raised concerns with me.

'Time off' suggested an employee and with Bergdis on the brain I couldn't help but read that line as Lawrence worrying that she and Sam would clash. Had Sam been packed off to rehab because Bergdis found her stash of drugs and reported her to Lawrence? That would have pissed Sam off, surely. Enough for her to finally want Bergdis dead? For James to do it for her?

The plane descends into Heathrow with my questions still unanswered and I pack the diary back into my handbag. I'll just have to look into it later and contact Lawrence. James is locked up, and as soon as the police know he had to have killed Bergdis alone, he might 'remember' where Sam has run off to, if only to try and weasel his way out of a second set of charges.

I terminated my rental agreement when I moved in with Ford, so I don't have a home to go to. Anything I didn't sell is in storage and I'll need to find somewhere to live and let work know that I'm coming back. Eventually, once I've recovered a bit from everything that happened. After leaving the airport I check into a budget-friendly hotel in town and decide to put flat hunting off for a week at least. I just need to rest.

Two days of watching terrible TV and eating instant noodles later, I get a text from Ford saying he's back in the country and I 'can pick my things up whenever'. Although the tone is light and breezy I can feel the implication behind his words. He wants me to get my stuff sooner rather than later. I can't blame him. We both have things we want to move on from.

I text back that I can come by tomorrow and Ford sends a thumbs-up emoji. We're communicating like strangers now. I don't have any right to expect more.

The next day I dress casually in leggings, trainers and a hoodie, all recently purchased from shops around Oslo Airport. Ford lets me into the flat and I put my key on the kitchen counter, looking around the flashy, pristine apartment. It feels like a dream that I ever lived here, that the handsome man before me was ever my boyfriend. Looking back I can't believe some of the things I did to get to this point, to find out what happened to Rose. It's as if I've been in a fog, thinking only of finding her, saving her. Nothing else could reach me. It's kind of horrifying.

'You're looking good, considering,' Ford says.

He doesn't look too bad himself. Well rested at least, if a little rumpled from travel.

'Did you only just get back?'

'Late last night, but I'm probably going to be heading back out tomorrow. Just came to pack up some things.'

'Oh?' I'm surprised, but Ford just shrugs, looking slightly pleased.

'Lawrence is still recovering but I think he's going to offer me a job out there, so I want to be there for him and Cecile while everything's still so chaotic. You know they haven't found Sam yet? I'm starting to think she died out there. It's not like she took anything with her, right?'

'No,' I say, shivering. 'She went into the woods empty-handed, except for the knife.'

For a moment we just stand there and then Ford gestures towards the bedroom.

'Right, so . . . I suppose you can just manage, right?' he

says. 'I'm just going to go downstairs and talk to the building manager about putting this place on the market.'

'No problem. I'll sort things and let you check before I pack them up.'

'No need, I trust you,' Ford says, smiling. 'Amelia . . . Whoever-you-are.'

I manage an awkward laugh and he heads downstairs to the manager's office. In the bedroom I put my empty backpack on the bed and start opening drawers. There's really not much I want to take with me. I brought very little from my old life, just enough to make it believable when I moved in with him. Most of that stuff was just what I bought to pose as Amelia Knox in the beginning and I pack that up: gold-plated rings, workout leggings, a velvet jewellery box of my mother's and my favourite coffee mug.

All my stuff is mixed in with Ford's and it gives me a pang to be untangling our lives, one charging cable at a time. I tug open the 'fine jewellery' drawer and find his watches in their boxes, velvet compartments with bracelets and necklaces nestled into them. I don't want any of it but I am looking for some sentimental bits like the handmade birthday cards Rose made for me. I hid them under the cushion in a box containing a really ugly acrylic necklace from some designer or other. He never asked me to wear it and to be honest I think he realized he hated it as soon as it arrived.

I'm lifting out the boxes in the way when I see it. Sitting there between two beige velvet rolls, where it must have been every time I opened this drawer. I've just never looked at it before.

A gold signet ring, bearing the Fowley crest.

I stand there, frozen for a minute. It doesn't have to mean anything, it's just a ring. But it isn't, is it? It's a ring like the one worn by the man in the picture of Rose at the university ball. With that one detail, I'm seeing everything differently, looking at Ford afresh, with his golden curls and his bone structure. All I can think of is, if you were a naive student who'd never met Lawrence Fowley . . . he'd be a pretty convincing doppelganger.

Sam said Rose never had Lawrence . . . Is that what she meant? That it was Ford all along, lying and using Lawrence's name? But if that's the case, then Sam wasn't angry on Lawrence's behalf but because of . . .

The front door clunks closed and I hear footsteps in the living room. 'Aimes? I'm back.'

I shut the drawer and turn to smile at him as he comes in, my heart racing. It can't be. I'd have seen it. I'd know.

'Want a cup of tea or something while we go through stuff?' Ford asks.

I smile again. 'Sure.'

Ford leaves for the kitchen and I slump against the vanity unit, thoughts going a mile a minute. Lawrence denied ever seeing Rose at the university ball, let alone kissing her. The man who did, in that blurry picture, had a gold ring on, the crest the only thing in focus. If that was Ford, what on earth was he doing there?

Unless he was visiting someone.

Someone like his cousin, Sam. Who went to the same university. It feels insane to even think it. I have no proof other than the ring and Lawrence's word that he didn't know her, and yet . . .

I think of Ford, so desperate to break into the family

business, watching Tom Slazenger get picked over him. How angry and frustrated that must have made him. Angry enough to get together with Sam and kill him? Both of them getting their revenge. Then, when Sam got sent off to rehab because of Bergdis, maybe she'd asked Ford to get rid of her while she had a perfect alibi.

But what about Rose? And Zak?

The words from Lawrence's diary leap out at me from my memory. *Checking RSVPs, realized Ford not coming.* How had I not seen the red flag? How could Ford RSVP if he had never been invited? He had lied to me. He wasn't uninvited the year Rose was killed, he chose not to go. Was he avoiding Sam? Possibly. I think about that video again, not the awful things I saw on it but the way it was made. Sam kissing at the camera, performing for it. Teasing him. Trying to regain his interest.

Had she remembered him kissing Rose at that ball? Maybe she'd assumed that by luring her to the party and killing her, she'd get his attention.

'Here, it's only decaf, sorry,' Ford says, coming back into the room with two mugs – our special Paris ones – and handing me mine before setting his down on the bedside table. 'Finding everything OK?'

'Just about,' I say, my throat dry. 'I, um . . . was just looking at your signet ring. I've never seen you wear it.'

'Sig . . . Oh, that.' Ford glances at the closed drawer. 'It's just something Lawrence did when he inherited. His father had this set made: cufflinks, watch and the ring. All in gold with the crest. He gave me the ring, as a gesture, I suppose.'

'That was nice,' I say, unable to tell if he's lying to me or not. He never wore it around me – odd, given how proud he is of being a Fowley. Perhaps it was too special for him to wear day-to-day, or it reminded him of just how far flung he was from the glittering Fowley fortune. If he is lying, he's doing it very well, but then he's had practice. Because if he was involved in the deaths, he's been lying to me as long as I've been lying to him.

'Mmm, it was,' he agrees.

'Did Sam not get anything?'

Ford's eyes fix on mine. 'I don't know . . . It's not like he was her real dad, you know?'

'Seems like she had a really bad time of it. That she didn't really fit in,' I say. 'Can't have been easy. Looking in at the amazing Fowley family from the outside.'

'I suppose not. But there's always been some distance between me and them so I kind of get it. But she was so ungrateful, throwing all that in their faces like she did,' Ford says. 'Are you going to drink that?'

I glance down at the tea and feel abruptly certain that he's drugged it. With loprazolam or something else.

'Yup. Oh, by the way, can you grab one of the suitcases from the utility room? I think I'm going to need more space to pack.'

It's a lie and Ford seems to realize something's up, but he shrugs. 'Of course. Be right back.'

As soon as he's gone I switch our mugs around and take out my phone, hands shaking. I tap three nines into it and hit dial, just as Ford returns, carrying a suitcase in one hand.

'Here you go, all . . . Oh, Amelia.' He sighs, looking at the mug on the bedside table. 'You were doing so well, but you're losing your touch on the details.'

I follow his gaze, realize the mug's handle is facing the wrong way, and dart for the door as Ford pulls back his arm and punches me in the face.

33

My head snaps back and I flounder, dropping my phone. Ford grabs me by the shoulders and shoves me towards the bed, letting the corner of it take my legs out from under me. I hit the floor, winded and panicking.

'You should have just drunk the tea,' Ford mutters, pinning me to the floor. 'Would have been so much easier. I'm not a freak, like Sam. I don't enjoy making people suffer.'

Trapped under him, his hands creeping to my throat, I glare up at him. 'You knew she killed my sister.'

'To be fair, I didn't know Rose even had a sister.' He's pinning me down easily, apparently very pleased with himself, in no hurry to take my life. He's won, after all. 'You did really well on your disguise, by the way. Even when I found the picture of her you kept in your makeup case, I could hardly see it.'

My stomach turns over. I'm struggling against him, but it's not getting me anywhere. 'You're the one who trashed the chalet?'

'Mostly I just wanted your passport, to be sure you wouldn't run after what happened to Zak. I had plans for you.'

'You killed him?' I choke out the words, feeling the pressure of his fingers on my neck. Toying with me.

'He killed himself.' Ford laughs bitterly. 'He started

bleating his accusations, and I knew as soon as Lawrence accused James, he'd tell Lawrence I was the one who'd been doing his work for him. So I invited Zak upstairs to James's room with the promise of evidence and offered him a drink. I thought he'd OD after I left him but that swan dive was spectacular.'

Ford tightens his hands and I struggle harder as he cuts my air off, looking down at me speculatively. As if he's genuinely curious to see what happens to me without air. I try and thrash but he's pinning me to the floor and everything I've learned about self-defence has flown out of my head. I'm too deep in shock to do anything. I stare into the eyes of the man I wrote off as harmless, the man I thought I had wound around my finger. They stare back, burning with unfamiliar intensity, with a deeply buried rage crawling to the surface like a mass of maggots.

'You had me fooled,' he says softly. 'For a while . . . There was something familiar about you but I couldn't place it. Then as soon as Sam saw you she realized who you were. Told me. She wanted us to do you together – bring the magic back – but Lawrence was never going to give me a job if I was with Sam. Even if we aren't related by blood. And she never inherited anything so no point in marrying her. But she was so insistent, killed Rose like a cat bringing me a dead mouse – expecting a pat on the head. I knew she had to go too, so I gave you plenty of time to snoop around. Either you'd catch her or she'd kill you and get caught red-handed.'

My vision starts to freckle with black dots and I realize that Ford has no doubt Sam'll keep his secret. Loyal to the end. She already took the blame for Bergdis, after all.

I flail my hand around under the bed, looking for

anything that I can hit him with. Finding nothing. My strength is failing me and I'm watching Ford's eyes as he waits for me to die.

My other hand twitches and I feel something hot and wet on the carpet. The tea I was holding in that dreadful, clunky mug. When Ford decked me, I'd dropped it. I fumble, find the handle and curl my fingertip around it, pulling the heavy mug closer.

'At least you're getting what you wanted,' Ford says through his teeth. 'You're going to see your sister.'

I hit him in the face with the mug and he jerks sideways, hands flying off my neck. Shards of broken mug scatter and I'm left clutching the handle. Gasping and choking, I wriggle under the bed and kick away from him. I can feel Ford grabbing at my ankles, trying to pull me back, but I clutch the leg of the bed to stop him.

When he lets go of me, I immediately pull my legs under the bed. Only a moment later, though, I feel fingers grabbing at my hair from the other side. Slashing out with the mug handle, I get free and roll out from under the bed.

'Bitch! Fucking bitch!' Ford snarls, cradling his bleeding hand. His face is cut, his eye closed protectively.

I leap over the corner of the bed, using it almost as a springboard to get out the bedroom door and into the hallway. I land with a thump on the floor and sprint for the kitchen.

Behind me I can hear Ford stumbling, yelling. He crashes into the door frame on his way out of the bedroom. I can hear his laboured breathing. But I've been going to the gym for a year and training for this. The shock is wearing off and that training is kicking in. He had the element of surprise, but now it's just the two of us on an equal footing.

I fling myself over the kitchen island, grab the handle of a knife from the block and turn just as Ford reaches me. He tries to get hold of my wrists but I block him with my empty hand and stab the paring knife into his side.

'You . . .' He grunts and stumbles back, trips over his own feet and falls on to the sofa, sprawling across it. His hands press around the knife and he grips the handle, then hesitates.

'Go on – pull it out.' I am panting. 'Bleed to death, or rot in prison – your choice.'

'I'm not going to prison.' He groans.

Over the sound of our ragged breathing, I can hear footsteps thundering up the stairwell outside the flat. Many feet in hefty shoes, accompanied by yelling.

'You sure?' I lean against the island for support and huff a bitter laugh. 'You're losing your touch on the details.'

His eye twitches. Blood runs between his fingers on to the floor.

'You missed my phone. I was still on the line to the police . . . They heard everything you told me – they record those calls.'

Ford pales as he registers the noises outside and the implication of my words.

'You're going away for a long time,' I rasp, my throat already swelling closed from the trauma he's put it through. 'No one's gonna care you're a fucking Fowley in prison.'

The look he gives me is pure hatred. The next moment he's pulled the knife out and blood is spurting across the sofa. I'm still standing frozen by the island when the police break down the door.

*

312

There is initially quite a lot of confusion over who did what to whom. I'm hauled outside to a van none too gently and for a while I'm worried I'm about to be arrested. But the police get their facts straight after conferring with the operator who took my call. I'm fairly sure my attack on Ford falls under self-defence and justifiable force but I've seen my share of bad calls by the CPS. I'm already steeling myself for bad news, preparing to handle it.

At the station I give my statement, which takes some doing. It's a long time coming but I have all the details now, plus they have the call recorded and Ford admitted to a lot while he was choking me.

I'm still struggling with the idea that for over a year I've been living side by side with a murderer. I might have lied my way into that relationship but there were times when I wanted him. When I took him to bed just because I wanted to, because he was handsome and kind and good to me. How had I not seen what he really was? I am sickened with myself. He may not have killed my sister, but he helped to kill others, and he lied to her, abused her trust. I'm just not sure I'll ever be able to trust anyone ever again. Not after this.

The police must have called Lawrence for confirmation, because after several hours in a side room drinking terrible tea, I get a phone call from him. A police officer brings me a cordless phone and leaves me to it. I roll up the sleeve of my borrowed sweatshirt – my clothes having been taken for evidence – and bring the phone to my ear.

'Hello?' I croak.

'Amelia.' His voice comes clearly down the line, and I feel the weirdest sense of relief. At least he can appreciate the insanity of what I've just gone through. 'They told me what happened. How are you?'

'Oh, you know, got a bit strangled but I'll be fine,' I manage. 'You?'

'Still a little stabbed but getting over it,' Lawrence says. 'I . . . I'm very sorry that I didn't warn you about Ford.'

My stomach shrivels. 'You knew?'

'Not about the murders,' Lawrence says quickly. 'I suspected him of the embezzlement. I've known for a while that James was outsourcing work to him, but I thought it was an innocent-enough arrangement until the money started going missing. I assumed you were in on his plan, that he'd brought you with him as part of another plan to rob me. But when we went out on my boat, you mentioned him not being invited to the party last year and I realized he'd lied to you about it. And if he'd done that, and you'd innocently revealed it to me, you were likely unaware of his guilt. Then in the chaos of Charlie's death and Sam's attack I just . . . I was distracted.'

'He admitted to poisoning Zak,' I say. 'So I suppose James was telling the truth. He's only responsible for one death.'

Lawrence lets out a long sigh. 'I'm starting to believe that my family might be cursed. But of course greed is a powerful curse all on its own. I had no idea Ford and Sam had any kind of relationship, or how significant it was. I didn't realize it was Ford in that picture you showed me. I just thought . . .'

'That I was crazy?' I shake my head. 'I wasn't exactly open to reason then but . . . at least, in the end, the truth came out, right?'

'As it usually does, I'm learning,' Lawrence says softly. 'I just wanted to apologize for the harm my family has done to you, and to your sister. And to thank you for, however inadvertently, exposing the evil I'd surrounded myself with. If there's anything I can do for you . . .'

'Just . . . do whatever you can to help the police find Sam.'

'I will. She won't get away with what she's done,' Lawrence promises. 'I know you came to my home thinking that I was some sort of predator with limitless resources. Well, I'm going to prove you correct. I won't rest until she's found.'

'Thank you,' I say, struck all at once by how strange it is that of all the ways I thought Lawrence Fowley and I would change each other's lives, I never expected that he would be the one to help me get mine back.

Epilogue

IT'S HOT AS HELL on the tube and twice as muggy. By the time I emerge to hail a taxi I'm glad of the frosty air outside. The flowers on the seat next to me are still fresh and perky, despite the chaos of the tube. I bought them as I was leaving work for the day, in preparation for this visit.

It's taken me a while to get back into the swing of things at the office – my extended leave left room for a lot of gossip in my wake, but things are improving. I'm not the old Amelia – people have had to get used to that – I think she died somewhere in the Norwegian forest the night I saw my sister murdered. Perhaps she died the moment I decided to take the path that led me there.

Physically I'm back to normal: my hair is dyed dark brown again and I've had my extensions removed, the fillers dissolved. The scars have healed. Perhaps my clothes are a bit more fitted now, a little more colourful, and I carry myself upright, looking opponents and hostile colleagues dead in the eye. The first time I dumped William's work back on his own desk when he left it for me, he looked so taken aback I actually laughed. I don't worry as much about being liked any more, or playing fair, not with those who don't deserve it anyway. I've heard at least two people call me a 'killer bitch', but in a whisper that held a tiny bit of awe. That would have made Rose laugh.

At the cemetery I follow the same route as always, around the small chapel and down rows of neatly kept graves. Rose's headstone is pale pink marble, her name engraved in gold. I bring flowers every few weeks now. It used to be every Friday, but my therapist said I shouldn't feel guilty about letting myself move on. I'm making an exception to my new routine because today is a special occasion.

I pause by her grave and pull out the newspaper from my bag. The headline reads 'Fowley Heiress Arrested for Serial Murder'. I fold the paper so the picture of Sam, wild-haired and half-starved, is upright. The manhunt for her lasted for weeks, but the police were relentless and Lawrence was as good as his word. He hired private security to comb the area and offered cash rewards for information. He even had helicopters scanning for heat signatures from the air. I saw it on the news.

According to the article, when they found her she was living in the cellar of a long-destroyed cottage – Tom's camping things were there, so she must've gone back to the cabin for them. She was filthy, bitten to pieces by insects and desperately hungry. She's currently awaiting trial for the murders of Elena, Tom and Rose, plus at least five care-home residents. It appears she kept herself busy between parties, causing a series of strokes, heart attacks and 'accidental' drownings in the hydrotherapy pool.

According to what I've seen online, Lawrence isn't commenting on the case. He's also not supporting her defence in any way. James, already awaiting trial for Charlie's murder, has likewise not received a penny from his older brother.

I know that, even if he'd kept hold of his inheritance, Lawrence wouldn't have given them anything. As it is, he's surrendered his claim to the Fowley fortune and chosen to come out. He is, I understand, doing OK financially. He's not a fool and he has money of his own invested in various places. As far as I know the estate is being sold, the money divided between distant relatives down the line. Ford, like James, having brought the family name into disrepute, has lost his chance to inherit.

Despite being arrested, Sam hasn't turned on Ford. As far as I can tell from the news articles, she is taking sole responsibility for all the murders, including Bergdis and Zak. Though Ford confessed to that on the 999 call, so he's probably going down for it too.

Although I've had no further contact with Lawrence, I actually bumped into Cecile several days before Sam's arrest. I was getting a coffee at King's Cross and she was sitting at a restaurant near the same platform. I felt the urge to avoid her but she acknowledged me and came over to talk. Apparently she was staying in London for a while and was in the process of applying to continue her training as a doctor.

'My father's absolutely furious,' she said, looking both nervous and slightly pleased with herself. 'He's already found someone else he wants me to marry, but I've told him I don't care what he thinks and I don't need his money. I'll be fine.' She put her hand on mine, her smile soft and kind, as if I hadn't deceived her and most of her future family. 'I hope you know you will be too.'

I place the folded paper on Rose's grave. There are already flowers on there, which is surprising. Her friends aren't the flower type, though they left pictures, candles and small gifts on her birthday. The flowers are gorgeous, a huge bouquet of yellow roses. I've become an expert in the meaning of flowers in all my weeks of visiting her. Especially roses, no surprise. I usually bring a dozen, half white, half ivory. White for purity and innocence, ivory for charm and grace. Yellow means friendship. I don't need to read the card to know that these are from Lawrence. Clearly he's also thinking of her in the aftermath of Sam's arrest.

Today, my bouquet is of blue hyacinths and sea lavender, surrounding two white roses. As she was wrapping it up, the woman in the shop told me that the hyacinths represented regret. I acted surprised but that was actually why I'd chosen them. I still regret what I said the last time I saw my sister. I will always regret it, but, since starting to see my therapist, I've allowed myself to stop taking the blame for Rose's death. Yes, I was unfair to her and I made assumptions which led to us parting on bad terms. But I wasn't responsible for inviting her to Norway, for luring her to her death. Rose had accepted that invitation because she was, at heart, a romantic. That was something to love about her, not something to regret.

'Shall we add some of this?' the florist had asked me, gesturing to the sea lavender.

'It's lovely . . . What does it mean?' I asked, not having come across it before.

'It doesn't really have a complicated message. It just means "I miss you".'

I nodded, not trusting myself to speak.

Now I set the bouquet down and squeeze the top of Rose's headstone in my palm. The pain of losing her isn't gone; I don't think it ever will be. But it's manageable now.

An ache like a wound slowly healing. I will always miss my sister, but she is, at least, no longer lost.

As I leave the cemetery and join the pedestrians weaving along the crowded pavement, I breathe in deeply. Beneath the scents of the city – exhaust, burnt coffee, metal and sour rubbish – I catch just a fleeting trace of roses. Then it's gone, and I hail a taxi, heading in the direction of home.

Acknowledgements

2023 WAS QUITE THE year – my first time writing three books back to back. For two separate publishers, no less. I couldn't have made it through without the help of all the lovely people mentioned below.

First thanks as always go to my family for largely tolerating my deeply stressed mood and the aversion to sunlight that came with my increased workload. I'm sorry you now have another name to remember on top of all the titles. I will at some point issue you all with a flowchart.

Thanks go to Dandy Smith, a fantastic author and even better friend. Not only was *One Small Mistake* an inspiring novel, but the support you've given my work is nothing short of humbling.

I owe everyone at Transworld a massive thank you for making the process of bringing this novel to publication as stress-free as possible. It's been wonderful getting to know a whole new set of names and faces, and you made me feel tremendously welcome at the Harrogate Festival brunch last year. Particularly Thorne Ryan and Emma Fairey. So, many thanks for that. Getting on board with a new publisher was so strikingly similar to being a debut all over again, and I greatly appreciate everyone who helped ease me in to it!

Special thanks go to Finn Cotton, a phenomenal editor – I am so glad we got the chance to work together on this and it was such a fun and rewarding book to write. It would be half the novel it is without your input and of course it was your brilliant idea and Transworld's fabulous cover that started the ball rolling. I had a fantastic time writing about this awful family, and watching this novel grow with each successive edit was a real pleasure.

Thanks as always to Laura Williams at Greene and Heaton, my incredible, indefatigable agent. Your input was, as always, invaluable to bringing this one together. Thank you for being so supportive and checking in on me during 'the year of three books'. It was a lot, but we got it done in the end, and thank you so much for throwing my hat in the ring on this one.

Slightly out of left field, but a big thanks to Arkane Studios and specifically everyone who worked on *Dishonoured* (2012). It's long been one of my favourite games, and as a devout introvert from a council estate in Hertfordshire with almost no experience of the rich and devious, the game was a big inspiration behind the Fowley party. A chance to really live the experience of sneaking around a mansion full of awful people. As a result there's a tiny nod to 'Lady Boyle's Last Party' in the book. Just to say, cheers.

Lastly, thank you to everyone who has bought, borrowed and read *The Serial Killer's Party*. I hope you enjoyed reading about the Fowleys and their insane party as much as I enjoyed writing about them.